PTO Art + Egotism

217 "You can get rid of a minister, but you're never cured of yourself".

218 "The success he longs for lies precisely in the myth he has made of his life, for it has given his existence a largeness denied to most lives".

134 " ~~your~~ pensive passivity which I sometimes likened to the meditation of a monk but which, most of the time, I knew was no more than a lack of real purpose".

113 "I was giving her pleasure. It is sometimes cited as proof of love, this desire to give pleasure to the loved one. But I knew that what I enjoyed was a sense of power".

CHIEFLY ABOUT HOOKE

CHIEFLY ABOUT HOOKE

Tony Sullivan

ANDRE DEUTSCH

First published in 1992 by
André Deutsch Limited
105-106 Great Russell Street
London WC1B 3LJ

CIP data for this book is
available from the British Library

ISBN 0 233 98777 0

Printed in Great Britain by
Billings Book Plan Limited, Worcester

For my friends

1

This is chiefly about Hooke. But Marion is also important and I shall begin with her; with the caprice which, in its consequences, drove us all to the brink of ourselves. That is how Hooke would have put it anyhow.

She went on holiday – but such a holiday! And at the height of the tourist season when she should have been tending her shop and making money – 'I'm sick of making money. I need a break.'

All right. But why a package holiday to the Pearl of the Tyrrhenian Coast? She had seen it advertised in the window of the local travel agents and had been seized by a sudden whimsy. I warned her that she would not enjoy it. She would feel out of place, smothered in cheery philistines. I described the vast hotel she would encounter, a pink nightmare modelled in concrete; its tedious technicolour patio and swimming pool; its Butlins dining room staffed with nose-picking waiters; the inedible food – 'You know how you love that pasta which looks and tastes like small rubber drainpipes. They'll give you lots of that.'

She merely smiled the patient smile she knows I loathe, putting all her waning loveliness into it. Her mind was made up and she was formidable. Having yielded to impulse she was determined to go through with it. I would never have shown such resolve, her manner implied; I would never yield to caprice. 'You're afraid to take a chance. You want the world all buttoned up tight around your prejudices.'

That pleased her; she turned from me with a self-absorbed smile. As a last resort, flinging caution aside, braving the

1

unknown, I offered to go with her. But she would not have it. 'It's no use, goggle-face. You'd only feel out of place.'

I wear spectacles. They are steel-rimmed. Without them I am quite good looking: my long pale face, my straight fair hair. I carried my face impassively when I drove her to Manchester Airport, saying little; but she was full of talk, anticipating an adventure with all the zest women bring to such things. On the bosom of her silken summer dress she bore a sparkling brooch in the shape of the letter 'M'. That was for breaking the ice. People would accost her, men probably, and try to guess what 'M' stood for. An intriguing relationship might develop from this.

The departure lounge was crowded with travellers, their excited gabble rising to the expansive ceiling, where a holiday sunlight shimmered. And they were all there, I pointed them out to her, the stereotypes she was doomed to suffer in the ensuing week – the Lancashire comic who would want to be everyone's friend; a muddle of elderly pensioners, vacuously cheerful; the fractious child with his automatic weapon; and the commercial traveller, insurance clerk or rally-driving bore who would set about trying to seduce her. 'You're such a snob,' she laughed, holding me and kissing me goodbye.

I watched her walk off with them – the bearded fanatic who collected 78s of obscure jazz musicians; the infant teacher with outsize breasts; the teenage lovers rapt in a haze of deodorant. They were all bound for a sunshine frolic in that place where Shelley's poor drowned body was washed up; and they were carrying my sister off with them, returning her smile and offering their mateyness, impressed by her looks and flattered by her manner, her serene accessibility, the interest she took in them, which they would not consider condescending.

She walked tall and slim. Her wonderful hair flowed tawnily and her stride was eager, her head tilted beckoningly. She was an elegant lady, forty years old and prepared to welcome whatever might arise. At the final gate she turned and waved – heart-catching, that lissom twirl from

2

the ankles. 'Enjoy yourself!' I cried, my smile urgent. I thought of terrorists and bombs, the superjet exploding, my love consumed in a rush of flame. . . I went to my car and drove home.

Yorkshire is a sort of uncle to Lancashire, a burly relative, wealthy and patrician where it isn't city-harsh or simply rustic. You have to take into account both Leeds and Harrogate. In addition there are those small snug towns locked into the Pennines where it is all stone: stone buildings and stone walls, rock piled hard within the neighbouring hills. I lived in such a town and Marion had spent most of her life there. Two or three years ago, finding herself divorced with a grown son to look after, she had rallied defiantly and plunged into activity. 'I know exactly what I'm going to do,' she had declared, quivering slightly; and in a short time she had created a thriving enterprise probably best described as a Gift Shop, for it has everything no one really needs yet everyone seems eager to buy. You will find it in the high street on the left as you enter the town, a little beyond the Wesleyan chapel (now a disco dive), the town jail (a vegetarian restaurant) and the Mechanics' Institute (an arts centre). It is close to the ancient packhorse bridge, recently restored to bear the weight of tourists – for this is a famous old town. It has appeared on TV endorsing the virtues of manly Yorkshire bitter and mass-produced wholemeal bread.

Leaving the bridge, tourists generally make for the open market, its stalls manned by itinerant Asians; and after watching the Morris dancers in the market square, they will move to the clog factory, the pottery and the antique shops. Many will discover Marion's establishment. It is set back from the pavement and you step down into a tiny cobbled forecourt decorated with potted shrubs. There are windows on either side of the low stone doorway and here you will find fine woollen dresses voluptuously draped over stripped-pine furniture, pieces of jewellery and glassware, a pair of handmade shoes perhaps and a couple of earthen pots sprouting dried grasses and flowers. Inside, hanging from the beamed ceiling, there are cunning mobiles and lampshades that seem made of spun sugar. Against the white roughcast walls, shelves and racks are piled with oddments chosen to attract the tourists' money – wooden toys and dolls, strings of barbaric beads, old-fashioned culinary implements of uncertain purpose, expensive chocolates and condiments, leather sandals fashioned by Third World peasants and vials of costly perfume innocent of cruel experiments on animals.

It is a fairytale emporium – feminine and frivolous, exotic and alluring, especially of an autumn evening when the lamps are lit: those mistily damp and hovering evenings culled from the pensive hills. . . Actually they can occur at any time of the year. And then, framed in the Dickensian windows, the jewellery gleams, the glassware scintillates, the homespun dresses radiate a warmth of brown and russet hues, passionate green, the luxury of the moors; and my secondhand bookshop, located in one of the narrow lanes that climb from the high street, seems decidedly drab in comparison. I am glad to get out of it, to enter the sprightly glow of Marion's presence, the airy smiling cynicism of her dainty commerce.

I reached the town about midday, an hour after leaving the airport, and went at once to her shop. Polly had been left in charge and she was busy; her young sister helped to serve the visitors crowding the place, waving their credit cards and champing restively. Polly was freckled and fair-haired. The large pink hoops that hung from her ears trembled with her anxiety to fulfil the managerial responsibilities suddenly thrust upon her. When she was free for a moment I told her I had seen Marion off safely. Then I left, feeling worn and thin, my aims diffuse and drifting in a vacuum.

By now she would be crossing the Channel, sipping a gin-and-tonic from a plastic container and smiling, perhaps, as someone tried to guess what 'M' stood for.

4

2

The bookshop had been my father's; his father had established it; now it was on my hands. The profit was negligible but my needs were few, a condition that displeased Marion. 'If you don't care to make a success of it, you should get out. You're nearly thirty. When are you going to start living your life in earnest?' At thirty she had been a wife and mother. By the time he was thirty, Hooke had written three novels.

It was, I had to admit – and her absence reinforced the point – a tepid life. A stillness had settled on me and I couldn't shake it off; wasn't sure I wanted to.

The shop was crammed with old books, a dark and suffocating place; but that wasn't the impression I had always had of it. In my father's day, when I was younger, it had been a cave of intellectual romance. I had an apartment upstairs now and went there, cooking an omelette for my lunch: a modest glass of wine and Leonhardt's performance of Bach's Cantata 106. *Gottes Zeit ist die allerbeste Zeit.* By now she would be in Italy, fastening her seatbelt as the plane circled Pisa choosing a spot to land that would avoid grazing the monstrous iced confection on the Piazza del Duomo.

The living room had a beamed ceiling, its angles narrowing to dormer windows at either end. The walls were plain, the better to feature the few pictures I prized. Hooke shrugged when eventually he saw them: they were watercolours. Beside the fireplace was a seasoned leather armchair with the disposition of an indulgent uncle. A desk stood in the corner, my notebook upon the desk. A chess computer was set out on a table to one side.

It was a place in which, these days, nothing happened but myself. Yet had I really wanted Lucy Armstrong, her dark hairs on the pillow, her damp knickers draped over the washbasin? 'You don't live!' she had cried, flinging off at last: 'You just make notes about it.' I had gone to my desk, making a note about it.

After eating, I washed the dishes – I wore bright blue plastic gloves for this – then went downstairs and opened the shop. Although the sun was shining with all the mindless aplomb of August, the shop was quite dim, but I did not switch on the lights. They were of low wattage anyway. The gloom was functional and my father had insisted on it, thinking that it gave the shop – its low discoloured ceiling, its uneven floor – an air of mystery, of exclusiveness and hidden wealth. In the dimness, his theory went, customers would take longer to decipher the titles on the shelves or to sample a page of the book they had opened, and the longer they lingered the stronger would grow the obligation to purchase something before they left.

'You hoodwink your customers,' Marion said.

'You seduce yours,' I replied.

The afternoon went slowly. When there was nothing to do I read Du Bellay, the *Poète courtisan*: not from choice. A tutor I had known at Oxford was editing a literary encyclopaedia and he had offered me the job of compiling the 'D' entries. I had got as far as Dryden but I kept going back to Emily Dickinson. *This is my letter to the world, That never wrote to me.*

A Japanese visitor looked in and I sold him *The Seven Pillars of Wisdom*, a pound a pillar. Then the telephone rang and I whirled to answer it: but it was only my father. He was with my mother in East Anglia looking at all the churches. Now that he was retired he spent his time travelling, frantic to see as much as possible of the world in his last years. When he died it would be from a surfeit of sightseeing. I spoke to my mother and asked how she was. She insisted that her heart wasn't troubling her. They were returning home soon, then they were off to Australia. All this coming and going, my parents, my sister, the urge to claim something before it was too late. . . I began to feel left behind.

When eventually, with the mild irony I loved, Sarah would enquire why I had become a secondhand bookseller – 'What drove you to it?' – I would tell her, hoping to impress her, that I had done so out of pity for my father; and this was at least partly true. The old man had carried the shop on his back all his life and it had grown about him like a horny shell out of which he peered and into which he retreated with a feebly petulant distaste for the changing world. I had urged him to get out while there was still a chance of living, admiring myself as an exemplary son nobly assuming his father's burden. This moral exaltation – the more uplifting in that I had never much cared for my father, who was too old to be my father and more like a misplaced grandfather – had not lasted long. Yet I hadn't then felt trapped in the shop, betrayed by a rash filial compunction. It was an easy life, providing me with time to read; and of course I hoped to write. I had published one book after all. But that was before I became a bookseller. Since then I had done nothing. The stillness.

Marion telephoned that evening. I had stayed in, hoping she would call, cancelling a casual dinner date with a girl of slight acquaintance. In any case the ethnic curry would have scorched my throat. *Are you there? Hello?* All the way from Viareggio, the neon-lit bars along the front, the soft southern night, the dusky beach and the sea running tirelessly. *What are you doing? Are you all right, precious?* She sounded drunk.

Later in the week I had a postcard from her: blue sky, blancmange hotels. Everything was wonderful, people were so friendly, she had danced the Hokey-Cokey. She did not say she wished I was there. Yet we had often gone on holiday together, driving through France and Spain, sampling the local vineyards, stopping where we pleased, laughing at anything. . . To hell with her. Yet I was elated when the week was over and I was driving to the airport to meet her, trying to guess the present she would have brought me. It was raining and she wouldn't like that; she would curse the decaying mess of England as travellers do when they return from countries where sunshine and splendour, the confidence derived from an assured culture, make living seem insouciant.

The plane was on time and soon the place where I stood waiting was full of holiday-makers returning home. They were sunburned and probably penniless; they wore bright clothes and carried exotic stuff they had picked up abroad. Some were disgruntled: a loathsome job, a miserable existence perhaps awaited them. A holiday was no more than an odd loop in life, closing at the neck and firmly returning you to where you had left off. A note for my notebook. But in Marion's case – I saw her from afar, appearing intermittently in the crowd – the holiday seemed to have entailed more than that, forcing a change between past and future; for there she was – I stared hard – kissing a man and being kissed by him while people eddied about them and swept on, hauling luggage and snarling at their children. Marion and a man clinging together in a paroxysm of parting, her arms about his neck, her dazzling hair hiding his face. Then they swayed apart; she patted him on the chest, stroked him lingeringly. He went off and was soon lost in the crowd. She looked about and waved when she saw me.

She must have guessed that I had witnessed the passionate embrace yet she did not refer to it when we met. And what if I had seen? It was her own private affair, her eyes declared even as her smiling lips kissed me. I grasped her luggage and we went to the car.

3

In the car driving home, my eyes on the rainy road, my glance sliding at times to her face as she sat beside me talking and laughing, telling me of her holiday and how wrong I had been: lovely people, gorgeous scenery and really not a bad hotel. She looked well, rejuvenated, full of animation. I had nothing to say. Sometimes her talk faltered and when I looked she was gazing through the smeary windscreen, her lips shaping a pensive smile. The rain persisted, clouding the hills. We reached the town at length and I drove to her house.

The converted farmhouse she had shared with Mark was sold after the divorce and she had come to live on a rise a little above the town, in one of a row of tall cottages. They were mostly occupied by moderately success-ful people who commuted to Halifax or Bradford, read the *Guardian* and fretted over the environment, placing their trust in vegetarianism and Green politics. 'Off-cumders' the townspeople call them. Anyone who comes to the town from anywhere else is an off-cumder. The cottagers they displaced – unemployed mill-hands, waitresses, minor beneficiaries of the tourist trade – had gone to live in comfortable semis in a council estate on the town's eastern edge where the valley widens. The off-cumders held the hill, cheerfully tolerating inefficient drains and rising damp. What mattered was that the cottages were stone-built and satisfactorily aged. Also they would hold their price in the market.

Like the rest, Marion's house had two storeys at the front and three at the rear where a garden trailed down the slope. It had been a weaver's cottage and sometimes of a black moorland night she swore she heard a ghostly loom at work in the topmost room, rattling the woes of the past.

I followed her into the house, carrying her luggage. She scooped up the mail and glanced at it indifferently. Beneath the rain, the morose sky, the house was dark and chilly. She gazed about and I thought she was probably missing her son. There was a postcard from him babbling of ouzo and the Parthenon. I wanted to stay – Should I make some coffee? Something to eat? – but she preferred to face alone the inevitable deflation that follows a successful holiday. Doubtless she would work it off by cleaning the house or hammering at her unruly garden. 'But come round tonight, won't you?' Her face was suffused with a delicate shyness. 'There's something I want to tell you.'

When I returned that evening she gave me a present: a bottle of *lachryma Christi* and an ornate silk scarf I would probably never wear. Hooke had not altogether approved of the choice, I gathered later; but I had no objection to drinking Christ's tears. And then she told me of him, sitting by the fireplace in her front room, its tall windows overlooking the dusky valley. She wore a long cotton skirt which fringed her bony ankles; her face was poised against the white walls. Here and there hung some of the pictures she had painted when she was an art student – a study of the moors beneath a melodramatic sunset; a portrait of Mark Tewitt with impasto to enliven the rugged beauty that once had stirred her. Now there was Vincent Hooke and her face was tender. If I wanted to be cruel (and it might come to that) I could call her smile a sentimental simper – 'The fact is I've gone and got myself a new man.'

She was a little afraid, I think, her appealing smile soliciting my approval, her dark eyebrows arched over the mystery, the man, love. See them in the plane sitting side by side (Fate!) smiling their fear at each other as they are flung thirty thousand feet into the air on a helter-skelter holiday. And the sun is always shining up there beyond the clouds; something she had never taken into account until he pointed it out to her. A gin-and-tonic apiece to celebrate the discovery, the sunlight streaming unceasingly. And then the Alps far below – 'Look Marion!' For he would already have guessed what 'M' stood for. Cruel black peaks skirted with gleaming white snow. He pointed them out to her. 'I've never known anyone quite like him before.' Her rueful laugh. 'He sees things other people miss. Of course he's tremendously intelligent.' She felt inferior, enjoying it. She had someone to look up to, rest her life upon. I was troubled, jealous, awash with Christ's tears. My fear for her. There have been others after all.

The studied casualness with which she produced the photograph, dipping into her handbag, raising her head and throwing back her hair as she handed it to me. Taken by some Italian street-photographer as they sat at a café table. Sunshine, heavy shadow: I couldn't gain much of an impression. A man of slight build, fortyish, open-necked shirt. (The way she excused his lack of style: 'He's not into fashionable gear'.) He seemed relaxed, gazing directly into the camera, unafraid of exposure, with nothing to hide. His mild self-possession. The broad dome of his brow, dark hair fuzzing out behind. She sat close to him, all in white, artful smile. They had their arms on the table and their hands were clasped lightly, with the negligence of intimacy.

They were in the same hotel, would eat all their meals together, their own special table: a bottle of vino, a dish of rubber drainpipes. Their heads drawing close as they shared a joke, some derisive comment on the other diners, the Lancashire comic, the fat lady from Leeds. Love. The way it reduces the rest of the world to objects of amusement or compassion. Hardly what I felt with Lucy. But Hooke and Marion were prepared to take a chance on each other. See them walking along the front past the lighted bars, the cafés, hand-in-hand. He talks, she listens: literature, philosophy, the state of the world. But he is carefree despite his secret sorrow. It makes him attractive and she is glad to be with him: the security of a man. Then on the beach in her bathing-costume, the two-piece she had such trouble choosing, her long white body glistening to a rosy tan. He sits beside her scowling: he doesn't swim, doesn't sunbathe, and the world troubles him, the noisy crowded beach, exuberant

11

Italians, dogs and transistors. Do people really know how to live? 'He can be very critical at times. A bit moralistic actually.' Thoughtful pause as she measured this against her love. What else did they do? Long walks in the hills, the Garfagnana – she *walked*? Since when had she been known to relish walking? But with Hooke it was different. His love of nature: flowers and butterflies, bunnies and squirrels. He had shown her the natural world as though it was an estate to which he had privileged access. And they had gone to Florence, to the Uffizi, the Botticellis. 'He really knows a great deal more about art than I do. Well, it's less a matter of knowing than a sort of instinct, an instant rapport. He saw all sorts of things in the pictures that I had never seen.' Oh my dear old innocent sister. But that was merely something else they had in common. 'There's really such a lovely innocence about him. He isn't . . . tarnished.'

Vincent Hooke, forty-four years old: comes from Liverpool but resident now in Halifax. Fate again: it's only ten miles away. Teaches at a college there, lecturer in English. They also have lecturers in Plumbing and Hairdressing but she did not thank me for pointing this out. 'In any case he isn't really a teacher.' Ah. He has written several novels apparently. That is what excites her. But none of them published; she doesn't know why. His secret sorrow. She had not intruded upon it. It was enough that he was a man with a romantic past, more than simply a boring old teacher. And what had especially impressed her was the fact that although his novels were unpublished he wasn't resentful, he didn't complain, his fury at the world had nothing to do with it but was purely the anguish of a morally sensitive nature. He accepted the situation and seemed resigned to being a teacher, dedicating himself to the humble task. . . She will see more of him, of course. 'I'm afraid it might be serious this time.'

Notes I made sitting at the desk in my apartment. My neat square handwriting, the words issuing blackly from my fountain pen. I will not use a pencil or a ballpoint. I love the balanced weight of my Parker, the smooth unyielding pressure of the nib. And when one has finished writing, to sheathe the precious point in its cap of polished steel. . . It gives a sense of accomplishment impossible to derive from the natty clerk's click of a ballpoint. There is authority in a fountain pen; no more than efficiency in a ballpoint. Taken once by my mother to a surgery when I was a child, I had quite forgotten my tummy-ache in admiration of the physician's penmanship, his gold-nibbed instrument dashing an esoteric message across the prescription pad. That was power, I had realized.

4

I met him the following evening for she was anxious to see him again and have my opinion; to place him in perspective. They had already eaten when I arrived and the dining room looked festive. She had lit a fire to cheer the rainy day – the old house needed warmth at the best of times – and firelight gave the room a succulent glow that glanced off the silken walls and nuzzled the heavy velvet curtains at the window. I seemed to see everything in a heightened form. I suppose it was the sex abounding there. The solid oak table was a glamorous ruin of plates and dishes, flowers and glasses, silverware burnished by candlelight. Was she trying to seduce him, corrupt his innocence, his austere distrust of luxury? There was such an air of indolence and wealth as though kings had been feasting! A languorous perfume mingled with the smell of cigarettes, the aroma of rich food – her exquisite quiches, her muscular Gallic stews, breathless soufflés and rare cheeses. She had prepared it all for him, wanting to serve him, serving herself up in a sinuous dress that left her arms bare, bold with the suntan of Italy. She offered me a cup of coffee.

Hooke put out his cigarette and rose to meet me. He seized my hand, wrung it sincerely. His eyes were bright, his smile hopeful; he wanted to be friends, Marion had told him so much about me. He was smaller than I had judged from the photograph, and sparely built. He wore a brown cord jacket and soft white shirt with a roll collar. (He never wore a necktie, had given them up years ago.) There was a compactness about his figure, a completeness, a singular

14

definition: once you met him you would always recognize him again. It was as though he had thoroughly lived himself into the shape he now possessed. His face was narrow, the features lean. Fine dark hair receded from his pale brow. I was a head taller and I could see the scalp showing through at the crown.

We went into the front room where there were earthenware crocks full of the large blooms Marion loved. Hooke was shrill with praise for the choice and disposition of the furnishings – 'I've never been in a house which so perfectly reflects the owner's personality!' It was as though he had made it up beforehand, tutoring himself in polite compliments.

I was embarrassed and Marion seemed uncomfortable, glancing at me with a timorous smile. He examined the pictures on the walls, concentrating upon those she had painted and marvelling at her dexterity, fondly chiding her for having given up art. Mark's portrait was missing. In its place she had hung a study of Ainsworth Crag, a local beauty spot. 'I'm sure I know it!' he cried excitedly.

When Marion had supplied the topographical details he requested, he nodded emphatically. 'It was the first mountain I ever saw. Of course it isn't really a mountain, I know that,' he went on, anticipating the objection I was about to make: 'but I was only a child at the time. It seemed like God! And I've never been near the place since. It must be thirty years at least.' He paused, appalled. He glanced at me appealingly. 'I'd really like to climb it. I only ever saw it from below. It was at a camp for boy scouts.'

'Oh your terrible old scoutmaster father!' Marion laughed.

'Why didn't you climb it?' I enquired.

'Bust my toe tripping over a guy-rope.' He ducked his face into a parody of shame. 'I spent the whole week gazing up at it. Perhaps it was better that way,' he added mysteriously.

'Well, you shall climb it,' Marion promised. 'Simon will take you, it will be an expedition!'

'I really would like to go.' He smiled at me.

I said nothing. Marion poured brandy into three glasses.

'Now tell me about this book you've published,' he said. He was lighting a cigarette and the words were indistinct. But he often mumbled when speaking of something that was of importance to him.

At Oxford I had chosen George Gissing for research and had made a critical biography out of it – 'Gissing,' Hooke said, 'I've not read much of him. I've read *New Grub Street* and – what's the other one?'

'There are twenty-six other ones.'

'I meant the other one I've read.'

'*Born in Exile*?'

'Indeed I was; but that's not it. Anyway it's your book I'm interested in. What did it feel like, actually being published?'

'Odd. As though it had nothing to do with me.'

'Really?' Marion reared her head. 'That wasn't the impression I had at the time. He was as excited as a schoolboy,' she told Hooke. 'For once he behaved like a normal human being. It was nice,' she added, smiling at me. 'It's not often you give yourself away.'

Hooke exhaled cigarette smoke. 'And was it rejected often, your book, before it was finally published?'

'Actually my tutor knew a publisher, so there was no problem.'

'Yes, of course,' he mumbled.

'It was quite an unimportant little book,' I assured him. 'Just one of a series of biographies.'

'But you were published,' he insisted.

'He's done nothing since,' Marion sighed, reaching for her glass.

'You went to Oxford and you've published a book,' Hooke recited severely, 'and now you're content to run a secondhand bookshop?'

'Oh he's hopeless. It wouldn't be so bad if he was a success at it, but he hardly makes enough to keep himself.'

'I don't care.'

'You're wasting your life!'

'I'm not so sure,' Hooke said wisely. He inclined his head, confiding in Marion. 'I think Simon is one of those people who have the courage to wait. Wait in readiness. He won't rush into anything foolish. He won't kid himself and waste his life.'

I wasn't sure that you could waste life. The concept seemed meaningless. 'You can waste time that might be better spent, waste opportunities, but existence goes on whether you like it or not.'

'Nevertheless,' Hooke urged, nodding agitatedly: 'that's the way people feel once they – once they've reached a certain age. You'll see. When they look back on their lives, most people feel they've wasted them. In a way, it's the best thing about people. I mean their desire to have done better.'

'It's true,' Marion murmured.

Hooke put out his cigarette. 'One is all the time haunted by an ever-so-desirable alternative; the better life that might have been yours.'

'That is why one writes fiction, I suppose. I'm very interested in these novels you've written,' I offered invitingly.

'Oh. . .' He swept them aside with a nervous gesture, again ducking his face into the gulping grimace that was perhaps more than merely the parody of shame.

'I'd like to read them,' Marion said.

'They're all in Liverpool.'

'Have you written anything recently?' I asked.

He shook his head. He had written nothing since leaving Liverpool and his wife three years ago. His secret sorrow. 'I'd like to read your book,' he said.

'I'm not sure I've a copy.'

'Oh you have,' Marion exclaimed roughly. 'Anyway I've got one here.' She rose and went to the bookshelf beside the fireplace. 'Yes, here it is.' She found the book and handed it to Hooke.

'But it's your personal copy,' he protested. Having opened the book, he had found the inscription I had written on the flyleaf.

'Oh that's all right,' she said.

He glanced at me wryly. An awkwardness settled upon us and no one knew what to say next. Marion refilled our glasses, then she and Hooke fell to reminiscing about their holiday, sharing a private joke. But I wouldn't be kept out. I wanted to know how it was that Hooke had gone on the sort of holiday he, no more than Marion, would be expected to enjoy.

'For the past three years,' he quipped, 'I've been trying to live the life of an ordinary person. Not an experience I can recommend.'

I was ready to challenge this but he was already talking of Florence and the glory of art. While Marion had investigated the souvenir shops on the Ponte Vecchio, he had visited the Accademia Gallery, encountering Michelangelo's David for the first time in his life. 'I'd seen photographs of it, of course, but I'd never realized its incredible size.'

Another colossal mountain towering over him like God. His face was alight with a mystical refulgence, his voice was hoarse with wonder. It brought out the trace of a Liverpool accent and made him appear slightly uncouth, a goggle-eyed prole nattering of aristocratic splendour. 'Of course the place was thick with tourists, Japs mostly, cameras stuck to their faces like the growth of some hideous disease. They kept bobbing about, having themselves photographed in front of the thing. But that didn't matter. The statue rose above us all – gigantic! It must be one of the very greatest works of art. And it was supremely alone, that was the point, as though it had cleared a magic space about itself. Nothing could intrude upon that beauty, nothing could violate it. There was this sense of a thing done once and done supremely, done once and for all.' He grimaced helplessly. 'Art like that shouldn't be allowed.'

The experience had cost him some despair – 'Did you know Michelangelo was only twenty-six when he created it? *Twenty-six!*' – yet at the same time it seemed to have granted him the reassurance of some profound insight. 'That's all that matters after all. Allegiance to art; creating

18

something, no matter what anyone thinks! Getting something accomplished that. . .'

I couldn't fully decipher his last words for he was lighting another cigarette and mumbling round it. It sounded like 'redeems the past'. I had the impression that encountering Michelangelo's masterpiece was almost the most important thing that had happened on his holiday.

It was growing late and Marion had more than once glanced at me, implying that it was time I left. But I sat tight, sourly relishing the situation, creating a situation of my own since I was shut out of theirs. At length Hooke said that he must go. He hadn't a car – he had never learned to drive – and he must not miss the last bus to Halifax. 'You already have,' Marion said. 'It goes early on a Sunday.' She laughed at his consternation, touching him fondly.

'I can walk,' he said.

'Oh, you're a great hiker, I know. But you're not walking tonight, my love. I can easily drive you there.'

He got up smiling at me apologetically. 'I hope we'll see a lot more of each other, Simon.'

I smiled.

They went out together and I heard her car start up, drive away. I was alone, yet the room seemed to be vibrating still with talk and the presence of the lovers. And she had given my book away to him. I didn't care what he might think of it but I couldn't help feeling betrayed. It was a while since I had felt anything of the sort and I made the most of it.

5

I had not behaved like a gleeful schoolboy when my book was published – not for more than an unguarded moment anyway. On the whole I had comported myself discreetly, my manner stiff with suppressed excitement, for I was unable to banish the hope that fame and an exalted career would follow. But the reviews were meagre and the expected commissions from publishers had not materialized. That was five years ago and the book was now virtually unobtainable. I had not realized that a book could die, disappear and never be heard of again. But I had faced the fact and, after some anguish, had accepted the bitter truth that I was not and would never be a significant writer. It was one of the few moral victories I had to be proud of.

Now I lounged in a chair in my sister's empty house, waiting for her return, surrounded by great blooms scarlet and white, their sickly perfume, and the picture of Ainsworth Crag reverberating on the wall above me. I was depressed, wished I had never met Vincent Hooke.

Marion was away for more than an hour – yet it would take no more than twenty minutes to drive to Halifax – and she was ill-tempered when she returned, finding me still there. Defensive, she at once launched an attack, standing over me and accusing me of rudeness towards her guest – 'Of course, I can understand you must feel pretty inadequate in face of what he's done in his life.'

'But what has he done? We don't actually know.' I removed my glasses and polished them. 'He claims to have written all these novels—'

'I believe him. But you will take nothing on trust. And what's particularly revolting is how you stand back, out of harm's way, and give nothing away. You let the other person give himself away, make a fool of himself.'

'Did you think he made a fool of himself? I didn't.'

'But he was nervous, anyone could see that.'

'Why should he care? He has your love.'

'Because you've published your wretched little book, that's why, and he's got seven or eight novels no one will publish. You've been to Oxford, you're an M.Litt. or whatever the hell it is, and he's only got his teaching certificate.'

'In other words, he feels inadequate.'

She gazed at me pensively. 'Do you remember the time I dropped you in the river?'

I was very young, for Marion was then no more than a big girl. We were in a meadow beyond the town where the river flowed broad and shallow between shelving banks pitted with holes where the sand martins nested; and I shall always remember the sudden swoop of her body upon me, the mothering female claim, her strong arms clasping me and lifting me up with an Ugh! of a heave, holding me out over the river as though it was a vast potty and impossibly dropping me into it, Oh the crashing splash and the icy shock! – 'You tried to drown me.'

She laughed carelessly, pulling off her outdoor coat and throwing it anywhere. She sat down and poured herself a drink. After a moment's hesitation she poured me one also.

'I want you to be friends. I really think he could be good for you. He's had so much more life than you have. Oh, I don't just mean age. Struggle, pushing against the odds, taking a chance. He's lived intensely – you know? And I hope you're not going to suggest he's unintelligent? He knows books, he's cultured. I thought it was fascinating, what he had to say about Michelangelo. Didn't you?'

'Oh yes. Fascinating.'

'He could be really stimulating company for you. You don't have any real friends.'

21

'Come now – What about all those people I sing with in the choir? And my customers. Some of my best friends are customers.'

'Wrinkled old men, fawning over books. The point is, you're in grave danger of stagnating. Oh, you've read a lot, I know; but a book can't answer back. You need a challenge. And I don't just mean intellectual back-chat. What's so fine about Vincent is that he is passionately open to life. You could learn a lot from him. I know I have. He's really opened my eyes. Mountains and flowers, great paintings, Michelangelo – Greatness, Simon! The sense of greatness in life. You've talked about such things and it taught me a lot. But when you discuss them – Well, you see, they're always put in a critical frame that somehow stifles the life out of them. Vincent isn't like that. Life is still an adventure for him, terrible though it might be. He is one of the few people I know who is really aware of life and feels compelled to do something about it.'

Restless, she got up and wandered about the room. 'He has made me think,' she declared. 'Who am I really? What do I imagine I'm doing with my life?' She kicked one of the earthenware crocks and a petal fell from a dahlia.

'Are you in love with him?'

She returned to her chair, eager to confide the wonder.

'Are you lovers?' I demanded sternly.

She laughed 'Well, of course.'

I squirmed anguishedly but she did not notice. She was mischievous, her voice rippled excitedly. 'I finally had to seduce him, actually. His background – boy scouts, tyrant father, Catholic Church – has left him with inhibitions.'

'He doesn't approve of extra-marital sex?'

'Sometimes I'm not even sure he approves of sex. I'm working on that, though.'

'Perhaps he doesn't like being unfaithful to his wife.'

'That has nothing to do with it. They're getting a divorce.'

I drained my glass. 'And what's the next step?'

'Well, I suppose we ought to have a go at living together.'

'Here?'

'Well, I'm certainly not going to share the miserable flat he has in Halifax.'

'Yes, but living together. . . Is that wise?'

'Oh God, you're such a spoilsport!'

'But you've only known him for little over a week.'

'You have such a conventional sense of time.'

'You feel as though you've known each other all your lives?'

'Shut up.'

'But have you really thought about it?' I pleaded softly. 'What about Willy? You can't just spring it on him. He'll be home soon, won't he?'

'In a week or two.'

'He comes home and finds his mother living with a stranger.'

'Willy will have to be told first, obviously.'

'And what will you tell him?'

'You don't really think it will last, do you?' she hissed, her face vicious. 'You don't want it to last!'

'I'm only thinking of you. Don't forget the other times.'

'What other times?' she enquired innocently.

The car salesman, the wine merchant, the aging hippy who peddled handmade jewellery (*My bit of rough*) – 'I just don't want you to get too involved before you're quite clear about everything.'

She stirred uncomfortably, like a thwarted teenager. 'What should I do then?'

I had worked it out as a compromise should all else fail. Above her shop there was a second floor which she used as a storeroom, although her stock could be accommodated on the ground floor, at the rear. Because of this she had sometimes thought of making a flat out of the upper floor and letting it. 'Why don't you finally get a flat made above the shop? Then Hooke could live there. In the interim, at least.'

She gazed at me. 'Why don't you call him "Vincent"?'

23

'I don't know. "Hooke" seems to suit him. It rhymes with "book". What do you think of my idea?'

'It had already crossed my mind. I'll see the builder tomorrow.'

6

It was too big for us, too ambitious a project, demanding greater resources and more passionate commitment than we could muster. Moreover, hardly anyone liked the work. 'The Committee have really dropped us in it this time,' Derek Parkin observed. 'We'll never do it' – 'It will be a fiasco,' Ben Sutcliffe agreed. They sat on either side of me.

The contraltos were dejected, unable to manage the correct entrance; the sopranos were pale with the effort of sustaining so many high notes. Some of the tenors had lost their voices and the basses were inclined to flippancy. 'He was stone deaf when he wrote it' – 'Blind drunk more like'.

Von Herzen – möge es wieder zu Herzen gehen. And Jones tapped the music stand with his brisk baton, rallying his forces for another assault on the *Gloria*. 'I love that *presto* at the end,' Derek muttered. 'Last time we tried it I nearly got a hernia.'

We had negotiated the *Kyrie* without too much difficulty but the *Gloria* was massively complex, and beyond the *Gloria* the peaks of the *Credo* reared threateningly: its cruel rocky intervals, its slippery ascents and sickening plunges to low D where my voice failed. 'Don't worry,' Ben said. 'The orchestra will drown us. All you need do is drone summat or other.'

'The orchestra will never play this bloody thing,' Derek asserted bitterly. 'I've heard Karajan do it.'

'Well, come December, laddie, you'll hear us fighting it out with the Calderdale Philharmonic.'

We sat in rows in an upstairs room in the Mechanics' Institute. There were about seventy in the choir. I sat at the rear. *You're a bass?* Marion had queried wonderingly – *I should have thought you'd be a tenor*, Lucy Armstrong said. But she no longer sang with the choir and her departure had raised considerably the average age of the sopranos, many of whom were motherly ladies who would have been happier, you felt, with a selection from *The Sound of Music*. Yet in previous performances they had tackled *The Messiah* and Verdi's Requiem and *Carmina Burana* without so much as mussing a wave of their rigidly permed heads.

The contraltos were a tougher and younger bunch, on the whole. They wore jeans, shapeless sweaters, T-shirts bulging with breasts, and their hair was defiantly ragged. They were mostly teachers or social workers and all seemed earnest feminists. Their swarthy Yorkshire faces. The tenors sat beside them, respectable trustworthy men who at all times professed a grave and orthodox masculinity; and the basses sat at the rear. Some of them were stout and all seemed imbued with a cynical aplomb. *You're a bass?* If anything I was a baritone, incapable of reaching either the glorying heights of the tenors or the profundity of a true bass.

I did not sit quite at the back, for the last row (and each jealously guarded his place) was invariably occupied by men of the working-class who all seemed to be either butchers or policemen. They took their singing seriously and would frequently glower at the basses in front, whose education and social standing gave them the right to disparage great art.

In Karajan's version of the *Missa Solemnis* the voices of the choir rush and soar in an ecstatic paean in praise of the Almighty – *Gloria in excelsis Deo!* – and there are the sopranos and tenors perched triumphantly on a high A, the contraltos and basses loyally supporting them from below. It isn't a long passage and the faster you take it the sooner do you reach the grateful descent to a lyrical *piano* at *Pax hominibus* – provided the basses, urging a low A from the depths of their bellies, have made a firm entrance at *Et in terra pax*. But the Calderdale Choir had trouble reaching that haven, for at the opening *Gloria* instead of ascending and soaring, our voices tended to stumble and collide while frantically searching for the right note, everyone ultimately collapsing in a muddled desperate heap.

'Im-poss-ible!' Jones screeched, whacking the music stand with his baton. 'Im-poss-ible!' And the accompanist blushed at her piano, her fingers tingling. 'Now just suppose Beethoven was to walk through that door now,' the conductor admonished. Derek looked round to see if there was any chance of it; a policeman glared from the back row and his neighbour muttered, 'I thowt we was on reight note anyhow.'

We went through it again, chastened and earnest, eventually with some confidence, although I continued to despise the magnificent banality of the composer's conception. *Pax hominibus* we took in our stride, the basses crooning soulfully. More running ascents at *Laudamus te*. We leapt and galloped then lapsed thankfully into the *pianissimo* minims of *Adoramus te*. I stretched plaintively for a high D and then an E at *Glorificamus te* – 'Piece of bloody cake,' the policeman commented scornfully; but even he became uneasy once we got entangled in the concluding fugue. *In glo-o-oria Dei Patris, A-men . . . A-men, Aa-men . . . Amen, Amen . . . A-men, A-men . . . A-a-a-amen!*

I was resentful and unhappy, loathing the work, immersed in a torrent of voices all bellowing the same rollercoaster tune at different intervals, the tenors breaking free and yelping sonorously only to be crushed by the basses, who in turn were torn to pieces by the shrieks of the sopranos. Jones lashed the air with his baton, his gaze raised ecstatically to Beethoven, and the accompanist was seemingly oblivious, engulfed in the crazy jangle of her piano.

The – Oh the dreadful teutonic urgency, the constipated effort to assert greatness! The *kolossal* and all the direly massive, emotive outpourings it had given rise to – Wagner, Strauss, Mahler, Bruckner: romantic elephantiasis. The strenuously majestic; the barbaric celebration of power, will, armed might! Thunderous bowels of national pride. Gigantic sprawl of a crazed ego – I was sick of the titanic, the gargantuan vomit: hellbent racketing orchestras and the howl of massed choirs. Alone and oppressed, I longed for the cool confident grace of Palestrina, Monteverdi, those artists whose work rose pure and sweet out of the security of an untroubled faith: Purcell, Vivaldi, Bach.

'He considered it his finest achievement,' Derek said as the rehearsal broke up. He nodded to various members of the choir who were hurrying off into the rainy night, the women clinging together and complaining. 'Are we going for a pint then?'

Ben's wife expected him home and he went to her. Derek's wife would wait passively, knowing her place. I went with him to the nearest public house, following in his wake as he shouldered his way to the bar. 'Two pints bitter!' be barked with a Yorkshire grumpiness no one considered objectionable (the barmaid even smiled broadly: he was a real man). We found a seat on a grubby wooden settle against the wall, beyond a congress of stalwart drinkers who stood like tree trunks, shouting conversation at each other.

'I sometimes feel he had a grudge against the text,' I said.

'Poor bugger thowt he were setting it in a new way, dint he?' Derek's dialect came to the fore when he was in a pub.

'He has no difficulty with the German of *Fidelio*, yet he seems to resent Latin. Do you think it's the influence of *Deutsches Wesen*?'

'Happen,' Derek allowed guardedly.

I sipped my beer and asked him to tell me what he knew of Vincent Hooke. They worked at the same college. Derek taught Engineering there. 'Hooke?' He glowered. But that meant little. It is merely the way a Yorkshireman looks when he is thinking. 'I don't have much to do wi' chap meself. But I've not been very impressed with what I've seen. It's his air of' – Derek took a great swig of his pint to clarify his analysis – 'toffee-nosed superiority. As though

28

he felt called to higher things and was compelling himself to submit to teaching as a kind of punishment.'

'That's very interesting.'

'How he got the job in the first place is a bit of a mystery. He's not got a degree, and they usually insist on that in Humanities. They reckon the Boss must've tekken a fancy to him. We've a Principal who has a fondness for oddballs. That's how we come to be lumbered with an RE teacher who's a raving atheist and assorted idiots who go weak at the knees when faced wi' a computer.' He drained his glass. I was barely a third of the way through my pint. 'How's your chess computer, by the way? Have you beat it yet?'

'Only at the lowest levels, and even then I feel the swine is merely indulging me. Incidentally, did you know that he's a writer?'

'Who, Hooke? Who told you that?'

'Hooke.'

Derek leered disparagingly.

7

Hooke called on me the following week. Everyone came to the bookshop eventually. I did not have to go out and meet them, I need only wait. It was rather like being a spider – 'Simon Cleaver!' He had his head tilted back as he came in, for he had been scanning the name-plate above the door.

I explained that I had the same name as my father and grandfather – 'You were named after the shop?' He glanced around in good humour, savouring from a fastidious distance the collapsed appearance of the place. Old books clung to the walls like bats; on the floor there were piles of out-of-date encyclopaedias and superannuated Bibles. In the dimness beneath the weary yellow ceiling, Hooke seemed even shorter than he had at Marion's house, where her presence had perhaps inflated him somewhat. Yet his self-contained air persisted in asserting that here was a personality to be reckoned with. It was the air of destiny he had, which he could never shake off.

Although it was Saturday afternoon, there were few customers. I wondered if Hooke would buy anything, but old books did not interest him. He liked crisp new paperbacks as fat as possible, crammed with fine print. 'So does Marion,' I said, and he laughed indulgently.

'Oh she's confessed that weakness to me! Harold Robbins, Jackie Collins – the sort of thing people devour to fill an empty life: lots of money and violence and soft porn. They fulfil a useful social function, preventing people from thinking. But I'm pretty sure Marion has lost her taste for them.'

'They're not the sort of novels you wrote?'

He shook his head briskly. It was like a bird worrying a worm. Yes, there was something birdlike about him. Not exactly an eagle nor yet a crow – 'I've sometimes wished I did,' he joked in answer to my query. He was at pains to point out that he did not scorn such authors, he did not grudge them their success; indeed there had been times when he had envied their fluency, their nimble incurious minds, their professionalism. He broke off to assure me that the fat paperbacks he preferred dealt with weightier matters, philosophy and psychology, history and religion. I mentioned a few names – Plato, Freud, Levi-Strauss – and he smiled and nodded. 'I've nearly finished your magnum opus, by the way. Very interesting! I would have got through it sooner but the new term has begun and the college is chaotic, as usual.' Apparently he mostly taught the rudiments of English to Catering and Technology students – 'They won't trust me with anything more demanding. Though one would have thought my peculiarly intimate acquaintance with literature would have proved useful. However, I have one A-level class this year. I've started them off on *Wuthering Heights*.'

A customer came to the counter and I turned aside to serve her: a Classical Dictionary and Emerson's *Essays* with a damaged spine – four quid the lot. Hooke glanced at his watch and said that he must be going: Marion was eager to show him the progress that had been made on the flat above her shop. 'I believe it was your idea?' He smiled warmly, thanking me for the interest I took in his affair. 'Once I've moved in, we'll be able to see a lot of each other. It's so good to have someone intelligent to talk to.'

'But at the college aren't there—?'

'Dick-heads for the most part,' he sighed.

I went with him to the door – an aimless courtesy – and we stood a moment outside. The pop-shop higher up the street was banging out its noise as usual – the canned chords of a synthesizer, the raucous howl of a vocalist – and we growled

31

in unison, Hooke and I; we had something in common. The shop had once been a handy chandler's where you could buy nails by the ounce and find practical implements for every task – at least so I am given to understand – but now it sold pop-records and played them incessantly, crouching behind windows plastered with posters raving of ecstatic gigs. 'Great God!' Hooke raged. 'If I had to stand that every day, I'd blow the place up.'

'I wish you would,' I whimpered. 'They're putting me out of business. It lowers the tone of the street. Many of my old and valued customers have been driven away.'

'Can you get the gelignite? I'll do it.'

The guttural crump of an explosion, a sudden sheet of flame and the air littered with falling bodies – youths in black leather jackets studded with steel; stout girls in short denim skirts – bouncing on the pavement amid a hailstorm of spinning discs black and gold. 'It's so hideous, so mindless!' Hooke ranted. 'And it's everywhere. They own the earth. Democracy serviced by gutter journalists and publicity punks, all polythened over with wrap-around pop! The end of beauty and innocence and greatness! The Dictatorship of the Proletariat.'

I looked at him.

'But what's the use,' he concluded. 'If you blew it up, from every fragment another bigger and even more crapulous pop-shop would spring. We are living in a cultural nightmare, Simon. The world belongs to the others. For them it's a candy-striped daydream. For us it's a nightmare.'

He paused. 'It's all over, I'm afraid. That's what I was trying to write about, you know. Small wonder I failed!'

He clutched my arm briefly then went off down the street. I stayed where I was, gazing at the pop-shop and trying to forgive it.

My parents were home again and on the following Monday evening I went with Marion to see them. When my father retired, they had given up the house in town where I was

32

born and had gone to live in a neighbouring village. It wasn't far away and I suggested walking there, but Marion insisted upon taking her car.

'I thought you'd acquired a taste for walking?'

'It all depends on who you're walking with,' she said tartly, unlocking the door of the Volvo so that I could get in beside her. 'Anyway, I've been working all day, rushed off my feet.' She started the car and we drove off. 'I enjoyed the shop once, it was like a game, but now I'm beginning to loathe it.'

'That's sad. Don't despise the lovely thing you created.'

'It takes up too much of my life. And it's so silly anyway. You shouldn't waste your life just making money.'

The village we drove to was a grim, close place high on a hill and there was a famous poet buried in the churchyard. It was a fine September evening, the sky dwindling from rose to dove-grey and I wished I was somewhere else, in a gentle forest glade with a rippling stream and a complaisant girl. We parked outside the cottage and my father came to the door. He greeted Marion effusively – 'Hello, glamour-puss!' – and gave me his hand. He looked like a tall thin monkey. He was spry and fit, his pipe clenched at a jaunty angle, his balding head weather-tanned and fluffed about with fine white hair. The stink of his pipe once more. He pranced before me like a visionary daft with the desire for immortality, his cracked old voice carolling the many glories he had seen on his travels, his manner fondly disparaging the unadventurous disposition of his stay-at-home son.

My mother looked small and frail. She sat quietly beneath his voice, striving stealthily to recover from the hectic whirl about the country. We spoke in an undertone while my father boasted to Marion that he had never felt better in his life – 'Are you all right, Mum? How is your heart?'

'Oh. . .' She smiled it aside.

'But do you really enjoy haring about like this?'

'Oh it's very interesting,' she assured me. 'And it's very good for your father. He thrives on it.'

They had been living in the cramped tourer my father

drove with heedless nonchalance, moving on from one place to another when he had seen his fill: King's Lynn and Swaffham, Thetford and Bury St Edmunds. 'Now this gateway, y'see,' he lectured later as we sat in the living room gazing blankly at the colour slides he projected onto a screen: 'this is Fourteenth Century. 1387 to be exact. The townsfolk were made to rebuild it as a punishment after they'd destroyed the old one.'

He had always crackled with a surplus of useless information, nosing after it with a burrowing enthusiasm and ruthlessly inflicting it on others – 'The castle mound is eighty-one feet high.' He had been forty-six when I was born, sixty-four when I left for university.

At some point in the evening Marion slipped away with my mother and I guessed what they would talk about. Later, as we drove home, I raised the point. 'Yes, I told her,' she confirmed.

'You told her everything?'

'Everything fit for her to hear.'

'That he was a writer?'

'That he is a good man. It was really rather nice,' she smiled, handling the steering wheel dextrously. 'I felt about eighteen, telling my Mum all about my boyfriend. Then she said, "Oh you'll have someone to look after you," and I felt about forty.'

'But you are forty.'

'Not in my mind I'm not.'

'A double negative. Things have come to a pretty pass. Are you going to introduce him to them?'

She was busy changing gear and did not reply.

8

I found myself thinking of him from time to time and I made an occasional note. I thought of him reading my book in his flat in Halifax – it was little more than a bedsitter; yet his salary would have permitted a better apartment, one at least with a kitchen rather than a two-ring burner, a living room whose window did not concentrate exclusively on back yards. I thought of him in his exile, his punishment cell, raising his fine dark eyebrows over a page, his pinched beak of a nose dipping into the lines I had written. Now and then he might titter or sigh as some feature in the life of my hero – his poverty, his desperate Grub Street authorship, his savage denunciation of society – caught his fancy and solicited affinity.

He returned the book eventually, drawing it from the pocket of his fawn raincoat and placing it on my shop counter as though it was a passport and he a refugee seeking asylum. 'Good!' he pronounced, giving me a deep look. 'I won't say how good,' he added archly: 'it would only make you blush.' There was something Irish about him. As he came from Liverpool, that wasn't surprising. The chuckling evasiveness of the Irish, familiar and faintly derisive.

He praised my prose style and the organization of the book; he commented ruefully upon what he termed the 'unblinking objectivity' of my analysis. Then he went on to draw a fleeting comparison. Like Gissing, he had himself massacred hundreds of pages in an endeavour to write well. Like Gissing, he was a thief, having stolen books from the public library when he couldn't afford to buy them. Unlike Gissing, he was never caught. But like Gissing he was a man who reverenced the greatness of the past and, Gissing again, loathed the present world.

'But now I must be off,' he concluded, leaving me no time to investigate the issue. 'I am to be presented to Marion's son, the young genius.' He grimaced forlornly. 'Is it true that he's eight feet tall?'

Willy was home from Greece and Marion talked of him when we met the following day in the vegetarian restaurant that had once been a jail. We lunched together once a week as a rule: she looked after the bill but I insisted on paying for the Perrier water. There was always home-made soup – I believe carrot tops were an essential ingredient – and the main course was generally something unctuous with lentils. However – somewhat like a saint helplessly collapsing into sin after a gruelling stint of virtue – the sweet was invariably luscious, debauched with dollops of whipped cream.

'And of course he thought it was meant for him!'

There was something coarse and full-faced about my sister – dare I say common? – when she spoke as a mother. You were reminded of washing and ironing and maternal rebukes. 'He thought you were having the flat built for him? Oh dear.'

'Yes, it was embarrassing. He got all petulant and spotty-faced when I told him it wasn't.'

I scraped the filling out of my lentil and asparagus pie, and ate it. The pastry shell was wholemeal and consequently inedible. 'What did you tell him?'

'That it was for a friend of mine, a very good friend.'

'He was suspicious?'

'Sullen. I had this adolescent thundercloud hanging over me. Oh but God! he does annoy me sometimes. I mean I love him to bits, but just then I wasn't in the mood. I thought, you're nothing but a spoiled brat! Expecting a flat of your own to have orgies in when half of Africa's starving.'

That was very Hooke.

The restaurant was not especially busy for it was the

36

middle of the week, and now that it was autumn, tourists only appeared in numbers at the weekend. It was a pleasant murmurous room, low-ceilinged and splashed with sunlight. There were flowers and curious pottery in the deep window recesses; the original stone of the walls had been exposed and varnished prettily. The diners were respectably clad and all seemed well-bred, applying themselves to their food with the decorous lack of enthusiasm typical of the middle-class English. I recognized Brian Hargreaves at one of the tables. He lunched at the restaurant most days in the hope of seeing Marion: a widower of fifty-five, the inheritor of a small woollen mill that now manufactured plastic toys; a strong patient undemonstrative man who for years had wanted to marry her.

'Well, then we had one of those nasty blundering arguments,' she continued. 'But it only made me feel miserable and heartless; and I won't be seeing him for ages once he gets back to university. So I made it up with him.'

'How?'

'I seduced him,' she said coldly. 'I'm good at that, you know. With money. I took him to Manchester and bought him everything – compact discs and a coffee machine and trousers and socks. He kept saying *Great! Great!* his hair flopping about and his eyes like saucers. Poor darling.'

'And then he met Hooke? How did they get on?'

'Famously.'

A waitress served the cup of decaffeinated coffee Marion had ordered. I brought my spoon to bear on a dish of cream-smothered trifle.

'What did you talk about?' I asked Willy when I saw him later.

'Football mostly. That was after we'd disposed of Adorno and the Frankfurt Mob.'

Willy was tall and thin, dressed in the usual sloppy duds of his generation: a strange puce garment like a peasant's blouse, ragged jeans and, for some reason, great clumping boots of macho hide. Beneath his abundant brown hair his

37

face was moodily intelligent, the flesh creamy with youth. 'He's all right,' he decided.

'He is familiar with the Frankfurt School?'

'No one ever gets *familiar* with the Frankfurt School.'

They had talked of Adorno and Habermas, at least Willy had; then with the gentle wearied smile of a man who has long since outgrown the earnest obscurities of neo-Marxism (I could see it!) Hooke had turned the talk to football, Marion having informed him of her son's devotion to the sport. 'He has actually seen the great Dalglish play at Anfield!'

'Who is Dalglish?'

'Philistine! We discussed the wisdom of buying back Ian Rush for three million quid. Might it not fatally disrupt a manifestly successful forward line?'

'Are you being serious?'

'Football is serious. Anyway I liked his lack of pretentiousness. It was a test really, the Frankfurt School; but he saw through it at once.' He glanced at me. 'He's her latest, isn't he? An improvement on the others, I reckon.'

'Do you know he's written novels no one will publish?'

'I don't hold that against him.'

When I told Hooke of the impression Willy had formed of him – the image of a moderately enterprising oddball who knew that to be lived fully life must be relished in all its manifold variety – he snarled bitterly. 'I handled him! I handle kids like him every day at the college, except that they aren't usually as intelligent. But you can usually exploit their innocence; they generally fall for a bluff, provided you are sufficiently brazen about it.' His face was small and shiny with self-loathing. 'The kid's so intelligent – in love with ideas. The Frankfurt School!'

'But aren't people of his age generally more impressed with honesty than with intelligence?'

'He scared me to death, that's all I know. I felt ashamed of the little I've been able to comprehend. If I read Adorno now I wouldn't understand him.'

'Few people do.'

'It's terrible, you know, when you begin to get old

and everything starts disappearing. And you're as bad,' he went on, laughing to take the sting out of it. 'Published at twenty-five. And your book would've been published even if your tutor hadn't given you a leg up. It's got the kind of authority a published book should have.'

'But it's only an uncontroversial, middle-of-the-road biography,' I felt obliged to protest. 'There's nothing creative about it.'

He seemed comforted. And a few days later when I was helping him move his belongings from Halifax to the newly-completed flat, he was elated and energetic, sporting a measure of confidence. We piled his stuff into the back of my car and drove to the flat, which Marion had taken pleasure in furnishing. He gazed about the spacious living room where a moss-green carpet lapped walls of a delicate apricot hue. 'It's too good for me! If you knew, Simon, the grotty dumps I've lived in in the past.'

'With your wife?'

'For the most part.'

There was a large new desk against one wall and he went to it like someone meeting his fate. Above it Marion had hung a rather bad self-portrait she had painted at the age of nineteen. As he gazed at it, Hooke seemed to be making some fervent promise. Then he turned to me, half-sitting against the desk. 'When I left my wife I decided to give up writing for good. Since then, for three barren years, living alone, seeking compensation where I could, I've stuck to my vow. I've tried very hard to live the life of an ordinary schmuck – be a good teacher, do a useful job, be content with my lot.'

He paused. I said: 'It hasn't worked?' It was what I was expected to say.

He moved from the desk, strolling briskly about the apartment. There was a living room, a bedroom, a kitchen and the usual offices. The builder, harried and supervised by a relentless Marion, had done a good job. Hooke wasn't fully satisfied, however. Standing in the living room, he rubbed his hands then clasped them tightly. 'Something's missing,' he declared. 'I shall have to go to Liverpool and get it. Would you like to come with me?'

At the time I believed he wanted no more than the convenience of my car.

9

I was not familiar with the city and when we got to Liverpool I had to rely on Hooke for directions, which were not always specific. It was Saturday and the town centre was a sluggish chaos of traffic piled up among people. Road signs seemed to point in every direction and one-way streets frustrated progress. I had a blurred impression of crowds and shops. Some large buildings asserted a hapless neo-classical dignity; others were dilapidated and seemed to have been looted and burned. There were also gimcrack modern structures like huge crates left on the pavement, with bits of plastic stuck on them.

The crowds eddied and flowed, clung in clumps and surged across the road. Most of the people were dressed in the shapeless transitory garments common throughout the world – jeans and a cheap nylon anorak, insignia of a mindless uniformity. 'Lets get out of here!' Hooke cried. He urged me to drive through the Mersey Tunnel: 'The great umbilical cord connecting depravity with mediocrity!'

He was excited and I couldn't tell how much of it was anger. When we reached Wallasey, at the other end of the tunnel, I parked the car and he took me for a walk along a promenade which began above a stout sea-wall hung with dripping green scalps of seaweed. 'I was born here, I'm afraid, not in Liverpool. It accounts for my lifelong inferiority complex.' The tide was out and the beach was an expanse of oil-streaked mud. 'Look!' He clutched my arm. 'An oyster catcher. Must've lost its way.' Downstream was New Brighton where Malcolm Lowry had been born (*Under the Volcano*. . ?) and some time later, the tallest man in Britain. Upstream, beyond Wallasey, was Birkenhead where Wilfred Owen had been educated. 'The place is full of fascinating literary associations,' he grinned.

It was a mild hazy day, early October. Hooke strode along elatedly, inflating his chest with what he took to be pure sea air. One needs to have faith, in Wallasey. But after all, if you think far enough ahead, there is the Atlantic, the vast ocean. . . I enquired about his family and his childhood, details for my notebook; and he was eager to talk. I began to wonder if he had not brought me here for that purpose. Perhaps he hoped I would write his biography. And why not? He was probably one of the foremost unpublished novelists of his generation. Whatever the reason, he was anxious to tell me about himself, he wanted to be understood. Perhaps then I would be able to explain him to himself.

We turned off the promenade and entered a small ugly council estate, its houses daubed with surly pebbledash. I asked if he had been born here and he laughed scornfully: 'Hell, no. But this is the Purgatory you have to cross to get to the petit-bourgeois Paradise where we lived.' In plain terms, there was an avenue of modest private dwellings on a rise above the council estate and he had been born there. His father lived there still, surrounded by scouting trophies – his high-crowned Mountie's hat; a signed photograph of Lord Baden-Powell – and looked after by his eldest daughter now that his heart was failing. She was a spinster who attended Mass every day and had a special devotion for the Little Flower – apparently a pet name for St Theresa of Lisieux.

Told me of his mother. I see her: a slight dark woman with a tense face, dressed in the postwar austerity of the early 1950s: a headscarf, drab coat, lisle stockings. Hooke on 'austerity'. The word once carried connotations of dignified constraint, moral severity; now employed to imply misery, destitution,

the lack of a microwave or package holidays to Viareggio. . .
He hankers after a spiritual austerity, the soul stripped clean
for action, a life stringently dedicated to some great aim.

His mother a frail dark embittered woman with a shamed
love of poetry (Housman, Walter de la Mare) and the conviction that she has never had her deserts. Sitting alone and
locked away in the cold bedroom reading the romances she
borrowed from Boots' Library. Her hard life: three kids
and another that died; marriage with a poorly-paid teacher who would never be a headmaster but gloried in being
a scoutmaster – the knobby-kneed fun and ethics devised
by the Old Chief. A man who could never give her the
tenderness she ached for.

When Hooke was a schoolboy – short pants, socks pulled
up to his knees and turned over at the top to show the
pattern, school cap with a badge on it, navy-blue belted
raincoat – helping his mother to carry home the groceries in
patchwork shopping bags made of 'American leather'. They
have to trudge through the council estate where snotty-nosed
kids yell after them derisively: *Fur coat and no knickers!*
Little Vincent wants to kill them but his mother restrains
him (They would have torn him to pieces). Her arm about
him, her face close. She tells him he is better than they are.
He is different, of an altogether finer spirit and destined for
a vastly superior future. *Different.*

'I wrote about it,' he said tiredly, 'in a novel that was
mainly autobiographical. My last novel. Different from all
the others I'd written.'

We stood on the pavement in the council estate. There
were children playing in the gutter. Then suddenly a gang
of them brawled past us, *Shit!* and *Fuck!* spilling from them
like poisoned dolly-mixtures. Hooke turned away, abruptly
starting back in the direction of the promenade.

'Aren't we going to visit your father?' I asked, hurrying after him. He shook his head dourly. We reached the
promenade and sat on a bench there. He lit a cigarette and
talked of his mother's death.

When he was sixteen. He found her dying. She had stayed in
bed that morning, wasn't feeling very well. He took her a cup

43

of tea hoping to cheer her: they would have a chat, discuss his glowing school report. But when he entered the bedroom he missed her customary smile, for she wasn't looking at him; she was staring at nothing, transfixed by the great clang that had gone off in her head. Her hair hung lank, her face was rigid and shiny. She wasn't lying down but was crouched up oddly, like a terrified child, against the head of the bed. It was meningitis or a massive stroke – he was never sure what killed her. But what especially distressed him was the waste, the appalling incompleteness, the pitiful lack of fulfilment in her life.

The sun had broken through the haze momentarily and sunlight glinted upon the grey industrial escarpment of the opposite shore, the docks of north Liverpool where containerization had supplanted the living skills of stevedores. The river was empty, there wasn't even one of those container-ships which, as Sarah would tell me, look like floating wardrobes. Hooke sucked his cigarette and spoke of the loss of God.

He had been a fervent Catholic as a boy, kneeling in church and pondering the holy mystery of the Deity, the priest at the altar transfigured with power, transcending humanity and bringing God down to earth. When his mother was dying he had prayed strenuously, praying from the gut as though with prayer he could fashion a fortress to keep her from harm – Had he lost his faith when she died? But his glance told me I was being simplistic. It wasn't until he was eighteen and in the Sixth Form that the crisis had occurred; and it was an agonized insistence on truth, he claimed, which had provoked it.

He faced me urgently, wondering if a lapsed Protestant could possibly appreciate the spiritual earthquake he had suffered. What could I know of the intellectual nausea, the profound disillusionment it had cost him? He had lost a personal Christ, the loving presence which had hovered in his soul since childhood; he had known the collapse of that grand scheme which for all Catholics spans the universe and alone makes sense of life. . . It gave him a certain distinction, especially as I had known hardly anyone who took God seriously. He was a man who had endured momentous crises, affording him a turbulent inner life, creating an unruly spiritual landscape not unlike the torn and battered Wagnerian sunsets Marion had once painted. . . Did I choose that flippant comparison to protect myself?

'That was why I never went to university,' he explained. 'I was certainly meant to go; my teachers were planning on Oxbridge, to tell you the truth.' But the loss of God had made a hash of his schoolwork and he had done poorly in the final examinations. 'My father believed I'd done it on purpose to spite him, and I couldn't tell him the truth. We've never been able to talk about anything important.'

His father packed him off to a teacher training college. Little intellectual challenge there, I gather. Three year course. The college was in Liverpool and it was the free and easy 1960s, the city was a radical funfair of popular art. He met people who pursued a bohemian existence and by the time he left college he knew he must be a writer. His father was under the impression that he was going to be a teacher.

See them together in the back garden of the little house, the sun going down in shadowy dusk. His father's fierce joviality. They are chums at last. The boy has disappointed him in the past – never took to scouting, failed to make university – but all forgiven now; they are equals, both teachers, brutally overworked and scandalously underpaid toilers in the shit-strewn farmyard of education. 'You've a good safe career ahead of you.' Then Hooke, doubtless jerking his jaw the way he does when he is frightened: 'I mean to be a writer.' His father standing on the shaved lawn, his stocky figure braving the fading of the light: 'A writer?' He sucks at the word, trying to extract some meaning from it. A *writer*? He laughs briefly, his tone assured: 'You're not a writer, old chap.'

We sat on the bench while Hooke smoked another cigarette. It was midday and I was hungry. The promenade was practically deserted, the broad stretch of concrete. The

45

river was before us and there were large old houses at our backs, shielded by ungainly shrubbery. Afar off, boys rode bicycles, wheeling in aimless circles. A dog ran about the beach barking frantically, a man calling to him in vain. Beyond the iron railing, the river was either leaden or silver depending on your mood. Perhaps silver, if you believed in God – 'I'd like you to see this,' he said, handing me a folded paper which he drew from an inside pocket. Had he brought it on purpose?

It was a letter from his father, *My dear Son*, written more than twenty years ago, limp with age and slightly torn at the creases. *Further to our conversation the other evening.* The handwriting was small and firm. *It was never my intention to distress you and there was no reason for you to storm off like that, although the fact that you did so suggests that you appreciated the force of my argument and simply couldn't face it. I only want what is best for you, Vincent! Why can't we talk it over calmly, man to man? For you are a man now and it is time you put away these romantic notions. Do you think we haven't all entertained them at some time or other? The gay Bohemian life! But you're not cut out for it, believe me. You're too unstable. Your failure to qualify for university proves that. So banish these dreams that can only lead to frustration and failure! To be frank, I've never suspected any literary talent in you, and I should think I'm qualified to judge. So please do forget all about it. Face reality! Get on with the humble but essential task fate has allotted you. Stick with teaching, settle down, marry some decent girl and raise children, thanking God for the contentment which rewards an honest and industrious life. . . Your loving Father.*

10

We were driving back through the Mersey Tunnel. Vehicles came upon us from the opposite direction, sliding smoothly past. The car's windows were shut tight against petrol fumes and this induced an eerie muffled stillness that would have been silence but for the prolonged rumble of traffic. I thought of the tons of rock and water pressing down on us – 'And now you're an atheist, I take it?'

'Oh no.' Hooke paused. 'No, I've never been able to manage that. I can't reject the idea that there's some. . . some spiritual power animating the universe. What about you?'

'I have never felt the need for religion.'

'Yes,' he sighed. He had already come to the conclusion that I was a soulless rationalist. 'Sarah's like that. She's a natural-born atheist if ever there was one. No spiritual dimension to her.'

I wondered if he had discovered a spiritual dimension in Marion – 'Oh yes. Of course it's overlaid by the usual meretricious rubbish people pick up nowadays, bargain-basement values – but it's there. Wonder in the face of life, that's what I mean. Already she is rediscovering it for herself.'

We swooped up out of the tunnel into Liverpool. Though weak, the sunlight was startling for a moment. There was a pristine brilliance as though flags were flying and everything had been renewed while we were underground. Then streets and traffic and people oppressed consciousness once more, the tedious congestion of the world.

We left the car in a car-park and walked through the town centre in search of somewhere to lunch. 'This'll do,' Hooke said. He pulled me into a large shabby cafeteria where you took a tray to the counter and were served with food that seemed drenched in glue. The place was full of people who could afford nothing better – middle-aged women with grainy faces, old men, youngsters who were probably on the dole. Everyone seemed to be smoking and talking, their heads bent confidentially. Hooke found a table and we sat down, our bodies bulky in the mean cramped space. A waitress having swiped a dingy cloth over it, the surface of the table was smeared with trails of damp like the tracks a giant snail might have made.

Hooke had sausage and chips, I had pie and chips and was hungry enough to consume more than half of it, helping it down with mouthfuls of lukewarm tea. ' I often used to come here,' he said. 'It's good value.' His face was the face of a man in some unenterprising occupation – shop-assistant, postman – and for an unguarded moment I loved his simplicity, his lack of pretension, his placid acceptance of cheapness and scanty living where it didn't matter – 'Aren't you going to eat the rest?'

I offered him my plate and he set about it enthusiastically. 'The pie is only fair,' he agreed. 'But the chips are excellent.'

Afterwards we strolled in the town centre where shoppers besieged the large stores, the slick new shopping-precincts, coming away with purchases as though they had been looting. There were street-entertainers – a man playing a banjo and singing hoarsely, the old favourites; a couple of coloured boys performing a break dance to the heavy rock of a ghetto-blaster. Vendors sold fruit from barrows, novelties from open suitcases on the pavement. It contributed to the liveliness. There was was a flaunting air abroad, a sense of excitement; and I was a provincial. The crowd seemed carefree or at least shruggingly derisive, gamely putting up with a rough-and-tumble life. They spoke with an accent heard nowhere else in Britain and when they weren't cursing they

48

were laughing. It was their vitality that I found attractive. 'Oh God, the old place has me by the heart-strings again!' Hooke cried, parodying the love he dared not express openly. Yet his attitude was perhaps ambivalent. 'There's a kind of purgatorial privilege to living in Liverpool, you know. I've never really felt at home in Yorkshire. But here the past stalks me like devils and angels.' He glanced at me furtively. 'D'you think there's any chance your sister might fancy living here?'

I thought of Marion, her elegant figure sweeping through these battered streets, her eyes hardening with impatience. No sentimentalist, she would be instantly aware of the less appealing aspects of Liverpool – the derelict slump of buildings, the loutish graffiti scrawled on barren walls, the rubbish littering the pavement, all the signs of a city collapsing into bankruptcy and ruin. 'I think she would probably like to give it a good shaking,' I said.

In a pedestrianized area there was a large concrete tub where dusty plants sprouted among empty beer cans and plastic bags, polythene trays scored with the snot of dried gravy. A wooden bench was fixed to it and we sat down, Hooke lighting a cigarette. About us, a crowd surged sluggishly. The man with the banjo cried out against the canned cacophony of the transistor: *Some a these days, Yeh gona miss me, Honey!* There was something faintly Yankee in the Liverpool accent – that came from seafaring – but most of it was Dublin Irish with a catarrhal inflexion. None of it was Lancashire.

'When you're rested,' Hooke said solicitously, 'I'll take you to the place where I used to live.'

'Will your wife be there?'

'Let's hope not. I've still got my key. With any luck, we can sneak in while she's out.'

His tone suggested a big-breasted threatening termagant. 'Why are we going there?'

'There's something I've got to pick up.'

'Something for your flat?'

'You could say that.'

We got up and went back to the car. I drove into a minor

traffic jam beneath the ramparts of St George's Hall; then we were free and heading uphill out of the town centre, past the Adelphi Hotel and Lewis's store where Jacob Epstein had placed a naked man who stared urgently out to sea. Soon we approached the university and the Catholic cathedral, a modern edifice in shabby concrete. 'Christ in a crinoline,' Hooke said.

A journey into the past, for he had scarcely visited the place in three years. Why he wanted me to come along. Not an altogether pleasurable homecoming. Something of an ambush, in fact. Each street, each building had its memories and I imagine him constantly accosted by the roles he had once assumed: young man of promise, scallywag bohemian, dedicated author, failed writer. The pain in his face as he stared through the windscreen at those great old houses in Victorian terraces: a warren of flats and bedsitters. He had lived in Liverpool 8, discovering it when he was a student in the 1960s. People he got to know then, undergraduates and artists, middle-class mostly. They had given him his first taste of high culture and stylish living: wine and olives, Picasso and James Joyce, all-night parties and girls in black underwear. They had finished off Catholicism for him, disembarrassed him of his virginity. They had confirmed his belief that he was a writer. The lively loving youthfulness that had once fluttered its bunting over these streets and houses – 'So innocent!' he cried with a hopeless laugh.

Some of the big houses had been demolished – here and there, entire streets had disappeared – and of those that remained, some had been restored to a stunned resemblance of their original splendour. These were reserved for an affluent and successful generation, however – computer specialists, business consultants, people in the media. The house in which Hooke had lived with Sarah was part of a terrace that had not been restored and was somewhat dilapidated. I parked outside – there were a number of old cars in the gutter, the sort that seem but loosely held together – and we mounted the steps that led to the front door. Small pillars supported the lintel. The door gave onto

50

a dim cavernous hallway. 'It's right at the top, I'm afraid,' Hooke said and we climbed flights of stairs, passing the doors of other apartments and picking up the muffled wail of a baby, a burst of pop music, someone complaining loudly. We reached the top landing and paused for breath; then Hooke pressed a bell-push beside a card that still bore his name. No one came to the door. Relieved, he flourished a bunch of keys, fitting one into the lock and manipulating it stealthily, like a burglar.

We entered the attic flat. Servants had lived here when a single family occupied the house. I saw them – the timid consumptive tweeny, the fat cook, saying their prayers at night, pulling on their uniforms at dawn, rushing in panic at the command of a bell. A self-indulgent fantasy. The living room was low-ceilinged and the windows were small. This made the light dim and misty, giving the place a chilly, abandoned air. The furniture was undistinguished, purchased for utility rather than appearance: a slackly-sprung couch, a small dining table, a large dresser against the wall. Assuming that it had not changed radically since Hooke had left, it didn't look much like the residence of an intellectual. There were books and pictures but the pictures were conventional – Cézanne and Monet in lifeless reproduction – and there was nothing that might suggest the presence of a forceful and original personality. It was the home of someone who worked for a living. It might have been anybody's.

'She's let the place go,' Hooke said. 'It was never as untidy as this.'

I guessed that when they lived together, he had been the one to insist on tidiness. It went with the constrained, obsessive side to his character. He stood before the fireplace, pondering, and I wondered if he was disappointed not to have found her at home. He had not seen her for three years, though they had communicated by letter and telephone, pursuing a half-hearted debate on divorce. 'Did you live here long?'

'Years and years. I wrote most of my stuff here.'

I looked for evidence of his wife – the thick jumble

of books, mostly dealing with social work, on the shelves beside the fireplace; a pair of shoes with medium heels, somewhat scuffed, one of them lying on its side. The *Guardian* was strewn over the couch. 'She never could fold it properly,' Hooke said, picking it up and folding it properly. The headlines featured Gorbachev, the PLO and the IRA. I went to the dresser. Its top was crowded with letters and junk mail, bills and professional journals, a pair of tights rolled up, sundry small ornaments of no great interest and Solzhenitsyn's *Gulag Archipelago* open at page 178. There were also framed photographs and I examined them, looking for her. 'Is this your wife?'

'She's no longer really my wife, you know. That's all over with.' Hooke peered at the photograph. 'Yes, that's her – though I've not seen this one before. Must've had it taken when she graduated.'

Sarah wore black academic robes hired for the occasion. She was smiling self-consciously but there was also a subtle triumph in her face. She had got her degree, she had done something for herself. It was Hooke she was looking at. Though not strikingly pretty her face was appealing, with a clarity of expression suggesting good sense and honesty. But any woman might have managed that in a posed photograph.

'This would've been taken two years ago. She loved university and they thought a lot of her. They like having mature students: it makes them feel grown-up.' He tapped the photograph with his forefinger as a detective might have done. 'Notice the hair, the urchin cut. She hoped it would make her look younger. No sooner had she started university than she was after another man.'

'Did she find one?'

'Had an affair with some clapped-out lecturer.'

'Is that why you broke up?'

He left my side and I followed him out of the room, across a passage and into another room. It was long and narrow. There was a window at one end, a view of roofs and chimneypots. Near the door there was a large desk, its surface bare. 'She's kept everything just as it was. What do you make of that?' There was some strain in his attempt at sardonic humour. 'Does it mean she keeps expecting me to return, or does it indicate total indifference?'

'Which would you prefer?'

He went to the far end of the room, where a squat metal trunk stood beneath the window. 'This is what I've come for.' I joined him and we stood over the trunk like pirates with a chest of treasure. It was fastened by a central hasp with a padlock through its nose. He went down on one knee, produced a key and removed the padlock. Then he flung back the lid. The trunk was full of manuscripts, handwritten and typed, thick wads of paper. They lay on top of each other, canted at angles like the slabs of a structure that had collapsed. . .

That simile is too artful.

11

It was true then. He really had written all those novels. He
had brought me here to prove it. . . I was conscious of some
discomfort, a lowering of the spirits. Hooke reached into the
trunk and withdrew the manuscripts one by one, rather like
a man fishing for crabs with his bare hands. He examined
each novel in turn, opened it and glanced at a page or two,
then passed it on to me with a brief dispassionate comment.
One was about the hope and failure of socialism, another
dealt with the loss of religious belief and its consequences, a
third told the story of a man who discovers the killing power
of material possessions and worldly success. I didn't look at
them, I simply held them, one novel piled onto another in
my arms. It was as though he was an inspector of suspect
goods and I was his assistant. At length my studied passivity
made him self-conscious and he became angry. Suddenly
wrenching the manuscripts away from me, he flung them
all back into the trunk. 'Fuck the bastards,' he laughed.
Then he kicked the trunk.

'Surely they're not that bad?'

'I no longer know what they are. Twenty years of my
life.'

'I'd like to read them some time. . .' But really I wanted
nothing to do with his novels.

'Maybe I was on the wrong track all the time, writing
in the wrong direction.' He lowered the lid of the trunk
and sat on it. He lit a cigarette and spoke, embarrassedly,
of his attempt to deal in fictional form with the decadence
of Western Civilisation – the destruction of traditional

values and the emergence of false gods radiant with the seductive promise of capitalist affluence; life reduced to meaninglessness, society rife with thuggery and fraud. . . A tall order. But again I am protecting myself from him. Why not admit that he was a good man who had devoted himself to a hopeless task, preferring to fail in a noble endeavour than make a fancy career for himself with novels that would please the undiscriminating, unserious majority. It was just that one was not used to such idealistic ambition.

'But is there no hope?' I asked.

'My work has been rejected over and over again.'

'I meant for the world.'

He shrugged. Then he said: 'I came here today to take all my stuff back with me. I feel meaningless without it. But now what I'd like best is simply to be rid of it!'

I was startled. 'You want to destroy all you've written?'

'Wouldn't that be best?' His face glinted feverishly. 'We could take it now and dump it somewhere. We could bury it out on those moors of yours where murderers bury their victims!' He put out his cigarette, his face bent away from me. 'Then I could make a new start,' he mumbled.

'Is that wise?'

He had no time to decide whether my remark referred to the destruction of the novels or to his belief in a new start, for at that moment we both became aware that someone had entered the flat. Hooke moved swiftly, his jaw jerking. He left the room. I stayed where I was. A woman's voice cried out fearfully. Then she must have seen him. 'Oh it's you.'

After a moment I joined them in the living room. They stood a little apart from each other. Hooke turned to me, welcoming the diversion. 'Ah, this is Simon! Friend of mine from Yorkshire.'

Sarah smiled at me. 'I thought it was burglars.'

I took her hand; it was soft and cool. Her eyes were bright and searching beneath level brows. Her hair was fair and it clung to her head, urchin-cut. Her clothes were undistinguished – an anorak, a dark-blue blouse, skimpy cord trousers – as though she paid little heed to appearance. But of course she had not been expecting us. She turned to Hooke. 'What are you doing here anyway?'

'I just came for something. Well, my manuscripts actually. I'm glad you kept them.'

'Did you think I would've got rid of them? What do you want them for? I thought you'd given up writing.'

'If you thought that, why didn't you get rid of them?'

'I knew you'd want them some day.'

I intervened, embarrassed. I was sure they would prefer to be alone. Would it not be better if I went off and called for Hooke later? They nodded in a preoccupied fashion, eyeing each other. I left the flat and walked about for an hour, zipping up my suede blouson against the chill of evening. There were few people and little traffic. It was too early for tarts and muggers. I investigated the backstreets which lay behind the great terraces on the main road. The houses were smaller, built about the turn of the century, some of them quite tastefully refurbished. It was growing dark and the atmosphere was autumnal. The quiet lonely streets suited my mood. The gloom was melancholy and intimate, almost confiding, as though a horde of invisible lives pressed close upon me. It moved me strangely and I felt at home, quite as if the city had been awaiting my arrival.

I returned to the flat and Sarah opened the door. She was pleased to see me. Her manner was fussily shy, perhaps even a shade deferential. She eyed me curiously. Hooke had told her I was a published author and she had never seen one before – 'George Gissing? The *New Grub Street* feller?' This was accompanied, confusingly, by the offer of a cup of coffee.

'You've read Gissing?'

'Don't look so surprised. Actually I've only read the well-known ones.' She was moving into the kitchenette and I followed as though pulled by the reins of her voice. Hooke remained in the living room, sitting hunched over the fireplace.

'His stuff is quite powerful, isn't it? Full of a cranky kind of energy.'

'His novels are the history of his opinions.'

She was impressed. I did not tell her I was quoting from the *Quarterly Review* of 1902.

'He's really a one-eyed writer,' she declared, filling the kettle at the sink. 'His lack of understanding of the economic exploitation of the poor is just incredible. And of course, his attitude to women. . .' She rolled her eyes deploringly. 'I'd like to read your book though.'

Her voice was bright, touched with a Liverpool accent. Her face was close to me, fair and slender. She smelled clean, of toilet soap. Turning away, she dumped spoonfuls of instant coffee into three mugs then sloshed boiling water onto it. We returned to the living room. *A one-eyed writer.*

Hooke smoked a cigarette as he drank his coffee. Perhaps it tasted better that way. In the kitchenette Sarah had spoken to me freely as though we were friends, but now that all three of us were together we were uneasy, dragging the conversation through a series of unimportant topics – Yorkshire and Hooke's teaching, my bookshop, Sarah's struggles as a social worker. Eventually Hooke said, 'Well, we'd better be getting along.'

'Don't you want something to eat?' she cried as though it was a crisis. She looked at me. 'We could go for a take-away.'

'No, we'd better be off – before someone pinches Simon's car.'

Hooke got up. He jerked his head at me and I went with him to the study. I measured the trunk with my eye, wondering whether it would fit into the boot of my car. Hooke sighed troubledly. 'Maybe we'd better leave it for now. I'm thinking of your car. The weight. It could bust the axle.'

I glanced at him. 'You're not going to destroy them then?'

'Oh certainly! But some other time. It doesn't have to be done right away,' he exclaimed irritably. 'I'll just –' He stooped to the trunk and rummaged among the manuscripts until he found what he sought. 'Marion insists on reading something. I'll take her this.' He showed me a large envelope crammed with paper. 'My last novel, the one I was telling you about.'

He secured the trunk with the padlock and we left the room. Sarah rose when we returned to the living room. She was anxious and uncertain, her forehead ridged with lines. Hooke said goodbye. 'I'll be in touch about what we talked about.'

'You can have a divorce any time you like,' she said coldly.

I wanted to take her hand again to recapture the sensation of something slim and cool and soft, but Hooke pulled me away with him. At the last, however, as the door was closing behind us, I glimpsed her face and caught a swift collision of words which, roughly interpreted as I followed Hooke down the stairs, suggested that she hoped she would see me again.

We got into the car and I drove off. Traffic lights and one-way streets, the bleak glitter of a city night. Hooke sat beside me, nursing his manuscript. His face was thoughtful. I asked if it had been an ordeal, seeing his wife again. 'Oh no. I was a bit apprehensive at first,' he admitted. 'We were married a long time. But she has her own life now. And I could never go back to that . . . conspiracy.'

'Is that all it was?'

'It's what it became. Marriages do, you know.'

'Did you tell her about Marion?'

'Not exactly. We talked about the divorce. That was difficult enough. It's a bastard when they start crying.'

He had stuck to teaching for a while, his father's strictures not without their effect. But ultimately the desire to write, to be a writer, to fulfil his destiny, had driven him to produce a novel. Sent it to a publisher who liked it and suggested a rewrite. He thought his future was assured, threw up his job and went to London, where he lived on scraps – 'Picking up dog-ends in the street like Jesus being scourged!' But self-deprecation barely concealed his rueful admiration for the folly and courage of youth. And the glory of it: those weeks of heroic hardship as he worked on the rewrite. But when the novel was rewritten, the publisher was no longer interested. Aghast, Hooke sent it elsewhere. Rejected over and over again. The anguish of failure.

He had returned to Liverpool, seeking the comfort of his bohemian friends; but most of them had vanished into good safe jobs. He was alone, felt hopeless. Decided to give up writing, the foolish dream: his father had been right. Then he met Sarah – quite as though he had been meant to meet her. It was at a party; someone had brought her, then abandoned her, a CND supporter. *That's the last time he takes me on a march.* She was eighteen. Hooke talked to her, poured out his woes. See them together: the tense scowling young man, the ardent girl. She was as if sent to convince him he must keep on writing. She believed in him utterly. Was ready to devote her life to him.

We reached the town. I drew up outside Marion's shop but Hooke did not at once leave the car. He smiled at me. 'Well, it's been quite a day, hasn't it? You've learned a great deal about me. If you'd care to know more – there's this.' And he offered me the bulky envelope, which bore the title of his novel in bold black letters. *Few Are Chosen* it was called. 'It isn't finished. I couldn't finish it. At the time, I thought I was finished.'

'It's autobiographical?'

'Yes. Quite different from anything else I've done and – dare I say it? – essentially superior. I wanted to tell the truth as it had happened to me. The agony of an unpublished writer.'

'The *agony*?'

'The absurdity then. Maybe I should have called it *Up the Pole* or *In The Shit*. Would you care to have a look at it, tell me what you think?'

But I wouldn't take the lump of paper from him. 'Shouldn't you let Marion read it first?' My tone suggested he was guilty of a minor solecism.

He looked baffled and chidden. I reached across and opened the car door for him. As he got out, he said: 'Don't forget next Sunday.'

I drove off.

12

I did not want to see Marion and I'd had enough of Hooke. To avoid them I spent the following day in York visiting a man I had known at university, his sharp-witted wife and precocious children, his house (the old Rectory) and his Hockney prints, bottles of wine and sprawling talk among the Sunday supplements in the living room; his job with the Ministry of Defence; her concern for handicapped children; how to make a fortune buying shares in privatized industry; the latest Bertolucci film; Iris Murdoch's latest novel. My friends seemed to have created a relaxed success-ful life. It wasn't what I wanted for myself but it made Hooke's grittily earnest ambition seem absurd.

On Monday I had to open the bookshop and Marion cornered me there, arriving before midday in order to find me without customers. I kept my distance, standing behind the counter. She expressed her customary impatience with the slovenly shop: 'Every time I come in here I expect to find you covered in cobwebs. Where were you yesterday? I phoned you seven times.'

'Are you familiar with Emily Dickinson's poems about spiders? There's a marvellous one where she describes a spider *dancing softly to himself*. A captious critic might suspect sentimentality; but really the language is too fine and exact for that. She writes of the spider's *theories of light*. Cobwebs, you know. Consequently it is possible to talk of transcendent knowledge—'

'For God's sake,' she sighed, 'stop wittering.'

I judged she would be a head taller than Sarah. The day

was cold and she wore a chunky woollen sweater with a collar like a halter. Head erect, her hair tumbled and glowing, she eyed me severely. 'What happened in Liverpool? You met his wife, I believe. What's she like?' A necklace of large dull stones hung from her neck, highlighting the exquisite daggers of her fingernails when she toyed with them.

'Friendly. A bit common, but nice. A good loyal wife, I would say. She cried when he talked of divorce.'

'Some women cry at the drop of a hat. It's like going on strike.'

'They were married for a long time, for the most part living in a highminded poverty that scorned the world. He wrote his novels and she was his devoted slave, supporting him financially for most of the time.'

'Good for her.'

'But the novels were never published.'

'You mean her self-sacrifice was in vain?'

'I shouldn't think she looked at it that way.'

'Of course she didn't. She was grateful. He'd rescued her from a dull safe life. She probably felt as though she'd won first prize at the Bingo.'

I said nothing. Marion's bright teeth gnawed her bottom lip. She looked – one could not say like a rabbit, she was too tall for that. But possibly an aristocratic hare. 'Why aren't you happy for me?' she cried petulantly.

'I don't know.'

'You don't think we'll hit it off, do you? I mean on a long-term basis.'

'I wouldn't like him to use you the way he used his wife.'

'Oh, child! everyone uses everyone else. There's nothing new in that. But where there's love, at least there's the chance it will be fun.'

'But how do you think it would go? Will you marry?'

'That's not essential; we could live together. And Willy won't mind. He was very impressed with Vincent.'

'They could play football together,' I agreed. 'But is Hooke to stay a teacher? Would you be happy with that? You expect him to start writing again, I suppose.'

62

'I don't see why not.'

'And if he fails again?'

'I wish you wouldn't use that word.'

'He uses it himself.'

'Because he's so self-critical – too much for his own good. But it needn't be like that. He's had three years away from it; time enough to get over the past.'

'And make a new start?'

She examined me narrowly. 'You don't believe people can change, do you?'

'Change? No. Develop – perhaps; even if it's only down-hill.'

'You're such a miserable pessimist!'

She turned on her heel and left the shop. I did not see her for a few days. I attended choir practice in the Mechanics' Institute – 'Now we're for it,' Derek said as Jones flung us into the *Credo*. In unison we bawled our faith: *Credo!* . . . *Cre-do! In unum, unum Deum, in unum Deum, in unum Deum.* I couldn't get the theme out of my head as I sat alone in my living room later. In the bass it sounds particu-larly turgid. I turned to my chess computer. We were in the middle of a game and a tiny, baleful red light reminded me that it was my move. Pawn takes Knight, Bishop to Q1. . . Why? Pawn take Pawn, Bishop streaks out of his lair and the swine would have me checkmate. I switched the thing off, erasing its memory. One can always have the last word.

Later in the week I called on Marion. It was after dark, she was alone and pleased to see me, her smile assuring me that she had known I would seek her out sooner or later. The front room was mellow with firelight. A manuscript lay open on a small table beside her chair, her reading glasses angled across a page. 'Yes, it's one of his,' she said proudly. His last novel. Autobiographical. *Few Are Chosen*. 'It's very good indeed. The writing is very powerful. The life he's had. . . What he's gone through! I really do think he has talent, you know.'

'Then why hasn't he been published?'

'Many writers are published who are totally devoid of talent.'

'I'm not sure that answers my question.'

'And some great writers weren't published for years. Look at James Joyce. *Ulysses* was rejected by every publisher in London.'

She meant *Portrait of the Artist* presumably, but I let it go.

'He said you refused to read it. That hurt him, you know.'

'It wasn't that way exactly. I merely pointed out that, as a matter of courtesy, he should let you read it first.'

'But he really wants you to read it. And you'll be impressed when you do, I can tell you. There are so many fine things—' She turned to the manuscript and put on her glasses. 'Just listen to this.'

She read out two or three passages, her voice low and intense. Hooke had called his hero 'Victor Hogarth' and I learned something of his struggles, his novels, his great love of humanity. One passage was devoted to a description of sordid city streets, another made a scourging attack upon corruption and injustice. The writing was clotted with colourful metaphors. Hooke's voice boomed in the words and I thought of him writing them, inspired and urgent. . . Do you detect a hint of lofty disparagement? But it is so difficult to be utterly objective! Even now.

Marion removed her glasses. 'Will you read it when I've finished it?'

'I doubt it.'

'You're such a wimp. What are you afraid of?'

'I just don't like being got at. He wants to involve me. I don't want to be involved. He wants me to read it only so that I will say how marvellous it is. It's a conspiracy!'

'But perhaps it is marvellous. This one has never been rejected—'

'It was never *finished*. Why didn't he finish it, I wonder?'

'Perhaps he was afraid.'

When I got up to go, she reminded me that I had promised to go with him to Ainsworth Crag on Sunday. I groaned. I had forgotten all about the wretched expedition

– 'You can't back out of it now,' she declared remorselessly. 'You promised. And it means a lot to him.'

When he was a Wolf Cub, twelve years old, stubbed his toe and could only stare up at the mountain from below. 'Perhaps it was better that way.' He was spoiled as a child, his mother holding him close with a vicious possessiveness (Yes, see it that way: a sore instinct for revenge). His father was unhappy, wanting a greater share in his son, eager to make a man of him or at least a boy scout. Became a Wolf Cub to please his father and went off with the troop to camp. Didn't enjoy it much: his Difference. Adolescent horseplay in the tented wash place, half-naked youths yelling and scampering as they belaboured each other with towels. And the practical activities for tenderfoots, learning to light fires and tie knots in preparation for life's great emergencies. He turned aside: Different. All that mattered was the mountain, gazing up at it, musing upon it.

Like God. He had never been so close to a mountain before. Its overpowering assertion of beauty and grandeur. It was a sublime mystery, radiant with promise, offering transcendence – a life beyond the life he had been born into. The great stone cliff like a mighty compression of music or the whole of history gripped in one massive fist; bearing down upon him yet at the same time, by some grandfatherly magic, raising him to its own height and setting him upon its bald crown, from there to view the world and choose the provinces he was surely destined to conquer.

13

The weather was unpromising: thin grey cloud hovered close to the earth and the atmosphere was damp – doomladen, one might say in retrospect. I had to rise earlier than usual; what's more, I would miss the morning concert on Radio Three. Feeling mutinous, I drove to Marion's shop and waited for Hooke. Fat stone buildings surrounded me, rooted in the vacancy of Sunday morning, and I thought of Liverpool, the murmurous life of its streets. The only source of activity was a newsagent's on the corner. People came away from the shop scanning thick newspapers, searching for sex and violence – 'Wankers,' Hooke muttered, opening the car door and getting in beside me. 'Our green and pleasant land is steadily wanking itself to death.' He did not seem to be looking forward to the expedition.

I started the car and drove out of town. Hooke lighted a cigarette, ignoring the No Smoking order I had recently fixed to the dashboard. 'A pity Marion hasn't come,' he remarked.

'She hates hiking.'

'Oh I wouldn't say that. Your sister has hidden depths. We walked for miles in Italy.'

'But then she was on holiday. It's an exception to the rule.'

'People can change, you know.'

He is annoyed, I thought, because I won't read his wretched novel. I was annoyed for other reasons. Neither of us really wanted to undertake the expedition. He wound down the window and tossed out his cigarette end, but it blew back again, burying itself somewhere in the rear seat. 'Whoops!' he laughed. I stopped the car, got out and clambered into the back, hunting about until I had found the beastly thing. He observed me with some amusement, his manner implying that I attached too much importance to mere material possessions.

I drove on, parking finally at a lay-by on a country road. From here a path wound over the moors to Ainsworth Crag. Hooke laced up his boots. They were of modern design, light and tough, an artful blend of suede leather and stout nylon webbing. 'Constructed on scientific principles. Notice how the heels are raised to bring the weight forward onto the metatarsus.'

'I'm impressed. I thought you hated everything modern.'

'Don't stereotype me, young man. I get enough of that at the college. If there's anything I'm not, it's a stereotype. I'm not against modern technology as such. It's the fuck-up we've made of it that maddens me.'

He got up and stamped his shod feet on the roadway. He stood bravely, like one about to commence an alpine assault. I said, 'It's only a thousand feet high, you know.'

'I shall choose the severest route.' He glanced at the old waxed jacket I was wearing, my soft-soled trainers. He wore an anorak of professional cut and his doughty cord trousers were tucked into thick socks.

We mounted a stile and set off over rising moorland. It began to drizzle. The air was cold and I wished I'd brought gloves. Hooke raised his head and snuffed the breeze gallantly, much as his father might have done. As his boots scoffed over the muddy turf and my trainers squelched through it, he spoke of his love of nature. 'One of the really great consolations, Simon. Once I'm in among nature I become wholly absorbed and am at peace.'

I gazed about. There was nothing to see but a few doleful sheep. A drifting mist withheld the Crag from sight.

'Of course, you country people – often enough you can't appreciate what's right under your nose. Not,' he added emphatically, 'that I include you in that category.

Though it wouldn't do you any harm to get your nose out of a book now and then, and bare your soul to nature.'

I kept clenching and unclenching and clenching my hands in my pockets.

'I have always been grateful for the gift – heaven knows where I acquired it! Hardly from the philistine crew I got myself born into.'

'What gift?'

'You always want to stick to the point, don't you? That's been my trouble, too. The gift is the ability to appreciate beauty, whether in nature or in art. The passionate aesthetic response! What more is there in life that really matters?'

He answered his own question. There were four things that really mattered. Natural Beauty and High Culture, Human Culture, Human Companionship and Creative Work. They constituted the good life. All the rest was a wasteland of materialist crap.

The rain misted my glasses and I couldn't see; but I refused to wipe them, I preferred for the moment to live in a solipsistic blur. The path was narrow and we walked in single file, Hooke in the lead although I had to tell him which way to go. His voice came to me from, it seemed, the back of his head and I couldn't always hear what he was saying, for I wasn't always listening. I kept my head down, stubbornly concentrating on the watery opacity at my feet. Then he stopped suddenly, staring into the distance. 'Is that it?' he cried.

I wiped the rain from my glasses. Ainsworth Crag loomed dimly ahead, buttressed with slabs of rock streaked black with moss and moisture. It rose above the trees of a gorge about half a mile away.

'It looks so insignificant! Of course, I've not seen it since I was a child.'

'Size is relative. You can make a mountain out of a molehill.'

'Equally,' he snarled, 'you can make a molehill out of a mountain.'

We walked on. The path ended at a stile which gave

onto a main road that must be crossed before we could enter the gorge. We had to wait while cars tore past, their tyres hissing on the wet tarmac. People were out on a Sunday drive despite the weather, peering at the scenery smeared blobbily on the windscreen. 'A drive!' Hooke raged as we stood at the verge like beggars waiting upon the mercy of clashing chariots. 'It's all they want from life. The Englishman's castle is his car!'

'But perhaps they are baring their souls to nature?'

We managed to scamper across the road eventually, finding sanctuary in a grove of trees, their boughs laden with the golden decay of autumn. We made our way down the side of the gorge and crossed a footbridge over a stream. 'I wish I didn't hate the human world so much,' he reflected penitently. 'I am capable of loving individuals, however. I love Marion very much, you know.'

'Did you love Sarah very much?'

'I loved her for loving me. You know how it is in some relationships. I was the beloved, she was the lover. Being the lover is the more positive and honourable role, of course, and you probably get more fun out of it. To have one's life constantly ignited by the presence of another! The excitement, the precious tension!'

'The mortification, the misery.'

We reached the foot of the Crag, the great stone grandfather, and paused while Hooke smoked a cigarette, squatting beneath a tree from which raindrops fell at thoughtful intervals. 'That's what I want to be with Marion.'

'The lover?'

'I want to try and be selfless for once, totally devoted to another. At her mercy! She deserves it, after all.'

'But isn't there quite as much egoism in being the lover? Possibly more.' I threw a pebble at a dandelion. 'The desire to possess is pure egoism.'

'In this case, I've no choice. I love her more than she loves me, you know.'

'How do you know?'

'I am prepared to commit myself without stipulating any

69

conditions. I'll take the risk. But despite everything she says – everything she gives me – I cannot feel she is irrevocably committed. Not yet, at least. I still have to win her love. But that's the position I want to be in. It's what I need.'

'You mean it will be good for you? Get you writing again perhaps?'

'That's not what I mean.'

'But there's a contradiction. You want to be the selfless, heedless lover; yet you also want to be loved – which is the privilege of the beloved.'

He glanced at me pleadingly. 'I do love her. You believe that, don't you?'

'Does Marion believe it?'

'You have this irritating habit of answering one question with another. It keeps you safe, leaves you totally uncommitted.'

'I'm sorry.'

'I know I'm a great egoist – I'm an artist, after all. Tried to be, anyway. And doubtless I took Sarah's love for granted, took all she gave and exploited her. Cruelly! But now I want to change, to transcend the self.'

I threw another pebble at the dandelion. 'You know, I suppose, that Marion has had other lovers?'

I had assumed he did not know. But he chuckled wisely, drawing on his cigarette, spurting out smoke in a controlled jet. 'I know all about that. We had a – well, rather a tearful scene on that score. She confessed to these other affairs. I have to admit I was a little hard on her at first. It was disillusioning, after all. My problem is, I'm a bit of an innocent: I always believe women to be as pure as they seem.'

'You forgave her?'

'Oh God, yes. I know how temptation can arise, the flesh is weak, etc. She was quite upset. Wonderfully dramatic, the way she flung herself into remorse, really wallowing in it! I calmed her down at length, told her it didn't matter, all is forgiven, etc.'

'Let's go,' I said. Striding ahead, I hurled myself at the stupid vastness of rock.

I chose a strenuous route – wasn't that what he wanted? – and began the ascent, climbing furiously and inelegantly, stumbling among boulders and heather, withered stumps of hawthorn. He followed. A rock face offered itself and I climbed up and about it. I wanted bitterly to get away from him. But he laughed, regarding it as a game, a challenge: Callow Youth v. Seasoned Experience. I heard him clambering busily after me – 'I'm right behind you! Look out: here I come!' His smart boots bossed the rock, his lean hard figure moved agilely. I climbed faster, panting, my glasses blurred with rain and sweat and possibly tears, my intelligence standing aloof and deploring the foolish contest. I have never much enjoyed physical activity and I was out of condition. I was unhappy with heights, moreover, and quivered with the fear of falling. Hooke soon overtook me and swarmed ahead, his booted feet triumphing over me. He was laughing and joking – 'See you at the top!'

I paused, clinging to something, afraid to look down. I was feverishly hot and heaving for breath. Nature in the form of stone and soil confronted me glumly. Then suddenly – But it all happened so quickly and impossibly! – there was an odd yelp from above, a slithering rush and I stared helpless as Hooke, arms and legs whirling, crashed down past me in a wild plunge.

14

It was his own fault; I was not to blame. But at the time, shaken with panic, I felt I was. I even wished that I had fallen instead. For if he was dead. . . So embarrassing!

He lay some distance below me, his body wrenched in an unnatural attitude. An outcrop of rock and heather had arrested his fall. He didn't move, didn't answer when, my voice quavering, I called to him – 'Are you all right?' Obviously he wasn't all right and it then became my fearful duty to climb down to him. I didn't want to, wishing it was all a terrible dream. Eventually, gaining some control over my legs and clinging passionately to the rock as though falling was contagious, I began the descent. With every step, beseeching some God I had never deigned to recognize, I prayed that he wasn't dead. I was dizzy with culpability and, like a whimpering schoolboy, scared of what Marion would say when she heard what had happened.

I got down beside him and touched him tentatively. His eyes fluttered open and he groaned – *'Oh Christ!'* He looked up at me from some great depth of despair, his face polished ivory beneath the mud that caked it. But at least he wasn't dead; though he might be dying. I asked if he could walk, I begged him to get up. His head rocked from side to side; he closed his eyes. He was unconscious. I looked about, searching for help, someone to share the responsibility: there was no one in sight. I tore off my jacket – *Keep the patient warm*. I must have read it somewhere, possibly in the helpful pages of the ladies' magazine Marion enjoyed. I wrapped the jacket about Hooke's body then set off down the slope, sliding and stumbling, wrenching my knee painfully – That was good. I was glad about the knee.

I came into the gorge, hobbling and crying for help. I floundered across the footbridge and up the other side, through the trees and onto the main road where the Sunday cars streamed past. I staggered into the road, waving my arms. A car pulled up and the driver wound down the window, a young man with the sort of moustache I loathe. I clung to the side of the car as though to prevent it escaping and made my urgent plea. The man got out and accompanied me back through the trees, the gorge, the footbridge. Hooke lay perhaps two hundred feet up the side of the crag but the man climbed to him easily despite the fact that he wore shoes with smooth soles. I plodded after him, feeling inexpressibly weary.

The man knelt and examined the body, his moustache drooping concernedly. 'Best get him to the hospital.' He fashioned a sling out of my jacket and we brought Hooke down. I was dazed and absentminded, hauling the body through a sluggish dream – the footbridge, the gorge, the trees: it seemed to take hours and Hooke groaned and cried out continually, his eyes shut tight with pain. 'Bust his ribs, I expect,' the man said.

We reached the car at last and he made room for Hooke on the rear seat, tossing aside some plastic toys. There was a joke sticker on the window: *If you come any closer, I'll fart*. We drove to Halifax – I believe I dozed a little on the way – and took Hooke to the hospital. He was at once surrounded by medical staff who asked questions in penetratingly loud voices; then he was despatched to an emergency ward. The man looked at me, raising his moustache in a smile, and I had the impression that he considered his Sunday well spent. He drove me to the lay-by where I had left my car and there we parted. I had no idea who he was, I didn't even learn his name.

The absorbing activity had dispelled my guilt, but it returned as soon as I faced Marion and told her of the

73

accident. She had always been ten years older than me and it was an advantage she would never relinquish – 'And, well, he fell.'

'What do you mean "he fell"?' She clutched her hands together to stop herself quivering. Her face looked haggard and fleshy.

'It wasn't my fault!'

She swept away, telephoning the hospital to find out how he was and I was suddenly cool with relief when I learned that, considering the uncompromising nature of the terrain over which his body had slithered and bounced, his injuries were comparatively slight: numerous contusions, a sprained ankle and two fractured ribs. We would be able to visit him later. 'You'll have to come along with me,' she said as though it was a punishment.

But when we visited the hospital and reached Hooke's bedside that evening, his first reaction – after grasping Marion's hand – was to thank me for saving his life. I didn't want that responsibility either and gave all credit to the man who had helped me – 'He really saved your life, you know.'

But Hooke wouldn't have it. 'Who would have gone for help in the first place?'

Marion brusquely put an end to this quibble. 'Are you in much pain, darling? You do look rather awful. I wish to God I'd never suggested that stupid expedition.'

'It was my idea,' Hooke insisted gallantly.

'But how on earth did it happen?'

'My foot slipped —'

'It was very wet up there,' I put in.

'It could have happened to anyone,' Hooke said, begging her forgiveness.

He sat up in bed, supported by pillows: a patient in a hospital ward, self-conscious, convinced that he had made a fool of himself and must look the part, a Stan Laurel character in striped pyjamas, his jowl unshaven, his hair scattered inanely. He was pale and limp, his body sagging about the great corset of bandages that held his ribs together;

74

but what I think concerned him more than his injuries was the fear that he was indistinguishable from the patients in other beds or the visitors who sat with them. These seemed for the most part to belong to the less enterprising section of the working class. Their faces were blunt and unimaginative or caved in with defeat – 'Oh God, he's fainted!' Marion cried.

Hooke's head had fallen onto his bandaged chest and his breath came snoringly. But it was no more than a drug-induced doze. 'He's still very weak,' said the nurse who came to look at him. Marion had risen as though to run away. The two women stood at the bedside gazing at the patient.

'Will he be all right?'

'Oh yes. Are you his wife?'

'Oh no.' Marion laughed confusedly.

We left the hospital and drove home. I followed her into her dark house and stayed while she made coffee, her face closed in thought. It was a time when idle comments were appropriate. 'I don't suppose anyone's informed the college. I'll give them a ring tomorrow.'

We sat drinking coffee at the kitchen table. She had not removed her topcoat and sat with it swirled dramatically about her. 'I hate those places,' she said.

'The hospital? I know what you mean. It's all right.'

'He looked awful, didn't he?'

'Oh I think, considering the —'

'No, I didn't mean awful in that way. . . Those pyjamas.' She shuddered.

We visited him again the following evening, waiting at the doors of the ward among a crowd of visitors: dumpy women with glasses, girls with pink hair-dos, craggy-faced men in clumping shoes, children with pudgy staring faces. When the nurse opened the doors they flocked into the ward and made for the beds, crying out a welcome, gripping the patient tightly and kissing him. Then they pulled bundles of food and other comforts out of the plastic carrier bags they had with them. I don't know why I found it so moving.

Hooke was feeling better and his smile signalled the news from afar. It was a knowing grin, mature and disparaging: his disability was a preposterous joke that would soon be forgotten. 'Why, you look really well,' Marion said, darting a kiss at his cheek while holding herself well away from the bed. 'You'll be able to leave in a day or two, won't you?'

'Well, it's a little more serious than that,' he laughed reproachfully.

But he was no longer looking at us; and Marion, still holding the salmon quiche she had specially created for him, was disregarded. I followed his gaze and a brief laugh erupted inside me. Sarah stood in the middle of the ward searching for her husband's bed, her smile coming and going as she encountered the faces turned to her enquiringly. She wore an anorak and an ordinary skirt – I learned later that she had come straight from work; yet to my eyes the casual outfit made her seem young with all the tousled, caught-out vulnerability of youth.

Embarrassed, Hooke told Marion who she was. We attracted her attention and she approached the bed, her gaze scanning our faces. 'What are you doing here?' Hooke croaked.

She regarded him a moment before speaking. 'Well, it seems I'm still your next-of-kin.'

He must have given her name and address when he had first been brought into the hospital. Perhaps in that agony of fear and pain he had wanted her, his next-of-kin – 'A policeman came and told me. At first I thought me Mam had been arrested for being drunk and disorderly.'

Her glance wavered between Hooke and myself while at the same time she examined Marion covertly. She may have sized up the situation at once – her perception was always swift and acute – and the reference to her Mam may have been designed to embarrass Hooke further, for she could see that he didn't want her there. 'I was going to come yesterday; but when I phoned up, they said you weren't in any danger.'

'You must be Sarah.' Marion smiled warmly and I introduced her, explaining that she was Hooke's landlady. We all laughed aimlessly at this: the idea that Marion – her faultless coiffure, her sparkling manner, her barbaric jewellery, her fingernails – could be anyone's landlady. 'You've come a long way,' she said, her unwavering smile hovering over Sarah's head. 'Did you have any trouble getting here?'

'It took me ages. I've been on and off bloody buses and trains since five o'clock.'

Yes, undoubtedly, she was bringing all her Liverpool swagger to bear on the woman she instinctively recognized as a rival. She turned back to Hooke. 'You're really all right though, aren't you?' She sat down, thanking me for the chair I gave her. 'Fancy falling off a mountain,' she exclaimed fondly. 'When I think of the peaks we've conquered in our time!'

'It could happen to anyone,' Hooke said.

'I brought you a few things.'

'Yes, well, just leave them—'

But it was too late, Sarah was already unloading the Tesco carrier bag she had with her, handing Hooke each item in turn: a limp bunch of grapes, a packet of cigarettes, two wrapped lumps which turned out to be bread rolls stuffed with ham, and a fat paperback – 'I've just finished it. It's fantastic. He's a really great writer. Oh Christ, it's so terrible what happened: the whole tragic perversion of socialism.'

Marion laughed uncertainly. I recognized the book and told Sarah I had read it. She turned to me eagerly, and at once – as in her kitchen a while ago – we were alone and absorbed in each other. 'It's really shattering, isn't it? What those people suffered. The injustice! It's hard to believe, yet it must be true.'

I nodded. 'I felt, however, that his irony was rather obvious in places.'

'Oh I wasn't worried about that.'

Hooke picked up the book. She had brought him Solzhenitsyn's *Gulag Archipelago*. He put it aside, raising his eyebrows at Marion.

'If you don't mind, I'll just grab one of these,' Sarah

said, taking one of the ham rolls. 'I've had no dinner and you've got that quiche.' She missed nothing.

'Oh you poor thing.' Marion crooned. 'You must come back with us and have a proper meal.'

'I've got to get back to Liverpool,' Sarah said with her mouth full. It was ridiculous, but I loved the way she suddenly thrust her wrist across her mouth and nose, sniffed and sighed then sat up straight and once more addressed herself to the ham roll.

'But will you be able to, tonight?' Marion wondered.

'You don't have a car?' I asked.

'Can't drive,' Hooke said.

'Yes, I can! I took lessons, passed the test first time.'

'You would,' he sneered.

'I even bought a little secondhand car.' She turned to me. 'Couple of weeks later, I come out in the morning, get into the thing – someone's pinched one of the wheels and propped it up on bricks! That's Liverpool for you. Never a dull moment. I haven't dared get one since, and those lessons cost me a fortune.'

'I don't see how you'll be able to get back tonight,' Marion persisted. 'Will she, Simon?'

'I doubt if there's a suitable train.'

We seemed to encroach on her like kindly guardians, tall and well-dressed, good-looking, well-spoken, practical and mature, taking her in hand. 'You can easily stay the night with me,' Marion said. 'Then you can go back early tomorrow.'

Sarah gazed at her.

'It's much the best solution,' I urged.

'I don't like taking time off.'

'Oh tush and piffle!' Marion laughed. 'Everyone likes to escape work when they can.'

'Do they?' Sarah turned back to Hooke. 'Anyway, what about you? I've hardly had a word with you yet. I've not even heard how it happened.'

'My foot slipped.'

'It was very wet up there.'

78

I took over, telling the story of the expedition and making the most of it. I doubt if I've often given a better performance. I was witty and deft, charmingly self-deprecating when referring to my own part in the adventure; and Sarah enjoyed it, she kept her eyes on my face. Then a nurse came down the ward announcing the end of the visiting period and we all got up to go.

Hooke looked cheated. I patted his shoulder, Marion touched his hand, Sarah grasped his arm. She stood over him, her manner uncertain. 'Look, if you want to, when you get out, you could come home for a bit. I mean to Liverpool.'

'Thanks, but it won't be necessary.'

We went down the ward, carrying off Sarah between us. She would stay the night. Marion would give her a bed in the top room where the ghostly loom sometimes rattled.

15

It was exciting, crouching in the back of Marion's car observing the two women in front. Sarah's head barely showed above the top of the seat but at times I caught a glimpse of her reflection in the darkened windscreen, her eyes and cheeks lit dimly from below and shrouded as in a veil. We were travelling back from Halifax and Marion was driving quite slowly, making the most of the opportunity to question Sarah while I was present. I wasn't sure whether she wanted me there for reassurance or to show me how easily she could dispose of Hooke's wife. She handled the big car with a languid expertness, expecting to do the same with Sarah. How elemental women were! My feelings kept jolting from one to the other. I admired my sister; I wanted to protect Sarah.

'I'm a social worker,' she replied when Marion asked what she did: 'struggling to hold together the rotten fabric of capitalist society.' She laughed awkwardly.

'Oh, but don't you think Mrs Thatcher – dear old ogress that she is – is really doing a good job? People have got to learn to stand on their own two feet.'

'Until they fall down a mountain.'

'We do need a government capable of compassion,' I put in but they ignored me. This was a subtle tussle between women; I was no more than a fey masculine squeak in the background.

The car ran smoothly on a country road, between stone walls. Trees appeared, glossed by the headlights, ragged branches hurled aloft like a preacher ranting a sermon;

then they were left behind. 'You're getting a divorce, I believe,' Marion said.

'Has he told you?' Sarah was mortified.

'Well, the fact is—' Marion swerved discreetly to avoid running down a rabbit: 'We're very good friends. I'm not simply his landlady.'

'Are you his girlfriend?'

It sounded so raw, her Liverpool accent making 'gurlfriend' out of it. Momentarily it placed Marion in a frilly setting in which engagement rings, Valentines and boxes of Black Magic figured prominently. I advanced Sarah's score at this point.

'Well – passionate friends, if you like,' Marion allowed. 'Gurlfriend' had unsettled her. She changed gear, the car climbing a hill. The moon's sharp sickle appeared in the windscreen. 'I think he's a really talented man,' she went on.

'Have you read anything he's written?'

Marion had prepared well for this. I awarded her a point – 'Oh yes. I'm reading one of his novels now. It's terribly well written.'

However – deduct half a point – she seemed briefly unsure of herself and was reluctant to engage in literary discussion with a woman who had read Solzhenitsyn. 'It's his last one. I simply can't put it down,' she concluded weakly.

'I've never read it.'

'Really? Why was that?'

'We were breaking up at the time.'

'Yes, that's always traumatic,' Marion agreed, her confidence restored. Besides, we were entering the town. Once in her house, there would be plenty of opportunities to patronize Sarah. 'I know from experience,' she added. 'But one feels a lot better once the legal formalities are completed.'

'Have you been divorced?'

'Oh yes. My husband wanted a faster car and a younger woman. Or was it the other way around? I was left with a growing boy to bring up. Of course, you haven't any children, have you?' Taking her eyes off the road, she smiled at Sarah tenderly. 'I really don't know whether that's an advantage or a drawback. A child takes up so much of your life. Yet despite everything, it's good to have someone to look after. A woman feels more complete somehow.'

I was crouched on the back seat, hot and urgent.

'Well, here we are.' Marion drew up at her house and we all got out, Sarah with her head bent.

'Look,' I said. 'There's really no reason why Sarah should stay the night. It's not yet nine.' I looked at her. 'I could easily drive you home tonight.'

'Oh would you, please?'

Marion was frustrated, tried to protest but knew it was hopeless. I left her standing beside her car and went off down the hill with Sarah. It was a mild evening. We walked along the high street and I pointed out the tourist attractions. She had never visited the town before and the shops interested her – the antique furniture and *objets d'art*, fashionable attire and glittering jewellery. But as Hooke would have done, she turned up her nose at the inflated prices, the sinful luxury. Then for the first time, she looked at me directly.

'It was a joint decision, you know, not to have children. We thought it wouldn't be fair on them while the future was so uncertain. We put off having them till he would be published.'

I smiled and said nothing. We walked side by side. Beyond a low stone wall, the river rushed softly in darkness. 'Actually I never really wanted kids,' she said.

'Are you sorry now?'

'I've got my work.'

We passed the packhorse bridge, the Baptist chapel – 'Sometimes I wish it had been different though. Some people have kids and they're living in dustbins. They love them though. Sometimes I wish it hadn't been so . . . mechanical.'

'Mechanical? Vincent?'

'It was like living with a machine, a lot of the time,

82

especially towards the end. All that mattered was writing, getting published. Life was just a means to an end.'

The things she said. I would have to remember them for my notebook.

'She's quite a character, your sister, isn't she? I always wanted to be tall and glamorous like that. Like a model. I can see why he's fallen for her.'

'It may not last, you know.'

'I don't care if it does.'

We walked up the cobbled lane. My car stood outside the bookshop. 'Is this your car?' she laughed. 'Well, it would be, wouldn't it?'

My car was – still is – a small neat saloon, a shiny modest receptacle. 'What do you mean?'

'It's like you.'

'Do you make a habit of judging people by their cars?'

'Oh yes.' She was teasing me. 'I didn't think you'd have a Porsche. I'm glad actually. I hate men who make love to their cars. And those huge things' – She meant Marion's Volvo – 'It's like riding in an upholstered tank. One of the things I liked about Vincent was that he never wanted a car.'

'Was there never one to suit him.'

'And this is your shop.'

She stood at the window examining by the light of a street lamp the volumes displayed: a frowsty set of Dickens tied with string, the complete works of H.G. Wells, the *Encyclopaedia Britannica* for 1959. I had not changed the display for some time and I was dismayed to discover how many of the books dealt with Edwardian mountaineering or the search for the source of the Nile. And those first editions: Warwick Deeping, Charles Morgan. . . 'Do you specialize?' she demanded.

'Only in dullness.' I was ashamed and enjoying it. 'Would you care to look inside?'

'All right. We mustn't stay long though.'

'It's not late, and I can get you to Liverpool in little over an hour. I drive fast but safely. You guessed that, of course, when you saw my car.'

Already we had a private joke to share. I unlocked the door and switched on the light. The shop was yellow and decrepit, cowering in its murky shell. She sauntered about. 'And this is what you do? This is your life?'

'What's wrong with it?'

'You know, don't you?'

'Would you care to see upstairs? It's where I live. We could have a drink before we set off.'

She followed me upstairs. 'Jekyll and Hyde,' she said when she saw my apartment.

'Downstairs is mostly my father, you know.'

'I prefer this,' she agreed.

'What would you like to drink?'

'A cup of tea would be nice.'

'You don't drink?'

'Everyone drinks. You have to, to stay alive.'

'I meant alcohol.'

'Oh God, yes. You know when you came with Vincent? I went through a whole bottle of sherry after he left.'

'Were you very upset?'

'I was very sick.'

I went into the kitchen, switching on the hi-fi in passing: a Bach Cantata. I filled the kettle and found the teapot. 'This is lovely,' Sarah called.

I returned to the living room. 'You enjoy Bach?'

'Is that what it is?'

I stood gazing at her and she became aware of her dowdy clothes, sensible shoes, lack of make-up. 'I didn't have time to change.' She scrubbed with her hand at a stain on the jumper she wore. 'That baby was sick on me.'

'What baby?'

'A client. I was holding him while his mother had a fight with a policeman.'

I made the tea and we sat drinking it while a soloist warbled the joys of a Christian death, *Heute, heute willst du mit mir ins Paradies*. Well, perhaps not the. . . However, Sarah was no longer listening. Restless, she got up and wandered about the room. 'You don't mind?' On my desk she found

84

the encyclopaedic entry I was compiling. She read from it, a roll-call: 'Dilettante, Dinesen, Dinggedicht' – She pronounced it 'Dinger-dicht' – 'Disraeli, Divine Comedy.'

I went to her, explaining what I was doing. 'I keep going back to Emily Dickinson. Do you know her poem about a spider?' I recited it, standing before her, feeling willowy: *The spider holds a silver ball, In unperceived hands . . . He plies from naught to naught, In unsubstantial trade . . . An hour to rear supreme, His theories of light. . .* 'It's a metaphor, of course. She's very transcendental.'

Sarah frowned. 'What's the last part mean?'

I repeated the final quatrain. 'For all his theories of light, you see, he ends up being brushed away by the Eternal Housewife.'

'Don't we all?' She turned aside. 'It was nice. I thought that was the way it was going to be when I married Vincent. You know – sitting on the floor, a bottle of wine, reading poetry to each other.'

'It didn't happen?'

'Oh we had a go. But he got impatient with my stupidity. Ey, what's this?' She had found the chess computer. 'Fantastic!' she breathed, poring over it. 'Can I have a go?'

I showed her how to operate the thing and she hazarded a few moves. The computer soon got the better of her. 'The rotten bastard!'

We returned to our chairs and she lay back in hers, regarding me speculatively. 'So here you are. This is your life.'

Her smile was inviting and I found myself telling her of the shop and the *Missa Solemnis* and Lucy Armstrong, my closeness to Marion and how she had tried to drown me, my interest in Hooke and my lack of ambition. 'You've said nothing about your book,' she noted. 'Aren't you going to write another?'

'I doubt it.'

'What's up with you?' she wondered.

'I must be afraid, wouldn't you say?'

'No, I think it's. . .' She screwed up her eyes in concentration. 'You've got this like weary sceptical attitude, as though nothing was worthwhile. That's your trouble.'

'The attitude of a coward,' I confirmed.

She glanced at her watch and got up. We left the apartment, I locked the door of the shop. As I handed her into my car I decided that I must make love to her as soon as possible.

16

I did not take the motorway, which was easily reached from the town, but chose a longer route across the moors. Sarah was beside me in the car and I was at the brink of her, in that early stage of a relationship rich in discovery and sensation, perhaps the best stage. The car seemed to travel soundlessly; the bluish night flowed past the windows; a great silence emanated from the moors beneath the moon. It was a romantic adventure. I wanted to surrender my sceptical self to a romantic mood the way other young men still managed it despite computers and space travel and the parody we have made of love. I felt the woman's gaze on my face as I drove. My gaze was held steadily and responsibly upon the road ahead. We spoke a little of Hooke – 'He was a writer all the time you were married to him?'

'Oh God, yes. He's never been anything else.'

'But he's written nothing now for three years.'

'Well, he may have come to the end of himself at last.'

The moors were left behind and we began to pass through small towns north of Manchester, places I had rarely visited, lumps of ugly building stuck together with neon signs and advertisement hoardings. It was difficult to sustain a romantic mood in such surroundings and I relinquished the rest of the journey to the motorway. At length a lighted sign signalled the terminus and then the city was upon us. I had not driven much in Liverpool at night and the sudden packed environment, the swarm of streets, traffic lights and traffic, was unnerving. It was like the time Marion had taken me on the Ghost Train at Blackpool, holding me tight and laughing at my fright as bogeys sprang out of the darkness. There was something of the same vengeful, female delight in Sarah now as she took charge and told me which way to go – 'Left, here. Left! Don't run into that bus, will you? He might not like it'– a teasing fondness as she discovered my anxious provinciality, mistaking it for innocence.

I stared through my spectacles, wrenching the steering wheel this way and that as I squirmed the car through a thicket of late traffic. She directed me down one street and along another. Finally we reached the terrace of old houses and I parked at the kerb. 'Come up for a minute and I'll make you a drink.'

We crossed the dark bare hallway and I followed her bottom up the stairs. 'It's right at the top, as you know. Vincent always liked to live above everyone else.' She unlocked the door of the flat and preceded me into the living room, tidying things away as she went, kicking a stray bottle beneath a chair and briskly snatching the *Guardian* from the couch, folding it properly. 'You'll have to excuse the mess. Most women rapidly degenerate into happy sluts when they live alone after having been married. It's a known fact.' She pulled off her anorak and fingered her hair. 'I never knew I could be like this. It's me Mam coming out in me. When I lived with Vincent I had to be really house-proud.'

They were not exactly poor, she said, but they were very careful, living on a strict budget. 'If there was such a thing as petit-bourgeois saints, we'd have been canonized.' A cramped existence, eventually, ruled by the mechanical routine of his writing. 'But don't think we weren't happy. He was really fun to live with – part of the time.' They had a fulfilled life. That was how people put it in those days. Their lofty ideals, their prudish disapproval of other people's muddled lives. Their isolation, eventually. No children, and they had little to do with either of their families. . . When she first took him home to the family house in Everton, her Mam smiling fatly, her sisters handing him round like a box of chocolates (*Ey kid, duzzen he talk posh?*) But they had

88

never really taken to him: *When's he gona gerra proper job?*

Standing beneath the light in the living room, she faced me with an appealing simplicity. Her navy blue jumper looked vaguely nautical; her skirt reached to her knees; her shoes were neat but creased with wear. I felt protective. There was something plucky and undaunted about her. With her short fair hair and delicate features she reminded me of a gallant little cabin-boy sent aloft, alone in her tatty crow's-nest, scanning the limitless grey wastes of the ocean. . . A somewhat extravagant image, I suppose. But it was the effect she had on me. From the beginning she made me feel lyrical and expansive.

I put my face to hers, conscious of the barrier of my glasses. She did not object to a friendly kiss but she kept her lips shut and they seemed to be trembling with laughter. She broke away. 'Make yourself at home. I'll get us summat to eat. I'm starving!'

I gazed about the living room: the rocking chair, the shelves of books, the cheap portable television. The place was rather battered and well used, but it was not un-welcoming. It quite lacked the air of tasteful contrivance that informed Marion's rooms. . . Yet I had never thought of her house in that way before.

I went into the passage, looked in on her as she worked in the kitchen slicing bread, cutting hunks of cheese. 'Have a look round,' she invited. 'Don't go in my bedroom,' she added as an afterthought. I went into the room Hooke had used as a study. Vincent. Sometimes now I thought of him as 'Vincent'. It was the women's influence. He came and went in my mind, sometimes 'Hooke' sometimes 'Vincent': the writer, the man. The man appealing for my friendship, the writer proposing a conspiracy.

I stood in the narrow bony room – the desk, the pad-locked trunk beneath the window, buried treasure: it was like being inside Hooke's head. There were pictures on the walls: Brahms glowering in his beard and one of the last self-portraits of Rembrandt. Two old men to watch over him; two great artists to keep him at it. On one wall there was an array of picture postcards, the sort tourists buy, medieval towns and views of the Alps. 'We brought them back from our holidays.'

Sarah had entered softly; she stood behind me. 'Did he have time for holidays?' I wondered.

'Oh we hitch-hiked all over Europe, in the early days; in search of Unspoiled Nature and Great Art. They weren't really holidays, I suppose. More like pilgrimages.'

I turned to her and she backed off with the gleam of a smile, assuming that I intended to kiss her. I followed her into the living room envying the naive earnestness of those holidays, sharing a tent with Sarah and climbing mountains that rose like great beacons of destiny. I could see Marion raising her eyebrows.

We sat beside the gas fire eating solid sandwiches and drinking tea from mugs. I watched for the moment when she would sniff and sigh and scrub her wrist across her nose and mouth. The revelation of Hooke's 'gurlfriend' still troubled her, though she did not refer to it directly. 'I thought he could've been a bit more welcoming, don't you? After I'd gone all that way to see him.'

'He was embarrassed. He isn't really badly injured but his self-esteem is dented. It's undignified, tumbling down a hill.'

'It's not a mountain?'

'We used to slide down it when we were kids.'

'He's getting old,' she lamented. 'I hope he'll be all right.'

'Oh a couple of busted ribs – he'll be out in a day or two.'

'That wasn't what I meant.'

I reached for another sandwich and asked how she had come to leave him – 'I didn't leave him. I'm still here, aren't I?'

'But you told him to go,' I guessed.

'It wasn't because he couldn't get published. You don't think that, do you? It was just that he wouldn't stop. I did it for his sake as much as for mine. I wanted to save both our lives: what was left of them.'

'Don't say that. You're hardly an old woman.'

'I'm older than you.'

'Seven years. It's nothing. And you look no more than. . . twenty-eight. There is a lovely fair delicacy about you. Age doesn't matter in the least.'

'Of course it doesn't.'

Perhaps one loves women precisely because they are so susceptible to flattery, loving their vulnerability.

He wouldn't stop. He could go on and on, writing his novels and having them rejected, plunging into despair and always resurfacing – as though he had found renewed determination down there – with another scheme for another novel which would surely, at last, be the one to succeed. But she could not go on. Her life disappearing with nothing to show for it.

She decided to make something of a life for herself. The university accepted her and it gave her status. She began to feel proud of herself; she had something of her own. She enjoys studying, loves ideas whether she understands them or not. Her intelligence grew, her confidence, and Hooke was diminished. She began to shut him out, gently and inexorably. He was disorientated, distressed. Wanting to save his marriage, desperate to prove himself, to regain her esteem, he embarked on his last great novel. She was unmoved, clung to her books, her new friends, the glamour of university. Something merciless about her now. Yes, I like that. The implacable woman coldly disentangling herself from an emotional encumbrance. And poor Vincent bashing out his novel, unable to finish it. *At the time, I thought I was finished.*

He resolved to do the sensible thing and give up writing, tear it all out of himself, the hateful poisonous gift. He would become an ordinary person; it was a kind of punishment. He wanted her to join him in an ordinary life, Darby and Joan with a steady job and a little car, package holidays, a semi on an estate, possibly even a child. She refused. An ordinary Hooke? It was a contradiction in terms.

It was past midnight. I got up to go. 'You've a long drive back,' she said worriedly. 'You can stay the night, if you like.'

91

The seizure of excitement one experiences on such occasions. It occurs in the solar plexus, the bunch of nerves there, sometimes mistakenly assumed to be the heart. 'Well, if you don't mind. It would be convenient.'

'You can sleep on that couch,' she realized, as though she had never before regarded the couch as an impromtu bed. She got up and left the room. I occupied myself polishing my glasses. She returned with an assortment of blankets and I helped her spread them upon the couch. We were laughing, tugging the blankets this way and that. 'You'll be really snug there,' she said, patting the bed absently the way a woman would. Her thin fingers. She wasn't wearing a wedding ring. 'Well. . .' She smiled frankly, heaving a breath. 'You'd better use the bathroom first. I must have a bath.'

She had gone by the time I returned to the living room. Ridiculous in underwear, I got between the blankets. The springs were slack and I sank down; it was like lying in a coffin. I did not attempt to sleep. I heard her come from the bedroom and enter the bathroom, then the dense rumble of water filling the bath. I lay in my coffin nursing an erection. At length the sound of water pouring away. When finally she emerged from the bathroom, I got up and went to her. I accosted her in the passage, which was dimly illumined by a lamp in the bedroom. The shadows made it easier; a light blazing overhead might have ruined everything.

She glanced at me in surprise – but I refused to take her expression into account. It is the only way. I took her in my arms and kissed her. She smelt wonderful, straight from the drenching hot sweetness of water. Her face was rosy, her hair damp. 'No,' she muttered as I removed her dressing-gown. Beneath, she wore a white cotton nightdress. I held her close, spreading my hands about her, the slim curve of her back and her rounded buttocks. 'Oh Christ,' she sighed, opening her mouth against mine and pressing her body close. I pulled up her nightdress until it was about her hips.

We moved into the bedroom, lay on the bed. I stroked

her belly, her breasts; she opened her legs. Vincent has been here before me, I thought as I fitted myself into her warm feathered nest. But there was no trace of him.

'Oh I love you!' she gasped, threshing about, staring at me wildly. The frenzy of orgasm, I suppose.

17

And then again halfway through the night when her timid stroking woke and aroused me, the woman hot for love. I slept heavily afterwards and the sun was shining when I woke. I lay for a moment in a eucharistic blaze of light, dazed with happiness. Sarah was already up and dressed, getting ready for work; I could hear her singing softly to herself as she made the breakfast. What is happening to me? I wondered.

I got up and went to her, swarmed myself about her. I nuzzled her neck, whispering wickedly. I was playful. *Playful*. I wanted her to come back to bed. She was dressed and I felt an urgent need to undress her, my body racing with sexual ambition. I was eager to repeat and if possible extend my repertoire of sexual skills and innovations; some of which, I had discovered, were entirely new to her and faintly shocking. 'Oh, for heaven's sake, Simon!' she laughed, shoving me away and searching for cornflakes.

I persisted, pestering her. I wanted to corrupt her a little, bend her to my will. I wanted to see her body get the better of her, lust burgeoning and overpowering her dutiful composure. Why did she have to go to work? She could tell them she was ill, we could spend the whole day together – Even as I babbled, I could see her harden into annoyance. 'Well, of course I'm going to work,' she said shortly. 'And I'm late, as it is.' I was suddenly aware that I was naked.

I went into the bedroom and dressed; then I joined her for breakfast at a small table in the living room.

She was whimsical and conciliatory, peering into my face – 'You have got a big one, haven't you? Somehow I thought it would be thin and twitchy.' The room faced west and the sun had not reached it yet. In the cold dim light she looked older, a woman with lines on her forehead.

I drove her to work. At night this had seemed a desperate area, surly with gangsters, seething with violence. But in the daytime and despite sunlight the streets were dreary, the houses unlovely, and, in general, Liverpool looked like a city on the morning after an unsuccessful uprising. The toppled barricades were everywhere – boarded-up shops, vandalized buildings, derelict cars, wrathful graffiti.

Sarah's office was somewhere in the suburbs and again I had to rely on her directions. She gave them in a clear practical voice that had nothing to do with the night before. I was disappointed and sulky. She smiled tolerantly and sought to divert me by talking of the clients she had to see that day: 'I've got this battered wife. Honest to God, I sometimes feel like battering her myself!' And there was an elderly woman terrified of eviction, a drug-happy couple suspected of abusing their children, an old man who needed additional benefits, an adolescent who lived on what he found in dustbins. It was an underworld I wanted nothing to do with, and my polite indifference turned her smile sour.

I drew up outside her office but she did not immediately leave the car. Absently she angled her head, peering into the rear-view mirror; and while tending her hair, she said that it would be better if we did not see each other for a while. Her tone suggested it was even possible we might never see each other again. My pleas only increased her firmness; and her remoteness – her clear cool presence, her angled head, compressed lips – made her infuriatingly desirable now that I had no right to her.

'The thing is' – Gazing at herself in the mirror, passive eyes meeting her passive eyes, her slender fingers thoughtfully twining strands of hair from her brow – 'I'm not sure I want an affair. You're really nice and I don't need to tell you how much I enjoyed last night. But I've never had an affair before and I'm not sure it's the sort of thing I want.' She opened the door, reached back swiftly to kiss me, then got out of the car. She smiled tenderly and I wondered if there wasn't a triumphant lift to her shoulders as she turned and walked away.

What had he said? Some wanked-out lecturer. . .

I drove into town and parked there. I strolled about, hands thrust deeply into the side pockets of my blouson. I was wearing a tweed hat woven from the fleece of Jacob's sheep. Perhaps it gave me a countrified air, for one or two people glanced curiously and a couple of girls giggled as they ducked and swayed past me. For some reason, this raised my spirits. I went to the Walker Art Gallery and enjoyed some of the pictures; found a secondhand bookshop and browsed contentedly.

> Despite everthing there is a saltiness in the air of Liverpool and – braving sentimentality – one thinks in terms of courage and derisive fortitude, a subversive vitality. It was invigorating. The place seemed to crowd about me, eager to claim me, unruly and disillusioned, jeering its Irish humour, promising marvels.
>
> At the Pier Head, the river glinting silver, dashed by a breeze. Astonishing array of buildings, great fortresses of commerce, towers and domes and pillared porticoes glorying in the sunlight, asserting a claim to power they no longer possess; for when one looked closer it was all grubby stone and cracked plaster, flaking paintwork, abandoned premises. Yet there was something appealing and familiar about their ragged grandeur, the spurious confidence with which they faced the broad river flowing to the Atlantic.

I drove home and opened the bookshop quite as if Sarah was at my shoulder urging duty. But then I closed it again and went along to Marion. Her shop wasn't busy and we were able to talk. She left Polly in charge and we went into the back where there was a little alcove for making coffee. She wanted to know what had happened.

'I stayed the night.'

'I thought you would.' She waited, smiling. For serving at the counter she wore a floral smock and it gave her a softened, almost motherly air.

'She has an old couch there, like a coffin. I spent an extremely uncomfortable night in it. Then we had breakfast together. Then she went off to work.'

She didn't altogether believe me. 'Of course she's terribly conscientious, isn't she?' She switched off the electric percolator but it continued to snort for a while. 'She's still in the same flat, isn't she? The one Vincent was so glad to get out of.'

'Was he?'

'Apparently it was less a matter of leaving than of scraping the place off him. Not that it was particularly slovenly. What he meant, I imagine, was a clinging mediocrity.'

'It's right at the top of an old house and the furniture looks as if it came from a jumble sale. It wouldn't suit you at all. It's altogether lacking in good taste. Yet it's a lively old muddle – like Liverpool.'

'And why wouldn't it suit me?' She poured the coffee, thin bangles sliding down onto her strong wrist.

I laughed, shaking my head. 'You couldn't live that sort of life. It wouldn't go with your nail varnish.'

'You mean I couldn't have stuck by him the way she did?'

'You wouldn't have stood for it. And quite rightly. It might have saved him.'

She did not seem to understand. Changing the subject she asked me to go with her to the hospital that evening, she wanted my moral support. 'It's really odd,' she confessed, 'and I hate myself for it. But when I see him in those stripy pyjamas, sitting up in that bed like someone perched on a woolly bed-pan. . .' She reached for her cup and bent her face to it.

I told her she would have to visit Hooke alone. 'Choir practice. I can't possibly miss it.'

'Oh come on!'

'They need me in the bass. I may not have much of a

voice; but it's musical intelligence that counts, and there I'm indispensable.'

'Bastard.'

'Make an effort,' I said coldly. 'Overcome your fastidiousness. The man will have been waiting all day to see you.'

After closing the shop and eating a meal while expecting the telephone to ring (I had given her my number) I went along to the Mechanics' Institute. It was an extra choir practice and most people turned up for it. The day was fast approaching when we would be arraigned in a public performance, perched above the orchestra in the concert hall, the men in creaking dinner-jackets and bow ties, the ladies in white blouses and long black skirts. We would be fatally committed; and in order to avoid the humiliation of a public disaster, everyone now cooperated urgently in a last mighty effort to master the work.

We had struggled through the rest of the *Credo* and had switchbacked over the brief entry in the *Sanctus*, throwing in a few *Nomine Dominis* for good measure. In the *Agnus Dei* there was little for us to do, other than alternately bellow and murmur Beethoven's disconcerting musical interpretation of the word for 'Peace' . . . Yet even as I write this I feel ashamed, loathing that flippant tone. The truth is, when we went over the *Missa Solemnis* that night, I found that my hostility to the work had weakened considerably. All at once it began to make aesthetic sense and my resistance crumbled. For instance, that moment in the *Credo* when, in dramatic contrast to the tumult of *Descendit in coelis* the tenors alone intone the tender line *Et incarnatus est*. . . Moved and astonished, I found myself yielding to the beauty the deaf old man had drawn out of his tortured guts.

A chastening experience.

18

'How was he?'

'Oh, quite well. He is taking little walks about the ward now. I took him a new pair of pyjamas – though he should be out by the weekend, if his spleen's all right.'

'His spleen?'

'Yes. It's one of those rather scruffy internal organs. They thought it might be damaged. While I was there,' she went on, her face tautening, 'I saw Mark.'

'He's back from Spain?'

Her ex-husband, once an architect and now a prosperous property developer, had been supervising the construction of a holiday village on the Costa del Sol; concrete cottages for time-sharing tourists. 'What was he doing in hospital?'

'He wasn't *in* hospital – he was visiting an employee who'd had a heart-attack. I imagine most of his employees have them, at some time or other.'

She smiled icily, surrounded by the glittering bazaar of her shop, her patrician head set against the tangerine sheen of a cashmere shawl, her hand toying with a stout wooden babushka – 'How was he?' I asked warily.

'Still a suave handsome ruffian; very friendly, oozing with cynical charm. He came over to the bed and I introduced him to Vincent.'

She looked away suddenly as though a customer needed her; but the shop was empty save for a couple at the far end who were merely sightseeing. She brought her gaze back to my face. 'I feel nothing for him now, you

99

know. Vincent is much the better man,' she insisted firmly. 'Yet they are curiously alike in some ways. Maybe that's what attracted me. They both go at life as though it was something you could hammer into shape; and I like men like that. They don't just wait for things to happen.'

'Vincent waited for twenty years.'

'Oh what nonsense! He was writing, struggling, engaged on a mighty task. There is all the difference in the world between him and Mark. Vincent's ideals are so high, so pure —' She laughed. 'That's probably why I hate to see him looking so lost and ordinary in a hospital bed, worrying about his spleen.'

When Sarah spoke you felt that she meant what she said. But Marion spoke mainly for effect, her words creating a charming suspension of meaning. And I was as bad. We had perfected the method between us. Speaking was a performance, an artful presentation of the self; a seduction, an evasion in which truth might be anywhere and meaning nowhere. A parody of communication that sought less to inform than to keep the receiver guessing.

'I'll go with you to see him tonight, if you like.'

'Oh would you? Better still,' she decided, 'you can go instead of me.'

It was preferable to sitting alone in my living room waiting for Sarah to phone. I wondered if he would look different now that I had made love to his wife, and whether I would feel different. I drove to the hospital that evening and joined the visitors as they streamed into the ward, bearing down on the beds and accosting the patients with a strenuous gaiety. Hooke had gone to some pains with his appearance. He wore his new pyjamas – they were mauve and silken – he was shaved, his hair was swept back from his brow and he was reading an improving book, Camus' *Myth of Sisyphus*. He laid it aside at my approach but his gaze slid at once from my face in search of Marion. I greeted him, offering a glib lie to explain her absence. He nodded glumly. 'She doesn't like to see me in here.

And – you're trapped! There's not a blessed thing you can do about your surroundings.'

I sat at his bedside in my chunky pilot-coat, the quiet distinction of my roll-collar jersey in fine white botany wool, the elegant planes of my hopsack trousers, the sub-dued power of my rawhide shoes. I was slim and healthy, no more than thirty, and I sat among beds that seemed monopolized by ailing old men. 'It might be different,' Hooke mused, 'if I had something awe-inspiring like cancer.'

'Then she wouldn't come at all.'

'She's a coward,' he agreed complacently. It was something else for which he could forgive her. 'But also, she's no hypocrite. She won't pretend to a gushing sympathy the way most people do, mainly because it's expected and looks good. I admire that,' he insisted. 'You wouldn't find Marion wearing a red plastic nose for the starving in Africa.'

'It would be unbecoming,' I agreed. 'How is your spleen, by the way?'

'Functioning perfectly. I met her ex-husband, you know – whatsisname.'

I would not help him.

'Mark,' he conceded. 'Did she tell you?'

'She mentioned it.'

'Christ! if he was in here, he'd still manage to look dashing – like D'Artagnan recovering from a sword thrust. He wore one of those big shaggy sheepskin coats. Probably caught and killed and skinned the poor beast with his own hands. And what I must've looked like, lying here with a bunch of seedy old dossers – poor sods – most of whom look as though they've been shovelled up off the road after life's great steamroller has flattened them!'

My brain was twitching irritably, querying whether I should have included D'Artagnan under 'D'. Perhaps a mention under Dumas was in order. 'She feels nothing for him now,' I said.

'A good job Sarah wasn't here to compound the embarrassment. I wish she hadn't come that night. She made such a fool of herself! Gnawing that ham roll like some deprived Bisto Kid. What Marion must've thought, I don't know. Thanks, by the way, for getting rid of her the way you did. That was very thoughtful. If she'd stayed the night with Marion, God only knows what she might have blabbed.'

'About you?'

'Don't let that little-girl innocence fool you. She can be as vindictive as any slighted woman; and it must have got on her tits, seeing Marion and realizing she was superseded. I had a letter from her this morning, about the divorce.'

'She wants it over with?'

'Humming and hahing for three years and now she wants it next week! There's all these bloody forms – she'll have to come and show me how to fill them in. I suppose one of us has to be the petitioner. I've as much right as she has; she committed adultery, after all. But that's unimportant compared with. . . It's the subtle way they get at you, y'see, Simon: making themselves indispensable, looking after everything – filling in forms, paying the rent, washing your underwear, arguing with the landlord. Protecting me. Genius at work, do not disturb! Oh we had a cosy little conspiracy, I can assure you. And it was all done out of love! I was the beloved. That's the way some women roast you, turning and lovingly turning you on the spit until you are done and done for. That's why, with Marion, I felt safe. I wouldn't have to perform the ill-starred genius day and night. I wouldn't have to put up with her pity! It would be a new start. I would be the lover.'

He stopped abruptly, glaring round. 'Hardly the setting for an ardent lover. This is the place where all the failures end up.'

'I don't agree.' I swept my hand about airily. 'There is success everywhere – survival, recovery! A constant

102

campaign waged against disease and death. It's a place of healing. One of the few institutions we can point to as possessing a truly altruistic purpose, devoted to doing good in the most sensible and practical way.'

Was it a parody? Hooke seemed to think so. But at that moment we were interrupted. There was a slight commotion behind me, a girl's voice exclaiming and then the sweeping rush of her presence. She stood above Hooke with her hands on her hips. 'Well, what have you been up to? Falling off a mountain – honestly! Who did you think you were – stout Cortez?'

'Good of you to come,' Hooke stammered.

She was a teacher at the college – Lecturers, I suppose I should call them – a thick-bodied young woman with a strained face and tied-back hair. Beneath her laughter and breezy manner, one glimpsed the brittle edge of anxiety and suppressed fury some women acquire when the teaching is tough. 'It's an official visit on behalf of the staff,' she announced, standing martially. 'I've been delegated to present you with this.'

She produced a large comic 'Get Well' card – the cartoon showed a bandaged patient leaping lustfully upon a nurse – on which his colleagues had inscribed their signatures. He showed it to me. Some of the signatories had appended a brief message: *Was it necessary to go to such lengths to avoid teaching Tech.One? – Missing you, you old sod (They're making me cover your Tech.One!) – Did you fall or was you pushed? –* 'That's Sandy Leach,' the girl laughed. 'And look at all the kisses Myra sends you, you lucky boy!'

'They're very kind,' he said drily. 'Give them my regards.'

'Hurry up and get fit, that's the point.' She glanced at me. 'We're short-handed enough as it is.'

'I think the doctor will insist on a few weeks' convalescence,' Hooke demurred.

'All right, but you can do some marking while you're at home, can't you? You've not broken your wrist; you can still manage ticks and crosses. Daniel said there was

103

a heap of stuff on your desk.'

She left as suddenly as she had arrived and we were both relieved. 'I've never liked her,' Hooke said. 'Beneath all her fun and bounce there's something sour and barren. Like the college itself.' He gazed at me. 'I don't want to go back. Being in here has corrupted me – being quite alone with myself, having the time to think things out. I've not been wasting my time, you know.'

'Of course not,' I agreed enthusiastically, boosting the patient's morale the way a visitor should; 'and once you get out, you'll have at least a few weeks to yourself. You'll be able to get a bit of writing done perhaps. Marion was very impressed with *Few Are Chosen*.'

'Oh it's a good novel. Good in parts anyway. If you read it, you'd have to admit that. But it could have been so much better.'

'Why didn't you finish it?'

'I was writing about failure and it got too depressing. The trouble is, the more you fail, the less confidence you're left with. So, although I know for a fact that, despite everything, my work was improving all the time – I couldn't take advantage of it, I no longer had the confidence to carry it off. I was writing with one hand while holding myself together with the other.'

I sat at his bedside, crouching forward like a priest hearing his confession. 'Will you finish it? If you could get it published all your troubles would be over.'

'Will you help me? You could if you would.'

I objected at once. 'Oh I couldn't do that, I really have no influence. I hardly know my publisher.'

He was staring at me. 'That wasn't what I meant. My God, d'you think I'd ask you to do that? How could you think such a thing?'

I said I was sorry.

'It's something I've never stooped to,' he protested. 'Get published by the back door, use someone's influence —'

Small wonder he had not been published.

104

Despite everything, he is convinced that he is lucky, he has
lived a lucky life – gifted with language, familiar with the
ecstasy of artistic creation. He cannot help feeling superior
to the other patients, for they will go to their graves – poor
sods – without ever having known a fraction of the joys he
has suffered. He was even lucky to fall down Ainsworth Crag,
and not just because I had saved his life. Something had
happened to him, something real, not the phantasmagoria
of failure. It had shaken up his life like a kaleidoscope,
fragments of consciousness drifting about in a glittering
mist, rearranging themselves in a promising new configuration.

In the ward, in the dark: alone with himself, pondering
his fall. For hours after it happened, apparently, his nerves
kept repeating the experience and he fell a thousand times.
Something put him through it again and again as if to make
sure he learned his lesson or perhaps simply to wear out horror through repetition. Think of him falling and pondering,
replaying the memory incessantly to extract the fullest possible meaning from it. 'I fell only halfway down,' he pointed
out. How much one might make of that! His life had been
saved and must be put to good use. His life had been saved
for a purpose. I think of him in the night, in the hospital
ward, lying awake: meaning returns to his life like a mother.

19

I got in touch with Mark – 'Do you think you could handle it?' I asked when he arrived on Sunday afternoon to inspect the bookshop.

'No problem. It's not my usual line but I'll be happy to serve you.'

'Will it be difficult to sell?'

'In this honeypot of a town? If I don't find you a buyer before Christmas, I'll buy it myself.'

'What would you do with it?'

'Wave a magic cheque and transform it into a catchy little boutique full of frilly purple knickers. Who wants books any more? Computers are much more fun. And your average citizen is perfectly content with a six-pack and a naughty video.'

He was wearing his sheepskin coat but the swagger it gave him was quite superfluous for he was full of it, even to the point of self-parody. 'It's an intellectual morgue,' he continued, strolling about and occasionally stamping on the floorboards. He picked at the plaster crumbling from rough stone walls and, raising his fine black head, inspected the dingy beams of the ceiling where I might have found dry rot had I known what to look for. A grey November afternoon hovered beyond the windows.

'Olde-world murkiness might have paid off in your father's time but in the modern world you've got to be clean. *Clean*! We rejoice in cleanliness, in hygiene. The Yanks have infected us with their neurosis and it's become our spiritual salvation. We worship the physical, the body. Why else the cult of Youth? We inhabit a playground of demo-cratic hedonism; and soon all your grubby Higher Culture will be relegated to a theme park of Quaintness, where chuckle-headed youths and young women whose brains have grown into their hair-dos will wander, hand in deodorized hand, giggling at the absurdities a few eccentrics cherished in the olden time.'

He handled these concepts, this vision of the future, with the fearless skill of a lion-tamer and they never bit him. They would have bitten Hooke and they should have bitten me; but Mark could smile at the ravening fangs, he could make the lions sit on their tails, armed as he was with an accommodating despair. He lived among nightmares – the despoilment of serious art; the earth choking with pol-lution; brute selfishness that left half the world to starve – and given the slightest provocation he would fling open the cage, let the beasts leap and roar. They had alarmed me, until he had taught me how to handle them. Then – leaving me with the memory of his handsomely tortured smile, the swashbuckling grimace of a man doomed to amorality – he had driven off with his new woman in his new Porsche while Marion had developed a passionate interest in the sale of expensive trinkets, her temples smouldering from the shock-therapy that had been burned into her.

He was dark and strong, compact with confidence, vibrant with the pouncing energy of an opportunist, and I had loved him once. 'Do you really intend to sell it?' he asked, smiling at me in the old way. 'What will you do then?'

'I haven't the faintest idea.'

'By the way,' he said as he prepared to leave, 'what price the rather seedy oddball Marion seems to have taken a fancy to? I saw them together in the hospital. You know him, of course. You saved his life when he fell down Ainsworth Crag.'

'So he maintains.'

'How can anyone fall off Ainsworth Crag? We used to slide down it. And what were you doing saving his life? Not the sort of thing you normally go in for, is it?'

107

'I can rise to the occasion when necessary. In this instance, I'm glad I did. He is a very interesting man, once you get to know him. Full of integrity.'

'Seeing her again, not having seen her for a while . . .' His smile strove to appear romantically ravaged. 'I sometimes wonder, you know, if I wasn't a fool.'

'Things haven't turned out well?'

'Oh she's a good lass,' he sighed, referring to his second wife. 'She suffers a lot from indigestion though; she's always chewing Rennies.' He went to the door. 'This goofball. . .Vincent. Marion's not really serious about him, is she?'

'I believe she is.'

'Dear-oh-dear!' He shook his head. There isn't a word for the soft snorting sequence of sound people make when they aren't really laughing.

I thought about him after he had left, leaning on the scarred wooden counter, the books huddled about me like children sold into slavery. I was no more than ten or eleven, a bespectacled schoolboy profoundly interested in cricket, when he had married Marion; and he was a prized batsman in the town eleven. Little boys loved the elegance of his leg-glance and cheered the sudden bounding vigour with which he would clout a full-toss for six – Oh there was such beauty in him then! And I had always wanted an elder brother or at least a younger father. Later, I felt the need for someone I could look up to, an embodiment of masculine virtue whose reproach would wither into contemptibility the murky sexual preoccupations that troubled me. I had admired him, loved him; I wanted to *be* him and was constantly seeking ways to earn his approval. He was an idealist in those days, an architect who yearned to design wholesome housing for the masses. But his rhetoric got the better of him in the end, and he had taught us how to do it, Marion and myself; we were his pupils. It was his flashy style we practised to this day.

Even after he left Marion, I was not free of him; he governed my embittered reaction, helping to create my present self. It was more than likely that the experience – ardent hero-worship followed by disillusionment and a reluctance thereafter to forfeit my trust – was responsible for some of my less appealing characteristics . . . I reached for my notebook, uncapped my fountain pen.

Later I went out, driving through the sombre afternoon to my parents' cottage. My mother let me in and clung to me. I put her aside and entered the front room, where my father sat in an armchair upholstered in floral chintz to match the curtains. His balding head – which had brown patches on it as though the earth was laying claim to him – was bowed over a heap of sound-cassettes as he tried to discover which piece of music he had recorded on which tape. In order to steal as much as possible from the BBC, he recorded a number of different pieces on the same tape – often without listening to them – then transferred them by means of a twin-cassette deck onto other tapes, isolating Beethoven from Bruckner, Mozart from Mendelssohn. But the system had broken down and he no longer knew where he was. He had recorded this on that instead of the other tape and now Stravinsky encroached on Delius and there were song cycles where there should have been oratorios – Ah the foolish old man! In any case he would be dead before he had listened to half of them.

I took over, sorting out the muddle with a controlled display of patience and toleration, transferring the contents of this tape onto that and playing a snatch of each to make sure, crouching at the cassette-recorder and punching buttons decisively, rewinding and re-recording, playing back and playing forward, creating order out of chaos while my father looked on helplessly, dully hating me, his skinny old body buckled in the chair. 'A pity you can't do as good a job with the shop,' he sneered at one point.

This gave me the opportunity to tell him I had decided to sell the place – 'We've discussed the possibility before, you know; and I think you indicated your agreement.'

He raised a few predictable objections – the shop had been in the family for three generations; bookselling was an honourable profession, a service to the town – but these faded to a yielding grumble once I disclosed the fabulous sum Mark had assured me the property would fetch. 'We can divide the profit equally: two-thirds for you and Mum, I'll take the rest. You'll have enough to circle the globe three or four times, I should think.'

He filled his pipe thoughtfully, his old eyes blurred with money. I left him and went upstairs to the little boudoir where my mother liked to sit and sew or read the *Daily Mail* with spectacles perched on her nose. She was sorting clothes in readiness for their next trip: they were off to Australia in a couple of weeks. There were distant relatives to stay with and my father would make field recordings of Aboriginal music chiefly in Sydney – 'But do you really want to go?' I asked anxiously. She looked frail and I feared she might not survive the journey.

'I'm looking forward to it,' she declared, her jaw grim. 'I shan't be sorry to get out of this miserable country for a while. England is going to the dogs.'

She wasn't much fun in this mood and I prepared to leave. She detained me, her voice sharp. 'What do you know of this man of Marion's? Why won't she bring him to see us?'

'But he's been in hospital.'

'He's out now.'

'I'm sure you'll meet him before you go away.'

'She says he's a lecturer.'

'Well, yes.'

'In a university?'

'Not exactly. But he's an intelligent man. And very fond of her. I thought you were pleased?'

'Yes, but who is he?' she persisted fretfully. 'Where does he come from? Who are his people? She tells me so little.'

'Isn't that her business? At all events, I'm quite sure he's more honourable than Mark proved to be.'

'Oh she made a fool of herself over Mark. She never did learn how to handle him.'

110

'You were the one who urged her to marry him.'

I left the cottage and slung myself into the car, feeling depressed. I drove out of the village, passing the churchyard where the famous poet rotted. Before I reached the main road, I stopped the car. I sat behind the steering wheel, gazing through the windscreen at stalky trees stripped bare for winter. Night was falling. Memory and desire lurched within me sluggishly. Then everything cleared suddenly and I felt bright, an instinctive grin shifting my mouth at the corners. Loving and reckless, I started the car and made for the motorway, driving to Liverpool fast and safely.

20

To have the smell of her naked, to bury my face in the creamy flesh of her belly – So fixed and intent was my desire, I hardly registered anything until I stood with her in the living room of the flat once more and she was in my arms, resting her head against my chest in a way that suggested helpless resignation; and the uncertainty with which she had greeted me – her surprised protest, the fleeting expression of pain in her face – was quite overcome and forgotten.

'I need you, Sarah! I've been terribly miserable without you.' Though hackneyed, it seemed the most suitable thing to say in the circumstances. But if I could have said it unselfconsciously, without calculation, without feeling a fraud. . . Yet I needed her and my desire was truth itself.

Above her bed, in the centre of the ceiling, there was an ornate plaster rose, grey and hideous. 'It reminds me of a dirty great scab,' she reflected, naked and gazing up at it. 'Sometimes while Vincent was making love to me I used to stare at it and plan how to get rid of it. I thought of – Well, could you scrape it off? But that might bring down the whole bloody ceiling!'

'You thought of this while he made love to you?'

'I shouldn't talk about it. It's not fair. The trouble was,' she went on nevertheless: 'I mean, I'd have him there, on my body; but often enough he seemed to be thinking about something else entirely.'

'His work,' I said, briefly envying his austere dedication to art.

'That's what is so terrible about you,' she laughed. 'When

112

you come to me, I feel I'm totally *there* before you. There's no escape. And when you – you know, lick me.' She drew in her breath swiftly. 'It drives me wild. I'm nothing but my body then, a randy old whore!'

She bent over me, kissing me solemnly, and I shall always remember the frivolous sob in her voice as she said: 'I'm in heaven, darling, when you make love to me.' How could something be both trite and beautiful at the same time? And did her words move me precisely because they revealed how vulnerable she was?

'I was so longing to see you again.'

'Then why didn't you get in touch?'

'I was afraid in case you weren't serious.' Her smile was timid and coy. 'You aren't really serious, are you? I don't care though,' she added at once, writhing herself on top of me as though to suppress an answer. 'I don't care what happens. You're here now and I've got you in my power!'

Naked, she straddled me and we did it that way, her body rocking upon me in a rapt incantation, her small hands gripping me, her woman's hips riding me, her eyes shut tight as if to prevent any pleasure escaping. I was giving her pleasure. It is sometimes cited as proof of love, this desire to give pleasure to the loved one. But I knew that what I enjoyed was a sense of power.

We left the bed at length and went to the bathroom, splashed in the bath-tub together. 'I never did this with Vincent. Oh God, Simon, I don't want to fall in love with you.'

It was about nine o'clock and we were hungry; I wanted to take her out for a meal. 'We can go for a take-away, eat it here,' she said. 'You don't have to spend your money. Anyway I don't want to share you with a restaurant full of people. I'm like Circe – is it Circe? I want to keep you enchanted.'

We ran like children – down the stairs, out into the street. Great barriers of buildings rose in the darkness; sodium street lights shed a brassy glow among harlot shadows. *Harlot shadows*? But I need a style suited to the

113

occasion, something exuberant yet falling short of literary refinement. I want something gaudy and vital to convey the romantic recklessness of that evening as we ran hand-in-hand, the shabby old city hunched about us and then a lighted thoroughfare like a fairground, where there were shops and eating-places and people. The Chinese take-away was crowded and everyone seemed happy. I rejoiced in the hiss and clatter that came from the kitchen, the swift rush of service at the counter: in my heightened state it seemed riotous. We ordered a selection of dishes and carried them back to the flat, ate them in the living room amid a litter of greasy cartons and cans of beer, a bohemian repast. I took a naive delight in it. 'Life is so simple and easy with you.'

'Do you have to go back tonight?' she asked, scooping up Chow Mein.

'Oh no. I love sleeping with you, you know.'

'What do you love about it?'

'I feel so relaxed and secure. It's blissful.'

'But what about your shop? I don't want you to neglect your business on my account.'

'There's nothing I can do about it. You're Circe; I'm enchanted.'

'Have some more sweet-and-sour pork.'

'In any case, I've decided to sell the shop.'

She gazed at me, a sticky spare-rib in her hand. 'You're selling it? Then what will you do?'

'Something outrageous, I hope. Come and live with you, if you'll have me.'

'You should write,' she said brusquely. 'You know how to do it. I read your book, you know. Got it out of the library.'

'I shall give you a copy for yourself, with a loving inscription written inside.'

'You should write another. It's not right to waste a talent when you've got one.'

'You really think I can write?'

'Of course. You're the dead opposite of Vincent. His stuff was all . . . passionate, indignant, as though he was

114

writing at the top of his voice all the time. But you're really cool. You never get sentimental or go over the top. And the writing is really precise, like it was engraved with a needle. I'm surprised the book isn't more well-known. It should be.'

I was inclined to agree with her.

'You give a very clear impression of your subject,' she went on. 'It's not always sympathetic; but that's all right. When it comes to an emotional part, you hold back and that creates a kind of vacuum, allowing the reader to fill it with feeling.'

'How well you put it.'

She forked the rice on her plate meditatively. 'The way Gissing worked, reminded me of Vincent. He would spend hours writing, day after day, buried alone in that room in there. I'd take him a coffee from time to time like someone feeding a lion.'

'Were you afraid of him?'

'Now and then, especially when he got mad and threw things at me. When you fail, you have to have someone to blame besides yourself. And he was ashamed, of course. All he'd promised me. All he'd promised himself.' She heaved a breath and scrubbed her nose and mouth with the back of her wrist. 'But when he got moody I could usually get round him by mothering him. That's really what he wanted.'

I refused strenuously to examine the implications of this. 'And what did you want?'

'Oh I was in awe of him at first. I thought he was a genius. Maybe that's partly why I married him, hoping some of his originality would brush off on me.'

'Do you still love him, Sarah?'

She shook her head. 'I love you now,' she mumbled. 'Ignore that,' she added hastily. 'It's this beer. I'm probably a bit drunk.'

'But I love you,' I assured her.

She put her plate aside, wiped her fingers on the paper towels we used as napkins. 'You don't have to say that, you know. We don't have to make any bargains.'

'If I am to write,' I pursued, 'what am I to write about? It's pointless to attempt to write seriously unless you have something worth saying.'

'My God, there's a million things! The struggle people have, to manage a decent life – You should meet some of my clients. And the corruption and cruelty everywhere, the injustice. Bad housing, poverty, the hypocrisy of these sodding Thatcherites!'

Was she going to prove boringly left-wing? I was irritable and depressed, partly because it wasn't what I wanted to write about and chiefly because I knew I wasn't capable of writing about it. In any case she had mistaken me. For a writer, having something to say means simply the imagination. I took off my glasses and polished them carefully. 'Now what's got into you?' she said, smiling.

'Do you remember Solzhenitsyn's *Gulag Archipelago*?'

'Of course; that's —'

'And don't you think it's a reasonable conjecture that what one might call creative opportunities are subject to history, time and place?'

She stared at me, her face on the brink of laughter. Perhaps she did not understand.

'I feel that those opportunities, that necessary cultural situation, no longer obtains in this country. We are played out, wearied by history and conquest, reduced to blandness. Art no longer seems capable of more than feeble pastiche. The creative opportunities are elsewhere – in Russia, South America, Eastern Europe perhaps: places where life is still felt intensely. They won't arise here. We can no longer summon up the necessary seriousness. Suffering merely embarrasses us.'

'God, you're intelligent,' she sighed. 'But that's all a load of bullshit, you know.'

I was suddenly joyful.

116

21

I called on Hooke and it was different now that I had made love to his wife again, establishing an understanding with her, an affair. I felt that I ought to confess. . . Is 'confess' the word I want? But the fact that she was no longer really his wife dissuaded me. There was no reason to feel guilty. In truth, I felt triumphant and thought that he must suspect the truth. Could he not tell from the swank of my manner, the shine in my face, that I had had her, that she loved me now? But his preoccupied air convinced me that Sarah had no place in his thoughts. Even Marion was marginal. What absorbed him was the burdensome obligation to write; he was gloomy and restless beneath the pressure to produce something.

He had been discharged from hospital – 'What a horrible expression that is! Bureaucracy dismissing its patched-up dependents!' – and it would be a while before he need return to teaching; with a little malingering he could eke out his convalescence until after Christmas. He had the time, the desire and certainly the motive to write. But he didn't know where or perhaps how to start. 'After more than three years,' he explained with a tired gesture.

His desk was primed for action – a pad of paper, a sheaf of ballpoints – and he sat beside it as though on the *qui vive* for inspiration, a man in his forties wearing a woollen cardigan and a nondescript shirt, his eyes dark and brooding, his face scarred with anxiety. Because of the rigid strapping about his ribs, he looked even more embattled and constrained than usual.

'Knowing where to start – charging myself up to take the chance! Lying there in hospital, it seemed easy and inevitable. I had everything to play for, couldn't wait to get started. I felt that the time was right. But now that I'm actually faced with it. . . I'm afraid,' he stated simply. 'Of it all happening over again. – Rejection. The same old kick in the balls. And Marion expects so much. She has such faith in me. It's a terrible burden. I have to prove myself.'

He got up and wandered about the living room, holding himself carefully. 'I feel really I should start at the beginning, at the bottom of the ladder. If only I *was* just starting out for the first time! If I didn't have the past to contend with. . . What I should do is simply practise my trade on some unassuming level. To hell with trying to write well, wrestling with themes that are too big and important to manage. I should regard myself simply as a craftsman, accept my limitations and write something – something popular, something simple and easy that offends no one. Lots of tits and bums and gratuitous violence.'

He paused and fished out a cigarette, looking at me expectantly. I shook my head. 'I think that would be the wrong course to take.'

He seemed relieved. But he would not at once relinquish the idea. 'I'm pretty sure Marion would think it was sensible. She wants me to be successful, obviously.'

'You're quite wrong. At one time a popular success might have appealed to her; but she seems to have changed. She's become rather weary of her own success, and it's one of the things she loathes about Mark. You have influenced her. She's never known anyone like you before, she told me herself. And what she particularly admires is your integrity. So you're. . .you're trapped, I'm afraid.' I laughed to make it easier for him. 'You've got to live up to her expectations. But they're also your own expectations, aren't they? Obviously then, you must carry on the way I'm sure you really want to – attempting to write something you believe is worth writing.'

I have since questioned the wisdom of this advice. But I doubted his ability to succeed in the marketplace of popular fiction. Perhaps also I didn't want him to collapse, after all his heroic struggle, into the banality of catchpenny authorship.

'That's what I hoped you would say,' he admitted, returning to the desk. Carefully resting his smouldering cigarette on the rim of an ashtray, he opened a drawer and drew out the manuscript of *Few Are Chosen*. He stroked it reflectively. 'I should really finish this and do it properly at last. That's what I'd really like to do. The trouble is. . .' He glanced at me shyly.

'Would you like me to read it?' I said resignedly. After all, I had made love to the man's wife.

I took it home with me, placed it on my own desk and looked at it. I circled round it, dipped into it from time to time, read a page and thought about it, made a note.

Childhood scenes often good. The stagnancy of Wallasey – those drowned scalps of seaweed; that promenade sorrowing in twilight mists, bewailing the absence of an ocean. The sensitive youth trapped in a philistine family. 'Victor Hogarth', his anguish and ecstasy. (Do I choose these words mainly for the play of assonance?) But difficult to gain a clear impression of the character, for Hooke's attitude is ambivalent, oscillating between admiration and self-pity, censure and praise. He doesn't know what to think of himself.

A turbulence in the writing like frothy waves coming at you, wave after wave breaking over you, his voice drenching the reader and bossing the narrative: one moment moralistic and wrathful, then gushing with a naive love of everything, then swinging a cutlass of sarcasm, then tittering unhappily over sexual love. *The roaring chasm of the vagina*. But the prose isn't always as bad as that. Plain and frank, at its best.

Victor's wife, based on Sarah? Grotesquely distorted. Did he ever see her as she really is? He fashions a crude stereotype – dull devoted housewife incapable of elevated feelings – that manages to omit everything I find attractive about her: her native intelligence and wit, her originality and sincerity, her lack of contrivance, capacity for love. Her blessed ordinariness.

119

I took the typescript with me when I visited her at the weekend. After making love – it had become a habit to strip off almost as soon as I entered the flat, her legs twining urgently about me – I showed her Hooke's novel. 'Would you like to read it?'

'You say he's going to rewrite it?'

'Well, he wants to write something.'

'I knew he'd go back to it.' She fingered the typescript, idly turning a page to see if there was a dedication. There wasn't. 'I never believed he really meant it when he said he was going to give up. He bounces, you see, that's the trouble. Bounce, bounce! One minute it's the end of the world and the next he's off on the old merry-go-round again. You try living with that for a few years.'

'And now he's prepared to start again. Think of the risk!'

'You admire him for that? I used to love him because he took risks – no regular job, no cosy pension to look forward to, living from hand to mouth. *Live dangerously*! as Nietzsche says. We took him at his word, not realizing the old fraud had a soft professor's job to keep him safe.'

I didn't want too much of this and reverted to Hooke's novel. 'Are you going to read it?'

'Have you read it?'

'Bits.'

'Only bits?' Her smile was ambiguous. 'Couldn't you bring yourself to read it properly? Didn't it deserve it?'

'I don't want to be more involved than I can help.'

'Does that go for me too?'

'Oh Sarah, my love!'

And it was necessary to kiss her breasts, etc. Then I tried to explain my attitude to Hooke, explaining it as much to myself. I talked of his hopeful dependence and my reluctance to be coerced into admiration and moral support. 'He wants me to accept his own evaluation of himself.'

'God, you're so simple, Simon. That's what everybody wants from a relationship.'

'But what do I get out of it? I don't need his admiration in

120

return. I don't want a conspiracy. But he persists in trying to involve me. Sometimes it's as though he was . . . predicating his future on my judgement, trying to make me a sort of agent of fate.'

'Are you really that important?'

'I saved his life, didn't I?'

'Yes, I daresay he'd make the most of that.'

'He's superstitious, isn't he?'

'Well, he was a Roman Catholic.'

'He invests life with more meaning than it warrants. He regards his own life as significant in a special sense.'

'Is that such a bad thing?'

She reached for the typescript, which lay half hidden among the bedclothes. 'What's it about?'

'Didn't he discuss it with you while he was writing it?'

'At that time, most of our discussions were slanging matches. Anyway he never talked about his novels until he'd finished them and could present them to me. With a flourish. He liked doing that,' she remembered.

I gave her a brief account of the novel, concentrating upon what I felt were – as far as I had read – the major events in the saga Hooke had made of his life: his mother's death and the loss of religion, writing and the struggle for recognition. 'The one arising out of the other, I suspect.'

'Am I in it?'

'Why not read it for yourself?'

'Why don't you give a straight answer for once?' She grabbed me. 'What's the bugger said about me? And he let your sister read it!'

Kissing her breasts, I assured her that no one would recognize her as Victor Hogarth's wife. 'It's a novel, after all.'

'Is it any good?'

'It may be very good, for all I know.'

'Oh let's forget about him!' Shoving the novel aside, she swarmed upon me.

Later I told her I wouldn't be able to see her the following weekend: it was the concert, I had to sing in the

121

choir. 'I'd love you to be there, of course. But it would be too awkward, don't you agree? I mean Vincent and Marion. You won't want to see them, I'm sure.'

'Why don't you want them to know about us? Are you scared of facing Vincent? The horror of embarrassment! Or are you just afraid your sister might not approve?'

I was irritated, frustratedly warding off guilt. 'All right, come to the concert. I'll get you a ticket. You can pick it up at the box office.'

'Do you mean it?'

Delighted, she kissed me; then she got off the bed and went to a large old wardrobe. 'What shall I wear? I need something that will knock her eye out. His too!'

She opened the wardrobe and stood before the wad of clothing hanging from a rail – her cotton frocks, simple blouses, practical skirts. Yet each (it was a lover's fancy) seemed unique because it was hers. She stood with her back to me, naked. Her shoulders were slender and vulnerable; but further down, her hips and bottom, her pale thighs, asserted a frank womanly fullness. She shook her head and turned to me. 'No, I won't come.'

'Why not?'

'It would be too embarrassing,' she laughed.

22

Writing and failing, at least in the world's eyes failing.
The experience of having your work rejected. He writes
of it with authority. So often, influenced by cinema which
simplifies to fit the pictures, failure is portrayed as something
merely drunk and disorderly. But real failure is hidden,
more often than not: someone cowering away in a corner
suffering a misery the world will never discover. Hooke
writes the truth, he knows it from the inside, the agony of
an unpublished writer. The sickening plunge into a despair
that threatens your very identity when your novel is rejected.
How often he suffered that ring at the doorbell and there is
the postman holding a package, cradling it in his arms and
grinning cheerily, thinking he has brought you a present. *A
dead baby*, Hooke calls it. He takes the package from the
postman and even grins in return to show how unconcerned
he is. Sarah is watching from some unobtrusive corner, her
belly writhing with guilt.

He conveys it so well: the crushing humiliation, the
shame. The fact that one has been tried and found wanting
(His father in the garden beneath a fading sky all those
years ago: *You're not a writer*) Maybe after all only failure
is *real*. Yet he went on and on, writing and being rejected
and writing again, year after year. Bounce, bounce! (Thus
she disparages his heroic persistence.) What kept him going?
What drives him now to start over again? I have to consider
the possibility of a genuine talent, deployed unsuccessfully
but refusing to be suppressed. And envy him. To have the
courage to pit oneself against the odds, daring failure time
and again, defiant to the last.

'Tell me the worst!' he said at once when I returned the

123

typescript. He was haggard and jovial, retreating into the kitchen to make coffee. 'I've nothing stronger, I'm afraid. Never was very interested in booze. It's rubbish, isn't it?' he went on, filling the kettle and staring at the wall.

'Of course not.' I found it hard to keep irritation out of my voice. 'It's very interesting.'

'But there are faults, of course? It's not a perfect novel?'

'Is there such a thing?'

'There you go again,' he laughed. He busied himself at the work counter, spooning ground coffee into a cafetiere. 'It's full of faults, I know. The trouble is, I write too quickly, I don't work things out beforehand, consequently there is always the danger of a muddle.'

'But it's only a first draft . . . I assume.'

'Well, yes,' he allowed hesitantly. 'If I'd finished it, I would have revised it thoroughly before sending it out.'

He wanted more. I sensed the tension of his nervous expectation and at the same time his horror of exposure. What would satisfy him? When I wrote a novel of my own I would know. Nothing the reader says is ever satisfactory. If the novel is published, the author no longer cares about your opinion. If it's unpublished, it's like having a conversation with a man striving to ride a bicycle in mid-air.

'There's a lot in it that's . . . very good. The childhood scenes. The experience of failure. Very good.'

He seemed absorbed in making the coffee. When it was ready he carried it into the living room and we sat down. 'Have a biscuit.'

There was a plate heaped with chocolate biscuits, of which he was very fond. He ate them rapidly, raising his coffee cup at intervals. 'Then your conclusion is' – he lit a cigarette – 'it's worth saving, working on and finishing?'

'Oh yes. But as you seem undecided about it and as it dates from a time when you were, as you said yourself, not at your best . . . might it not be better to put it aside for now and write something else, something that isn't autobiographical?'

'You think the autobiographical element spoils it?'

'I didn't say that. I just thought —'

'Many of the best authors are autobiographical: Lawrence, Joyce, Thomas Wolfe —'

'Céline, Proust, Solzhenitsyn: I know. I just thought —'

He exhaled smoke, shaking his head emphatically. 'I have to get this out of the way first. I hate to leave anything unfinished.' He glanced at me keenly. 'I want to draw a line under my past, ruling it off once and for all.'

'I see.'

'What should I concentrate on?' His head was bowed, his hand hovering over the biscuits. 'What needs improving most?'

'But I'm not an authority, you know. There may be nothing radically wrong with it. And if there is – only you can decide.'

'Have a go, anyway,' he mumbled.

'Well, there's your protagonist, Victor,' I offered. 'One doesn't get a very clear impression.'

'He's complicated,' Hooke agreed.

'I meant – he's supposed to be "different"; you make the point a number of times. Yet there is very little evidence of it. He's sensitive and intelligent, but so are thousands of others. There is little sense of a truly original personality.'

He wasn't expecting this. 'It's what he does that counts,' he objected numbly.

'And that's another thing: the novels he writes. We learn nothing about them other than that they are "remarkable".'

'Well, one can't bore the reader with a detailed account of each one.'

'My point is, if they are truly remarkable —'

'— why haven't they been published?'

We were on dangerous ground. He stared at me haggardly, sagging within his corset of surgical strapping. I tried to prop him up with praise but it wasn't very successful. 'The rendering of failure – the shame, the anguish – is really the best thing in the book.'

'I know that.'

'But why does he fail? The point is never cleared up.'

He put out his cigarette. 'There is a difference, you know, between "failure" and "lack of success".'

'Whatever you call it, the problem remains. Why doesn't he succeed and how is he to recover from failure? Judging from the last pages, it seemed you meant to end with him achieving some sort of success.'

'That's right.' He tilted his cup up against his face.

'How do you propose to do that?'

'Well, I thought. . . He leaves his wife, of course.'

'Yes, he's already done that. I felt, incidentally, that you were less than objective there. You could have shown more sympathy for the wife.'

He waved this aside, concentrating hard. 'Also I thought maybe his father could die.'

'That enables him to write a successful novel at last?'

'It releases him from the iron hand of the past – not only the tin gods of petit-bourgeois respectability but also the steel-tipped dogma of Roman Catholicism. But is that enough?' he wondered. 'Would it convince the reader? I take your point about his failure, too. Why exactly does the stupid bastard fail?' he raged.

I took another biscuit. 'I felt that at times, especially towards the end, you were forcing the narrative in a direction that was not perhaps imaginatively logical.'

He looked at me suspiciously.

'What I mean is, why does Victor have to succeed?' I was excited. I bit my biscuit forcibly. 'Might it not be more satisfying, more convincing, if he failed utterly and you ended the novel there? Then you don't have the problem of engineering his eventual success. I'm thinking in terms of a tragedy – the story of a man who believes he is a great writer. A tragedy of self-deception!' I exclaimed, spraying crumbs of biscuit.

'Isn't there enough tragedy in the world as it is?' Hooke said at length, eyeing me earnestly. 'I do feel, you know, that a writer has the duty to provide the reader with some hope. We need writers who will show the better side of humanity:

126

courage and self-sacrifice, dedication and integrity. Why have the usual dreary collapse into hopelessness? It's such a cliché. Art should be life-affirmative. Why not be daringly unconventional and for once show a man overcoming failure and achieving a genuine moral success?'

'You mean, out of hell into paradise?'

'Purgatory,' he chided gently. 'Out of purgatory.'

'Where you are purged of your sins?'

'Where you earn paradise.'

But I was uninterested in the quibble and anxious to leave, eager to get to my notebook. I made some excuse and he did not appear displeased; if anything, he seemed relieved. 'You've been a great help,' he assured me. 'If you'd found the novel hopeless, I would have destroyed it on the spot. As you seem to believe it's not altogether bad – suddenly I'm convinced it's worth finishing. I can't wait to get started on it!'

He came with me to the door. 'I knew that sharp-edged brain of yours would locate the weak spots. And I agree, there are problems. But I feel I can solve them now – I know I can. You've given me back my confidence. And this time I shan't rush into writing straight away. I'm going to work everything out and get it right before I start. I'm going to really *think* about it.'

I went home and made a note, two pages of notes, writing faster than usual.

23

Marion had discovered that I meant to sell the shop and she didn't know what to make of it. She had often urged me to take the step; yet now that I had done so, she was disconcerted. She had grown accustomed to sighing over me, savouring the romantic charm of my wasted life – the elegant spider limply dangling in the meshes of his own web, trapped in silken filaments of scepticism. She assumed Hooke's forthright example must have prompted my decision, and that gave her satisfaction. But she was offended because I had not consulted her beforehand, seeking her advice, her encouragement, her permission. 'And what will you do now, pray?'

I grinned lamely – last flicker of my discarded, enervated self – and made some evasive answer. Once the shop was sold I would have enough money to keep me for a while. Perhaps I would travel – 'Travel? What do you mean, travel? What sort of a life is that? You're as bad as your father.'

She sat in my living room, drinking whisky and looking forlorn, brusquely denied a role in my life. She wanted me to confide in her the way it had always been in the past, the time I had wept in her lap over my failure with Lucy Armstrong and the hours we had spent together when I was writing my book. Her eyes pleaded for recognition. 'Something's going on, isn't it? Don't think I haven't noticed. You've been away such a lot recently. I've not been able to find you when I wanted you.'

'When have you wanted me?'

128

'Oh you silly little brother! It doesn't make any difference to *us*, the fact that I have Vincent now.'

'Well —' I raised my glass. 'I have someone too.'

I told her of Sarah, observing her reaction as I did so, the procession of expressions across her lovely face which yet remained composed, as though the procession was taking place in a church. At first she seemed titillated as by a lewd joke, and there was a female knowingness in her malice – 'She's a fast worker!' But at length she settled for an airy, amused indifference. 'I wonder how long it will last? Of course, it's none of my business; nor indeed of Vincent's, I suppose, now the divorce is under way. You can hardly be said to have made a cuckold of him.'

'That was never my intention.'

'You're quite sure of that, are you?'

'I never expected it to happen. But I'm very glad it did.'

'You've made lots of notes about it, I'm sure.'

She drank her whisky, holding the liquor in her mouth a moment to prolong the fierce tingling. 'Isn't she a little old for you?'

'She's younger than you.'

'That isn't the point surely.'

She let me see that she was hurt. The droop of her red mouth took care of that while her eyes glinted fury which some trick of her nose modulated into mature disparagement.

'Age doesn't come into it,' I maintained. 'What I like about her is that she is – unfinished, somehow; and never will be finished. She is open to experience, doesn't bring a predictable response to it. She isn't trapped within herself, the way people often become as they grow older. She's a person, that's the point, not a contrivance. A warm, affectionate person.'

'An interesting analysis,' she conceded; 'but hardly the outpouring of a passionate lover. Are you in love with her?'

'Well – it comes and goes, doesn't it? I'm not sure what the words mean anyway.'

'I'm not sure you ever will. I've often thought you were

too detached and analytical, too careful with yourself, to fall in love. You can't let yourself go.'

We left it at that. She seemed convinced that I would tire of Sarah once my notebook was full.

The next day, Mark telephoned. He had found a purchaser for the shop. *Ready money. This fool is bristling with it.* The bookshop would be converted into an amusement arcade and Mark was prepared to invest some of his own money in the scheme. *Fruit machines. Space Invaders. It will go well with that record shop you've got at the top of the street. They'll reel out of there, brains soggy with pop, and empty their wallets in our establishment.*

I replaced the receiver, numbed. The die was cast. Life had me by the throat. A sudden gulping panic reduced me to cliché.

The concert took place on Sunday evening. Sarah telephoned and wished me luck – *I love you, darling.* The performance wasn't due to start till seven-thirty but the choir had to assemble earlier, for great attention was paid to the way we lined up and filed onto the stage, where ladies and gentlemen would segregate themselves meticulously, facing the audience in a petrified bouquet of evening dress. Our entrance must be orderly and dignified, giving the impression that we knew what we were about, that the choir and Beethoven were on the best of terms and everything was under control.

We waited, huddled in shadow at the back of the stage, greeting each other with suppressed hysteria. We were companions in distress, embarked on a hare-brained enterprise. Derek grasped my arm warmly and even the policeman ('Piece of bloody cake') seemed glad to see me. In the darkness, rueful murmurs and giggles fluttered about: 'Did you hear yon trumpets at rehearsal? I've heard better from a ragman's bugle' – 'Nice, isn't it? I got it from the Oxfam' – 'Is'll never reach those high As. Need a bloody stepladder' – 'I've no voice left. I've been sucking Sanderson's all day.'

We filed onto the stage, which was banked high in rows.

Sopranos and tenors sat on the right, contraltos and basses on the left. I stared out over the orchestra, the lights hot on my face. There were perhaps three hundred in the audience. Most were relatives and friends of the performers: elderly women in glasses with a gutsy appetite for a rousing chorus; respectably dressed men chastened by the prospect of an evening of serious music. There were also some off-cumders, generally bearded and garbed in tentatively unconventional attire. They were loyally supporting a local artistic venture comparable, in their view, with a village fête. Marion and Hooke sat together near the front, their arms and shoulders touching.

The soloists entered to a rattle of applause and we stood up. The National Anthem roared out absurdly and I kept my mouth shut: I would not sing on principle, refusing to countenance such banality. There was a moment's silence while England's empty boast echoed into vacancy, then Jones raised his baton. He smiled indulgently at the orchestra, stared imploringly at the choir. With a sonorous chord, the *Missa Solemnis* rose into sound.

My task is to entertain you, I appreciate that, but I am not going to be tempted into facile satire at the expense of my friends in the choir, most of whom are still alive and leading a blameless existence. Easy enough to caricature the concert as a catastrophe (alliteration alone might take care of that) but in fact, when it came at last to a public performance, we made an honest job of it and the result was about what you would expect of dedicated amateurs. We sang lustily, with great conviction – an amateur is someone who hasn't lost his innocence – and the orchestra banged and bellowed as required, sinking to a plaintive pianissimo in tender lyrical passages. The soloists were not outstanding but they did what they could with a cruelly demanding score.

And I was wedged in the midst of it, my awareness heightened, my defences lowered. I sang for Sarah but could scarcely hear my own voice in the din. Behind me, the proletarian basses boomed profoundly while at my side the altos sang with that candid, schoolgirl tone I much prefer to the reedy shrieks of sopranos.

We reached the *Credo*, that vigorous bounce into an opening chord and then the loyal male declamation, *Credo . . . Cre-do*! after which you swing into the rhythm of *In unum Dominum*. The choir has it all. The soloists warble a quartet at one point but essentially it is a hymn for the masses and the voices roll and soar through it with a kind of awakening splendour. After the *Crucifixus* and the dragging mournful theme of *Passus et sepultus est*, the tenors shout their triumph – *Et resurrexit tertia die*! – and a lively accompaniment carries you into *Et iteram venturus*. Then the complementary voices make their great acclamation, *Vivos! Vivos!* It doesn't appear to have much in common with Christ judging the living and the dead but it has everything to do with life itself, *Vivos! Vivos!* And once the altos began their exalted chant, *Et unam sanctam catholicam*, moving steadily through the forest of voices like a procession bearing candles and images – I was lost, I was carried away, my voice no longer mine but part of a vast articulation, an element in an immense constellation of sound.

Flushed, fervent, bestowing glory, I looked out over the audience, a scintillating mist before my eyes. I saw Marion and Hooke and felt myself pouring out over them in a loving benediction. Then for a moment, engulfed in the ecstasy of music, my own life seemed transfigured, piled high with possibilities, and my future was like a fairground whirling with merry-go-rounds, prancing horses and romping tigers, with laughing showgirls and droll clowns all with their faces turned towards me, welcoming me to an enthronement garlanded with love and joy, the rapture of fame . . . Such music is bad for you.

Enthusiastic applause brought me to my senses and then it was the interval. We filed off the stage knowing that the best was over, for the concluding sections of the *Missa Solemnis* are decidedly inferior to those which come earlier. There is less for the choir to do and too much for the soloists to express with sustained conviction.

I wandered into the foyer, bemused and unsteady, swaying a little as though I had been at sea in a storm. Marion found me and clutched me, her face glowing. She praised the performance – 'I do like something with lots of guts and noise to it' – and Hooke added his congratulations. He was accompanied by my parents; he had met them at last and they seemed prepared to like him. Had they not been flying to Australia in a couple of days they would have invited him to tea. 'I think he's quite charmed them,' Marion claimed as we followed them into the bar. She talked of his novel and was pleased that I had read it. 'I knew you'd enjoy it. He said you were very impressed with it. I'm so glad. He's already begun rewriting it, and it's so good to see him working at something he really understands and loves. It gives him a kind of authority.' She laughed confusedly. 'As though he'd suddenly grown two feet taller.'

There was something different about her. Her hair was looser, no longer cunningly contrived about her head but falling soft about her face, making her chin and cheeks seem rounder. Together with the dress she wore – not the stiff satin I expected but something in figured linen, the line blurred and flowing – it gave her rather an impudent appearance that seemed on the point of relaxing into a carefree, amused acceptance of middle age.

I liked it. The freedom, the warmth.

24

After years of pensive passivity which I sometimes likened to the meditation of a monk but which, most of the time, I knew was no more than a lack of real purpose, my life was all at once filled with business. It was alarming and exhilarating, a billowing experience – Freedom. As soon as you are aware of it, you want to clamp it down with sensible decisions. I had to leave the shop and contrive something of a future for myself.

I strove to be practical. The sale of the property was out of my hands – a bookworm solicitor would take care of it, sighing as he made out his bill, but I had to get rid of the stock. I slashed the price of books – large orange posters announced ruinous reductions – but it was early December, raining most of the time, and tourists would not visit the town again until Christmas. I sought purchasers of the stock in bulk and had some success, disposing of books as though they were so many sacks of potatoes: Shakespeare and Homer and Plato and Tolstoy, all the unread masterpieces – Warwick Deeping and Louis Golding, Daphne du Maurier, all that dead weight. I flung it off me, other people's books. (The image of a well-preserved corpse heaving aside the grave-loam occurred at this point.) I was agitated and elated. Whatever compunction I felt was smartly overcome by tough-minded resolution.

So much had to be fitted in before Christmas, for I hoped to begin my new life in the new year – no one is entirely free of superstition. And Sarah had to be fitted in. I still managed to see her most weekends, and one Saturday she took me to the Albert Dock. 'You'll either love it or loathe it.'

It was at the Pier Head and I wanted to take the car but she preferred to walk. 'It's such a lovely day. I used to walk everywhere with Vincent in the days when we had no money. It's much more interesting that way. You don't see anything from a car.'

We walked downhill to the centre of town. What was there to see? The shops and the crowds, the battered vitality of a city that increasingly urged itself upon me, the rogue Irish midden of Liverpool. We looked in at the shops, the secondhand bookshops. In Bold Street, buskers played guitars and croaked the blues. In the Walker Art Gallery she showed me her favourite painting and I kissed her for it. Then she took me to the Albert Dock.

Disused for years, it had been converted into a nautical theme park with authentic cobbled quays and redundant winches. Sundry museums offered the usual half truths and there was an art gallery which appeared to specialize in exhibitions that had failed to amuse London. The inner basin of the dock was flooded and various craft were moored there. Sarah grabbed my arm. 'See that old sailing ship? They have a group on board sometimes, singing sea shanties. And they let people climb up the rigging' – 'Have you climbed it?' – 'Christ, no. These days it takes me all my time to get into my tights.'

The place was crowded with people who seemed to be enjoying themselves – parents with children running about, young lovers arm in arm, a party of old-age pensioners who appeared to be drunk. They congregated in the vast hall of the main warehouse where cursing dockers had once laboured for a living. Now the interior was given over to shops and novelty stalls, prettified handcarts where you could buy decorated chamberpots and porcelain plaques (*This is It!*) to hang on your lavatory door. Some of the stalls offered scented bouquets of artificial flowers, homemade fudge straight from the factory and ballpoints with your name engraved on them. Others displayed mementoes of

135

the Beatles and sepia photographs of yesteryear, the squalor of Victorian slums in a frame of simulated walnut.

The outer wall was a series of great arches through which one caught a glimpse of sunlit water. And beyond, ranged against a cloudless sky, the Liver Building and the heroic barricade of the Pier Head. Sunlight glanced off the water and shimmered upon the warehouse ceiling, endowing the monumental structure with an ethereal grace. I observed politely that it was really quite Venetian – 'Venice in wellies!' Sarah laughed, but she was pleased. 'It's good, isn't it?' She gazed about happily. 'I think they've made a really good job of it.'

'Quite splendid.'

'I'm so glad you like it. I was a bit afraid you wouldn't. I know if Vincent was here, he'd have a sneer on him you could hoover the floor with.'

'Oh no, it's . . . pleasant.'

'It's good to see people enjoying themselves, isn't it?'

The odd thing was, once I had claimed to like the place I found much to admire and enjoy. My senses were quickened, my sympathy aroused. It was the effect she had on me.

We visited the art gallery – an interesting Magritte; acres of turgid Rothko canvases – then had a scrappy lunch in one of the eating-places. I wanted to offer her something choice and expensive but she was altogether content with a meat pie and a sticky mess that pretended to be coleslaw. After lunch we left the Dock and she took my arm, leading me across the wide deserted square of the Pier Head. We went down a covered gangway to the river. 'This is a floating landing stage we're standing on now. It's unique. You may think you're on solid ground but really you're floating.'

'We have no such marvels where I come from.'

'We used to catch the ferry from here to New Brighton, me and our Josie and Linda. The funfair and the sands.'

'I'd like to meet these sisters of yours.'

'No chance. Our Linda stole a boyfriend off me once.'

I wanted to learn of her background – 'Anything about

136

you interests me' – and she talked of the overcrowded terrace house in Everton, the three little girls in one bed and the song they used to sing. She sang it for me, twirling about at my side: *'There were three in the bed and the little one said – Move over! Move over! – And they all moved over and one fell out.* That was me, more often than not. Actually we had two beds between the three of us but we liked to all snuggle in together, telling dirty jokes and shrieking until me Dad shouted up the stairs, threatening to give us down the banks if we didn't shut up.'

Her father had died some years ago but her mother was still alive. Sarah visited her dutifully, taking her cans of Guinness. 'She doesn't much care about me though. All that matters is her latest grandchild; you'd think it was the Infant Jesus. I was there the other day and she was slobbering all over it. I'd just been promised this promotion and I told her about it, all excited. She didn't take a blind bit of notice! All that mattered was, the bloody spastic baby had fallen over. And then after Stan and Linda had carried the kid off in their nearly-new BMW she turned on me, said I was jealous. For God's sake! She doesn't give me credit for anything. I mean after all, I haven't exactly wasted my life. I got to university – the only one in the family – and I've got an important job. But our Linda just has to lay a fat lump of a kid and she's the Queen Mother!'

We walked along the floating landing stage and the river glowed with sunlight. The opposite shore was no more than a grey smear against the sky. The landing stage was deserted; it seemed bereft of purpose and might have been suspended in mid-air. 'There were ships here once, weren't there?' I had seen photographs in the Maritime Museum: the towering hull of an ocean liner roped to the quay and a file of passengers mounting the gangway, men in homburgs and overcoats with velvet collars, women in cloche hats with fox furs about their shoulders.

'Oh the place was rotten with ships at one time.' Sarah nodded ahead, downstream. 'All along there, as far as Bootle. There was an overhead railway and it took you

137

along the docks. Everywhere there were ships and men working on them, big derricks hauling the cargo out of the hold.'

'Do you remember that?'

She flushed. 'There was still a bit of it going on when I was little. Vincent saw more of it than I did. And that's what would have enraged him about the Albert Dock,' she realized. 'All that contrived nostalgia.'

'Post-modernism for the masses. It's all we've got left.'

'But you didn't seem at all concerned.' She gazed up at me speculatively. 'Vincent would've been spewing black bile. All the kitsch – people's lives and their misery tied up in fancy ribbon, in that dock where men had to stand in line for a job, bribing the ganger with a drink and fighting each other for a day's work. And out here —' She indicated the empty landing stage, the empty river: 'there's nothing. No ships, no work. No reality! He was a pain in the neck sometimes,' she concluded unhappily, 'I don't deny that. But at least he got angry about things that mattered.'

'Including, doubtless, the world's indifference to his genius.'

'Oh shit.' She stopped and faced me. 'We're not going to quarrel, are we?'

'Must we never quarrel?'

'Never. We can have a good bursting row, if you like; but I hate nasty little bickering quarrels.'

She drew me to a bench set against the wall of something disused, and we sat down. She took both my hands in hers and smiled into my face. She wore a woollen hat pulled down over her hair. Linda, her wealthier sister, had given her the muffling coat she wore. It was a hand-me-down and too big for her but she wouldn't get rid of it, not a good camel-hair coat, cost you two hundred pounds in George Henry's, with a lovely big collar to warm your ears.

'You're different from what I imagined when I first met you. You're not really an innocent little boy at all, are you? It's a change, being involved with someone who's really hard. An innocent little boy in glasses; he removes his glasses in his debonair way and suddenly you find you're dealing with a grown man.'

'Does it alarm you?'

'Well, it's a bit unnerving when you're not sure whether he loves you – Don't say it!' she added at once. 'Don't ever say it just because you think you ought to.'

We sat on the bench with our hands clasped and I was no longer quite sure which flesh was mine. Was it only a matter of years – no more than seven, after all – which prevented me from committing myself entirely to her, escaping at last from the sceptical, uncommitted stranger who stood in my way? I knew that I needed her; but that wasn't all she needed. Yet I longed to confide in her, to release myself to her by telling her my plans – the reckless project I yet hardly dared confide to myself. I began by telling her of Hooke, the fact that he had begun to rewrite his novel and was determined to finish it – 'Really? Well, he's sure to succeed now he's got your sister behind him, isn't he?'

But this wasn't what I wanted. It was the man himself and his past that interested me. 'You've said I should write something,' I muttered self-consciously. 'I would really like to base something on Vincent, you know.'

'A biography?' She appeared to find it amusing.

'Not exactly.'

'You're not thinking of writing a novel, are you?'

'I started one once. Wrote ten chapters.'

'What was it about?'

'Old men. I think I was trying to dispose of my father.'

'And you never finished it.'

'Everyone is entitled to one false start.'

She said nothing and somehow her silence diminished me, her past association with Hooke and the Alps he had climbed. He seemed to loom over me, two feet taller, a giant of heroic endeavour girded with suffering and genius, a genuine writer no matter what the scorned world might think. At length she said: 'I don't think you should try and write another. I don't think it's your field really.'

'Why not?'

Her face seemed gilded with a patina of hard-won wisdom, though the setting sun probably had more than a little to do with it. Her smile was both remote and compassionate. She said I wasn't a novelist. My mind was too – 'It's a very good mind, don't get me wrong. But it's too logical, too *hard*. And you don't really seem to feel very much. Oh you're lovely and passionate with me,' she added at once. 'I meant for other people and . . . things in general. What's more,' she concluded, heaving a breath: 'you've not been hurt enough to write well. It's like what Vincent used to say: Writing is a throbbing bruise.'

The giant loomed in her life also. He might be dead as far as marriage was concerned but he wouldn't lie down.

25

I divided Christmas between Yorkshire and Liverpool, spending Christmas Eve with Sarah – 'It's much better than Christmas Day anyway, which is always an anticlimax; too much food and the Queen's Speech to give you indigestion.'

Knowing that it would please her – indeed she shrieked and hugged me – I bought a small tree and we set it up in the living room, draping it with tinsel and hanging glittering trinkets from its branches. Hooke would never give house room to a Christmas tree, considering it bourgeois and a waste of money. On the other hand, he had always insisted on a Christmas stocking, unwrapping with childish glee the presents he found in it. We followed the same procedure and bought each other a heap of small gifts, some of which – you could tell from our exaggerated whoops – were inappropriate: the exotic perfume I gave her; the gaudy boxer shorts she gave me. We unwrapped the presents sitting up in bed after a prolonged and innovative yuletide copulation. On the radio a Cambridge choir sang traditional carols, the boy sopranos fluting soulfully, as though nothing had changed in two thousand years.

We ended the day with a banquet at a notable Chinese restaurant. There were twelve courses, and round about the seventh, with the air of someone recalling an unimportant piece of news, Sarah informed me that she had told Hooke of our affair. 'I wrote it on his Christmas card. Well, I wanted to have it out in the open and done with,' she cried, as though I had expressed dissatisfaction. Something may have showed in my face; a quiver of reproach perhaps, implying betrayal.

I called at Marion's house the next day with some trepidation, for Hooke would be there; but he greeted me with an indulgent smile, shaking my hand and grasping my arm to emphasize his bland forgiveness – 'Why did she tell him?' Marion wondered, drawing me aside for a moment. 'Did she want him to know she was doing quite as well as he was?'

'I think it was a desire for honesty,' I said stiffly.

'It ruined his concentration.' Her tone was proprietary. 'He couldn't write a word for a day or two.'

'Something of a shock,' he admitted later as we sat together in the front room while Marion worked in the kitchen ('I want absolutely no interruptions') and Willy was busy with a girlfriend upstairs. 'But she has her own life now, of course.'

He sighed, sipping sherry. He wore a bright new pullover, his shirt collar turned over at the top. With his shapely head and lean features, it gave him an unpretentious workmanlike appearance suggesting that he had left his desk for only a moment to participate in a meaningless convention. His shoes were disappointing, however. I have never understood the pleasure some men take in pointed black Italianate shoes, the toe-caps swarming with filigree. 'She's a bit old for you, I would have thought. I suppose it's the usual thing – the attraction of an older, experienced woman. A surrogate mum.'

'No, it's because in essence she is younger than me.'

'There was always something childlike about her,' he agreed.

'No, that's not what I mean.'

But he shied away from the point. It was discomforting, the thought that I may have discovered in his wife some precious quality he had missed. 'In a way, you know, I'm almost glad,' he asserted. 'It shatters another link with the past; makes things definite and final. I only hope she doesn't let herself go entirely.' He drained his glass, his mien thoughtful. In imagination, he was charting her decline into tragic whoredom.

'Oh I think that's most unlikely. Her sense of humour would always save her.'

'I'm glad you appreciate her.' He might have been her father, obliged to entrust her to my safe keeping. 'You'll have to watch out for her though,' he added with an elderly teasing chuckle. 'She'll want to rub all that middle-class shine off you. I know her. I'm sure she's itching to take you in hand and make something of you.'

He shifted in his chair, drawing from his hip pocket a crumpled Christmas card. He opened it and read from it. 'Yes, she says here, you see. . . Mmm, yes: *I know he's miles above me intellectually but I still feel I can give him something. . .*' He gazed at me over the edge of the card. 'I assumed at first she meant her body. But sex never really meant a great deal to her.'

'Oh stop it!' I laughed, wishing I could have shown him a nasty video of us devouring each other in bed.

'Ah but I must read you this bit,' he protested gaily. '*He still. . .* Yes, this is it: *He still isn't enough aware of what life is really all about and I can help him there, I think. Already I feel he is starting to change. He's not ashamed to be serious now.*' He offered me the card, the inside covered with her handwriting. 'Here, read it for yourself.'

I refused, pouring myself another glass of sherry, though what I needed was some long draught to cool me. 'Don't take it too much to heart,' he laughed. 'She's a dear girl, really. You won't find a better. And I trust, of course, you'll do the decent thing by her.'

'Marry her?' I yelped.

He tittered maliciously. I changed the subject, hoping to embarrass him by asking how the rewrite of his novel was progressing – 'I'm not rewriting all of it, you know. One must have some faith in one's work. Much of what I'd already written seems quite acceptable.'

'But have you solved the problems?' I persisted.

'I've made some necessary alterations.' But then he abandoned caution and spoke of his work with a glow of excitement. 'They seem to have done the trick. And the writing is so. . . I've never written so well before. I just can't stop! Everything is flooding out so smoothly and inevitably. The novel is writing itself. God! I've been waiting so long for this. To have the power! To be able to write at last with freedom and authority.'

I didn't want this – I didn't want it!

Willy came down with his girlfriend. She looked in and wished us a Merry Christmas then left the room, and for a moment I was distracted by the bold flash of her thighs in an abbreviated skirt, the trailing skeins of her blond hair, the dazzle of her sex and the freshness of her youth. 'We've been bonking,' Willy said when he returned after parting from her. He yawned absently.

'She seems a nice girl,' Hooke ventured.

'What is that supposed to mean?' Willy laughed rudely.

Marion called us to the dining room and we sat down to Christmas dinner, feeling obliged to make the most of it after she had gone to so much trouble: the flowers and lighted candles, bottles of wine, the array of cutlery and glasses. The main course was a brace of ducklings served with a sauce that seemed in love with them, so ardently did it cling to the meat and hosanna the flavour. But it bores me now to describe my sister's famous meals. In any case, the dinner wasn't the success she hoped for, her first Christmas with Hooke, the nativity of her smiling lapse into a bohemian ease and expansiveness. Although she strove to summon liveliness and laughter to the feast, our response was sluggish. Willy seemed obscurely at odds with himself and I could eat little after the Chinese blow-out the night before. I was sated with rich food, indifferent to vintage wines. In future I would confine myself to meals that were simpler and less ceremonious.

Hooke was preoccupied, uncertain which implement or which glass to use and probably despising himself for submitting to the bourgeois ritual. At times he raised his head and gazed at the opposite wall as though a mural was scrolled there depicting his true self and only life, the dedication to austere artistic duty. Once the pudding was out of the way,

Willy got up and went to his room claiming there was an essay he must write. We remained at the table cracking nuts and drinking port, offering conversational items in turn, none of which survived for long. Hooke smoked cigarettes while doubtless writing his novel in his head. Then the doorbell rang and Marion rose to answer it. I saw Hooke's face stiffen as he heard her at the door, her hostess welcome and then the smooth rolling baritone of her ex-husband.

I was not surprised by Mark's visit. It was the season of goodwill, after all, and he liked to keep in touch with his discarded family. Marion sometimes sought his business advice and he was genuinely proud of his son's academic achievements. 'What's he want?' Hooke whispered hoarsely, eyeing me like a fellow conspirator; and his ill-bred reaction disposed me in favour of Mark, whom he sought – it seemed unwarrantably – to exclude.

He entered with Marion, talking and laughing, paying her a compliment with a glad catch in his voice. 'You look lovelier than ever.'

'Oh don't be a fool!' she giggled, falling behind as he advanced on us, hand outstretched, his personality burnished for the occasion. The room seemed to shrink about him, so strong and positive was his presence; and for a brief astonished moment I was his devoted slave again, the pale goggled youth who had loved his beauty and grandeur, his seigniorial appropriation of the world – 'Yes, we've already met,' he smiled, standing over Hooke as they shook hands. Though he was not in fact an outdoors man, preferring a smoky bar and gamey jokes among the whisky, his manner – matched by his smart hacking jacket, his sumptuous canary-yellow sweater – suggested that he had spent the morning striding over hills.

'You're at that college, aren't you?' He sat down, hitching up his cavalry-twill trousers, and gazed at Hooke intently. 'Get more than your share of dunderheads there, I imagine. What do you teach them?'

'Oh, but he isn't primarily a teacher,' Marion had put

145

in before she could stop herself. Hooke stared at her imploringly but there was no help for it; Mark had seized on the qualifier and she was forced to assert that her lover was really a writer.

'Published?' Mark enquired at once, though I was convinced he already knew the truth. He had seen Willy recently and must have questioned him.

I chose a walnut, cracked it open and picked its brains, concentrating upon the task while Hooke, like a man staggering upstairs with an enormous parcel, explained that although he had written a number of novels, none of them was yet published. Mark nodded sympathetically. 'It's a racket,' he agreed. 'In that business, the only gift you really need is people with the right influence. We all know the scenario—' His smiling cynicism drew us all into his orbit. 'Giles meets Jeremy over a glass of fine sherry at the club, and twelve months later another tremulous distillation of middle-class twittery hits the bookshops.'

'Is that how it's done?' I sneered, reluctantly lurching to Hooke's defence.

'Well, it wasn't far from that with your book, was it?' Mark laughed.

Hooke challenged the scenario and Marion watched keenly as he sought to uphold the probity of publishers. He began with a broadminded concession. Granted, Grub Street was a traffic jam of Porsches nowadays and journalistic expertise set the literary standard; the dollar was dominant, takeovers were common and many fine independent publishers had been wiped out. Nevertheless! he insisted while Mark laughed softly and shook his head – here and there, in coy Bloomsbury enclaves, publishers survived who were devoted to good writing, the honesty of true art; firms of integrity who were prepared to squander cash on a promising talent.

'You can't be serious.' Mark turned from him to gaze at his ex-wife helplessly. 'This man has the innocence of a saint!' He sat between Hooke and Marion, lolling negligently in his chair. He turned back to Hooke. 'It's a fairy-tale, old son.

You're living in a dream world. If your novels lack the zip and sparkle the punters expect, you'll never be published. Publishers are businessmen: first, last and always. If they don't make money, they go out of business. You may be the reincarnation of Virginia Woolf for all I know; but if you can't compete with the telly – you're out. A point the publishers seem already to have made to you in no uncertain terms.'

Hooke tried to argue, his mouth opening and shutting, but nothing coherent emerged. I could have gone to his rescue; I knew that some publishers still subsidized good but unprofitable books with the money they made on bestsellers; but I was too absorbed in the struggle to want to intervene. In any case, if the man couldn't defend himself. . . It was strange, an illusion based on the dull congested flush in his face, but I seemed to see him wrangling physically with Mark and getting the worst of it. They were comic-book schoolboys, the captain of the First Eleven and the fifth-form sneak, Hooke with his head trapped in the muscular crook of Mark's arm and his face crimsoning abjectly, his bottom squirming, as he strove to escape. From her expression, it seemed Marion was afflicted with a similar fantasy.

26

The weather turned wintry after Christmas and the hills were covered in snow when the time came for me to leave. The country was giving me the cold shoulder. My apartment above the shop was dismantled, I gave Derek my chess computer and stored my furniture temporarily in Marion's top room. She considered this significant. 'I thought you would have taken it with you to Liverpool.' But that would be tactless, I pointed out, a slight on the long-suffering furniture Sarah had accumulated. In any case, I wanted to go as it were naked into my new world, and vulnerable.

I called on Hooke before I left. He had returned to teaching but it was Saturday and he was at home catching up on his marking. 'Doing what I can for my poor dunder-heads,' he laughed, giving the impression that he and his students were united in scholarly integrity, braving Mark's malicious sneers. I had scarcely seen him since Christmas Day and he had not sought me out, but I felt that must be because he was working hard on his novel. While she served in the shop, Marion had heard his old-fashioned typewriter hammering hour after hour. I said that writing must be difficult now that he was teaching full-time and he gazed at me in surprise. 'But it's finished. Didn't Marion tell you? I've sent it out.'

I was nonplussed, having assumed he might spend as much as a year in revision before it was ready for publication. He shook his head authoritatively. 'You can work a novel to death, you know, and lose all sight of it. You have to know when to stop. And it had finished itself, you might say. All the problems were solved, all the characters toddling off to their various destinations.' He gestured complacently. 'I've sent it to a publisher I've never tried before. A small firm, but I've studied their list and they seem the right choice. I think they'll take it.'

My reaction gratified him, for I was both envious and admiring. He, on the contrary, was mature and decisive, a man who knew what he was about. The clash with Mark had not damaged his composure – if anything it had hardened his resolve – and his self-confidence was impressive. He rested secure in the belief that he had finally written something which was both exceptional and publishable.

I wished him good luck. He wished me good luck. Neither of us meant it. 'You're off to Liverpool?' he surmised, smiling sourly. 'Give Sarah my love.'

I went to the bookshop, entering it for the last time, and picked up my luggage: a suitcase of clothes, a box of books, my notebooks and the work I had done on the 'D' compilation, which had to be finished by spring. I locked the door and took the keys to Marion. She was not in her shop – Polly could take care of what few customers there were – and I found her at home, she was cleaning the house. Her hair was tied up in a headscarf, and her working clothes – long-legged jeans, a check shirt – made her look bony and hardbitten. She did not stop working and I was obliged to follow her from room to room, speaking as best I could against the grinding howl of a Hoover as she scoured the carpets, her face bent stubbornly to the task. When I expressed surprise at Hooke's rapid despatch of his novel, she switched off the machine and leaned on it, examining me pensively. I had assumed she would be pleased by the proof of his industry and confidence but she seemed indifferent. 'Does it really matter all that much?'

'But if it's published—?'

She switched on the cleaner, dourly forcing it over the carpet. 'If it's published it will sell about sixteen copies and then disappear forever, like most other books. Like your own book. So what's the point and why all the fuss?'

Bewildered, I stood watching her as she worked. The noise of the machine bellowed about me, her voice coming and going in the din: 'Gnawing his fingernails to the elbow . . . going hot and cold whenever he thinks of it . . . terrified of another rejection slip . . . life in the balance.'

She switched off the Hoover and carried it out of the room, a warrior of housework, grim and relentless. I followed her upstairs to the bedrooms. 'He can think of nothing else!' She thrust the snarling machine under a bed. 'He's so obsessed – so absorbed in himself. He doesn't really need me. All he cares about is his damn book.'

'You're jealous,' I laughed, misunderstanding.

She swept the Hoover across the floor like a deadly scythe and I stepped back hastily, my toes threatened. When she had finished the room, I told her I must go. 'Yes, she'll be waiting for you,' she agreed grittily. We went downstairs. She confronted me in the hallway, her face flushed with exertion and the skin tight across her cheekbones as though with the effort of suppressing something. 'What do you hope it will do for you, living in a slum in Liverpool? Do you expect some miraculous change? You won't change. No one changes. The older you grow, the more you turn into yourself.'

When I kissed her goodbye, she was unresponsive, a grieving statue. Her level gaze insisted that I was deserting her in an hour of need . . . They can never let you go!

I drove away through the snow, beneath the embittered trees, the indifferent hills: a winter journey into the future. And why should I be ashamed to admit that she was right? I expected to be changed by the experience. She might raise her eyebrows despairingly, but it was precisely that naive posture – Hooke's unsophisticated response to life – that I wished to adopt. It involved, after all, greater risk than the deployment of scepticism I had learned from Mark, the art of self-protection derived from disillusionment. I wanted to be different – innocent. The exaltation I had felt briefly during the concert – sudden belief in myself; the thronged fairground of the future – encouraged me to believe that I could become, with Sarah's help, a less wary and more trusting, more open and impulsive person; one finally equipped to pursue – and this was the main point – a creatively active life.

There was no snow in Liverpool. 'That pretty white stuff?' Sarah said. 'Oh it wouldn't fall here, get itself all dirty.' She was nervous. We faced each other in the rumpled living room high above the city streets, uncertain how to proceed. 'I wonder what will become of us?' she laughed.

Without a planned future, she felt insecure; it was something she must have acquired from Hooke. In their case the future had not arisen as it did in most lives, simply as an extension and consequence of the past – steady progress in a secure career; the kids growing up; a life designed by society and lived by habit. They had wanted more. In their case the future had been a meaningful construction projected some distance ahead, towards which they had travelled in hope and longing. It had never materialized; he had not been published, fame had eluded him; but the impulse remained for both of them, the moral imperative to live to some end. 'Can't we just love each other and see what happens?' I suggested.

We loved thoroughly for a while and she had her fill of me. Living together had been my idea, I pressed for it. She had been hesitant – *Well, of course* Marion would have interjected at this point; but I felt that Sarah's reluctance was genuine; she had the look of a woman conscious that she was putting herself at risk. And now that I was installed in her life and she must accommodate me, it pleased her to adopt the role of a seduced woman helplessly surrendering to desire, her existence mindlessly concentrated upon what in the good old days they would have termed lust. This lasted for some time and was generally pleasurable. Sarah thrived on it. Sexual fulfilment gave lustre to her flesh. Her body preened itself in physical pride; her breasts rode high

151

and her bottom swayed a little wantonly when she walked. Living with a man who wasn't her husband gave her an illicit thrill. Eventually however some atavistic morality, derived from her traditional working-class background and reinforced by Hooke's puritanism, made her aware of herself and she became uneasy. This was about the time when orgasm had become commonplace and my sexual force had begun to wilt. Then life righted itself and assumed an everyday course. She went out to work and I sat at Hooke's desk in his study completing my encyclopaedic chore, finding platitudes to fit *The Dream of the Rood* and struggling to say something sensible about the *Duino Elegies*. Finally the task was finished, the pages neatly typed on the electronic marvel I had purchased, and I gave it to Sarah to read. She was not especially impressed. 'Most of it you've just copied from what other people have written.'

'That's show business.'

'What will you do now?' she wondered, standing at the desk and gazing into the narrow gulf of the room where Vincent had worked with such passionate earnestness year after year while the world ignored him. 'I'm sure you're going to do something really good now,' she said in her bouncy way, kissing me, and I felt that I must not disappoint her.

Meanwhile we did things together – read poetry aloud and, with greater enthusiasm, played *Scrabble*; dug into Chinese take-aways and got drunk occasionally. We walked the streets a great deal, for I wanted to know the city thoroughly; we visited well-known pubs and joined the mob at Anfield where Hooke had stood, watching Liverpool play their devastating football. I made copious notes and Sarah anticipated the day when I would translate them into some serious piece of prose.

She had friends and I wanted to meet them but she seemed reluctant to introduce me. Then there was a party at someone's house and I finally met Dick the social worker and Alan the teacher: big men with blunt snubby honest faces. They talked about Hooke, claiming that the reason he had not been published was that he had insisted upon writing about working people, which was not fashionable. After ascertaining that neither had read anything he had written, I argued that the working-class experience was perhaps better conveyed in drama and in song than in the novel, and they looked at me narrowly. They asked what I did for a living and my idle grin, hovering above my fancy accent, confirmed their suspicion that I was a social parasite.

I did little better with the women – Sally, who was Green and vegan; Andrea, another social worker; and Jessica, a single parent rejoicing in an ideological motherhood. They talked about Hooke – leaving Sarah had been the greatest mistake of his life – and asked what I did for a living. They eyed me curiously and at one point in the evening, when I was half drunk and defenceless, took an amused feline swipe at me with the lash of a feminist argument. When Sarah intervened protectively, they glanced at her with pity.

I did not suggest meeting her friends again. Finding me subdued and thoughtful, she assumed I was preoccupied with some important project and I fostered the delusion by spending long hours in Hooke's study, sitting at his desk and staring at his padlocked trunk while Brahms and Rembrandt sneered loftily from the wall. Eventually, as the winter passed and spring began to make a crumpled appearance in the trodden local park which was all I had in place of green and uplifting moorland, she grew restless. She wasn't used to having about the house a man who wasn't engaged upon some mighty task. She wanted action. Ordinary life – even ordinary loving – wasn't enough for her. Her expectation pressed upon me clammily and occasionally I caught her out in a puzzled glance, a tiny exasperated sigh. She seemed to be thinking, searching for something that would make sense of the future.

Coming home after my usual trudge about the sterile streets I found her in the dusk-laden room. She had not switched on the light and it was as if the darkness flowed out from her into the room. Somehow I had never imagined she could be depressed and it wasn't fun. I couldn't get to her, buried brooding as she was in some impenetrably private part of herself. I didn't *know* her. Did what I could to cheer her up, trying to discover what ailed her. Had she had enough of me? I found myself stammering excuses, pleas: I was sure I would start work on something soon, etc. An undignified display. But that wasn't the point, it seemed. She raised her head and stared about the gloomy room with loathing. She hated the place, she said. And what of the future? Discounting the possibility that we would remain together forever, she wondered what was to happen to her, oppressed by age and loneliness. Was she to live on here for the rest of her life, with nothing more happening to her? I suggested moving to a new place, somewhere bright and tasteful; but it failed to cheer her, for that wasn't the point either. Finally she confessed her strange longing, stroking my hand wistfully. 'You know what I'd really like?' Her sudden daring smile. She wants a baby.

27

She went out to work, I stayed at home; sometimes I stayed in bed pretending to be asleep, but generally we breakfasted together and then the morning's *Guardian* proved convenient. We crunched toast and scanned its pages absorbedly. She read the news section – full of murder and riot, child-abuse and political corruption – snorting indignantly and occasionally crying out in exasperation as the horror and folly of the world rose up against her. I read the magazine section, the review pages, the sunny side of life. There I discovered a host of people who seemed to be having a good time. They were generally young and good looking; but you could be plain and old as long as you were successful. That was the sole criterion. Everyone was successful in these pages of small print hung with photographs. Writers, photographers, liberated women, fashion designers, enterprising gourmets, philosophers, travellers and pop stars. They were in the news, they were what everyone wanted to be. They won prizes, they made money, they gave interviews and seemed to live in an environment of constant excitement. They were famous, they were the blessed. And even if one discounted much of it – Hooke would have discounted all of it – as chicanery and frivolity, the assiduous self-publicity of modern mountebanks, there remained an impressive residue of talented and intelligent people engaged on significant work. I envied them and it was excruciating. They rode the crest of the current world and I longed to be up there with them – 'I'm glad you're putting that section to good use,' Sarah said. 'Vincent would never read it.'

Once she had left for work – after telling me what to buy at the supermarket; and if I'd nothing better to do, I could clean up the flat – I was free to slump wearily into the hopeless apathy that began to overtake me at this time, a period of profound depression sometimes scorched by fires of panic. I felt it was something I had to go through, as Hooke must have done; and when it became unbearably boring, I escaped into reading. Poetry mostly, something to hang my mind upon. Great novels were too fatiguing and every time I opened one – Tolstoy, Stendhal, Joyce, Kafka – it was like being lectured by a severe headmaster.

Meanwhile Sarah was busy doing what she could for battered wives and abandoned girls, smelly old women wandering in their wits, dull-faced youths who were always in trouble and troublesome old men whom no one wanted: inhabitants of the ordinary fallen world of Liverpool. I knew of them because she insisted upon telling me; but they failed to excite my interest or compassion. This was unfortunate. Had I written of such people in a book that boxed the reader's ears, I might have taken my place among the cheerful and successful gallants in the review pages.

At the weekend, when Sarah was at home, I took to the streets and tramped miles in the hope of wresting something out of the city, all its piled lives, striving to wrest something out of myself. And always – his slender dark figure, his brooding intensity – Hooke seemed to be walking ahead of me. It wasn't that he was leading me but as if I was trying to catch him up, to fall in step with him, to discover what he had found in the city, the grubby bricked-up arena where all his drama had taken place. Did I want his life? It was the stern uncompromising alternative to the jackanapes' fame enjoyed by the others, and on my best days I preferred it. Not the failure, of course; but the innocence of his dedication, his proud indifference to the world. But the more I came to know the city – the hapless, artless muddle of buildings and traffic and people, the streets often devastated by huge gaps where the past should have been – the less it had to say to me. The barrenness, however, was in myself.

Often I went to the park and you might have seen me there one bright high breezy day in late March, inspecting the crocuses growing among discarded beer cans and plastic detritus: a tall thin man in spectacles, wearing an absent expression. My straight fair hair, the angular slabs of my pale face. A man of thirty, of no fixed address or beliefs, wondering what was happening to his life.

Sarah was preparing Sunday lunch and I didn't want to return to the flat, to endure her fond compassion, her helpless smile, her growing conviction that I would not after all produce the resounding piece of work she had hoped for. What was more, at any moment I expected her to announce – doubtless with that fearful air of smug acquaintance with a profound female destiny which women assume on such occasions – that she was pregnant.

Inevitably I had felt trapped when she had first declared her need. *You know what I'd really like?* But it wasn't a ruse to bind me to her. Quite the contrary. And once I understood that this was her practical womanly way of resolving the situation – by introducing a third, unforeseen consideration that would take precedence over both of us – I had nothing but love and admiration for her. She wanted the baby *for herself*, that was the point. At the same time, this new obligation increased the pressure that caused my depression; for if I couldn't even produce a baby. . .

I returned to the flat at length, anticipating without much enthusiasm the conventional roast dinner she liked to provide for Sunday lunch. We would spread the *Observer* over it and she could read long dense articles about American involvement with the Middle East or the growing restlessness in communist countries while I concentrated upon the book reviews, hoping they would prove censorious. A diatribe rejecting literary pretension on the grounds that the novel was dead would aid my digestion considerably. But when I entered the living room I felt at once that something had happened; I knew it from Sarah's alert, caught-up manner when she met me, her face stark with news. 'Vincent's been here!'

157

I thought at once that something must have happened to Marion, some terrible accident – 'It's his novel,' Sarah said. 'It seems it's going to be published.'

A shock sometimes sends you reeling back to childhood and for a moment I was a little boy full of bitter sobs and the conviction that life was unfair. 'That's wonderful,' I said. 'Where is he?'

'He's gone to see his father. He's coming back later.'

She stood before me, mechanically wiping her hands on the apron she wore. Her hair hung limp about her slender face and I loved her, she seemed so defenceless, assailed as she was by a horde of conflicting emotions. When I asked for further details – Was it a *fact* that he was to be published? – she was scatter-brained, laughing ruefully. 'Well, he seems to think so. This man phoned him up – one of the editors. Said he liked it. He's going to London to meet him, tomorrow.' She broke away suddenly and ran into the kitchen. 'The fucking meat!' she screamed.

It was only a little burnt but it could have been charred to the bone for all I tasted of it. We said little, sitting at the flimsy table in the living room and poking at our plates. At one point, forking a chunk of beef and plastering it with a poultice of peas mashed with gravy, she said: 'I only hope he hasn't gone for an easy popular success and that's why they're publishing it.'

'Betraying his principles, you mean?'

'I'll bet your sister's over the moon.'

She returned to an article critical of Mrs Thatcher's leadership and I finished reading a review slobbering praise for the genius of a Latin American author who dabbled in magical realism. When the meal was over and we had to face each other again, she said: 'It's marvellous. Five minutes with her and all his dreams come true.'

'But we don't yet know that it's a *fact*,' I reminded her.

We waited for his return, confounded and nervous. 'Did you think it would be accepted?'

158

'Oh I felt, you know, there was a good chance.'

When he arrived we rose to meet him, crowing congratulations and wanting to know everything at once. I felt uncomfortable: he looked so pleased, never doubting the wholeheartedness of our response. But he kept his excitement pretty well under control and his joy expressed itself, for the most part, in a bemused serenity. He was vindicated at last after all his years of struggle and failure. 'But when the moment of vindication finally arrives,' he reflected, 'you find you no longer need it. That's what I discovered when I told my father the news.' His face looked small and rosy as though his head was a knot tied in his body to keep elation from escaping.

'Was he pleased?' I asked.

'Nonplussed. And what was best of all – suddenly I found I was no longer afraid of him. After forty-five years!'

'But is it really, I mean, definite?' Sarah asked anxiously. 'Are they definitely going to publish it?'

'Well, obviously,' he explained heavily, 'they haven't yet committed themselves. I have to go down there and – I suppose they might want me to make some changes, some cuts maybe.'

'You won't make too many compromises, I hope,' she said.

'Surely you know me better than that?' He gave a wistful smile. Then he gazed about the flat as though it was unfamiliar, presumably the doleful retreat of some nonentity. 'Are you happy?' he asked in an undertone.

'I'm happy for you,' she said; and it was true. More than I could ever have managed, she was capable of transcending the situation and genuinely rejoicing in his good fortune. 'And you're going down to see them tomorrow?'

'Yes, I —' He glanced at his watch. 'I'd better be getting back actually. I don't even know how I'll get back, Sunday travel being what it is.'

'I'll take you, if you like.'

I wanted to see what would happen and to discover Marion's reaction to the news. He accepted my offer and stayed another hour, talking trivialities. He shifted about on his chair unable to keep still, barely attending to what was being said. Mrs Thatcher's leadership, magical realism, the possible disintegration of the Soviet Empire – they were no more than gnats dancing above the surface of his mind. All that mattered was the great fact that he was to be published; and he couldn't keep away from it, it kept bubbling up in his talk. 'Of course I'd always felt reasonably confident; I knew it was a good novel. But so often I've deceived myself. . .' Now that he was vindicated and there was no longer anything to fear, he could admit to having deceived himself. 'It feels unreal,' he went on. 'That's actually what convinces me that this time it's really going to happen! I felt exactly the same when I fell down Ainsworth Crag – that it couldn't be happening. Yet that was real enough.'

When we left, he said goodbye to Sarah and I tried to decipher his expression as, clasping both her arms as if to hold her upright, he kissed her cheek, letting her see that he knew he no longer had a right to her lips. There was a gentle toying compassion in his glance and perhaps the merest hint of gratified malice.

We drove out of Liverpool and onto the motorway. The sun was shining as though summer had come already. Cars raced past, hurrying to reach somewhere before all the light and warmth had vanished. He was silent for a while and I wondered if he was thinking of Sarah. I had seen him gazing at her with a look of remote betrayal and I felt he was troubled by the realization that another man had made love to her, that she had given herself to me on the hallowed marriage bed beneath the ugly grey scab of a plaster rose. Indeed, when at length he spoke, it was of her. 'You can never have everything, of course.'

'But you have Marion.'

'D'you really think so?' His sceptical smile was as good as anything I might, at one time, have fashioned myself.

It is the way his mind works that fascinates me; the fact that he believes in a meaningful universe ruled by an even-handed (however tardy) justice; where vindication comes at last to those who deserve it, suffering is rewarded and loss in one respect is compensated by gain in another. He is always prepared to strike a bargain with fate. One cannot have everything and he has lost Sarah. But in exchange fate offers success, perhaps even fame. He accepts the bargain readily.

28

He sat beside me in the car, musing upon tomorrow's crucial meeting. Occasionally he raised his face to the sunlight as though God was in it somewhere.

Sarah had not objected when I had proposed driving him home. She was as eager as I was to discover what would happen. Also she probably welcomed some time to herself in which to confront the confusion that had suddenly rushed upon her. I thought of her sitting alone in the flat struggling to balance her joy in his success with the mortifying jealousy she must feel now that Marion was to reap the benefit of all the years she had faithfully endured with him. She would not find much consolation in the thought that she possessed Marion's brother in exchange; and her troubled reflections would almost certainly come to rest at length upon the wistful hope she placed in her untried womb.

I had not been out of Liverpool for more than two months and it was like escaping. The top-floor flat had lost some of its tumbledown charm and I had begun to feel confined, much as Hooke must once have done. Now as green moorland appeared, golden in the sun's haze, and familiar hills rose up on the horizon, some of the excitement packed so tightly within my companion began to infect me. I looked forward to seeing Marion again.

We reached the town and I parked outside her house. But when she came to meet me, holding out her face to be kissed the way women do, I realized she had mixed feelings about Hooke's promised success. Her eyes gazed into mine, conveying a meaning I could not comprehend.

He told her at once of seeing his father and the moment of vindication – 'After forty-five years!' He rubbed his hands, disposing of his father. Marion raised her eyebrows. We sat in the front room where a large window divided the outlook into six equal panes: two for the glowing sky, two for the hills and two for the grey stone huddle of the town below. Hooke got up and wandered about, lighting a cigarette as he stared out of the window, seeing only the future. For what was clearly not the first time, he consulted Marion about the train they should catch tomorrow and the clothes he ought to wear. 'I wish I had a decent suit.'

She turned to me, telling me that my parents were back from Australia. My mother was in surprisingly good health, it seemed – 'She got a good rest while she was there' – but my father was morose and listless. Perhaps the immensity of the continent, the impossibility of encompassing that barren world, had done for him at last. 'He looks really old and frail now, as though he's finally given up.'

'Did you tell them about me?' Hooke interjected, nodding and smiling.

Marion didn't answer. She sat erect on her chair, her face impassive. Eventually, reaching a decision, she told him she would not be accompanying him to London after all. 'I never said I would, you know. You took it for granted.'

'But I thought you'd want to come,' he said plaintively.

'I really don't see the point. And I'm needed at the shop, especially with Easter practically on top of us.'

'But I thought you'd want to come,' he repeated, distressed.

She smiled. 'It's your day. I want you to have it all to yourself.' She was like a mother idly beguiling a child.

'I could drive you there,' I said.

'Why, you're a regular taxi service!' she said crossly.

'I'd like a day in London.'

Hooke thanked me in an absent-minded manner and I arranged to call for him in the morning. He left soon afterwards and Marion saw him to the front door. When she returned, her body was tensely clutched together, her hands were clenched as if to keep her claws from tearing something to pieces. 'Oh he's such a fool!' she raged.

I didn't know what to say. She sat huddled in her chair. Then she raised her head and looked at me. Her expression was harsh with contempt. 'He's been going on and on and on about it, ever since the publisher's editor phoned.'

'When was that?'

'Friday – Thursday! He was born on a Thursday, you know. Did you know that and can you appreciate the earth-shaking significance of the coincidence? That's the sort of thing I've had to put up with.'

'What did the editor actually say?'

'Why, just that he'd enjoyed reading the thing and would like to meet him.'

'It isn't a *fact* then, that —?'

'Of course not. But straight away he jumped to the conclusion that everything was settled. All the signs were there! He was born on a Thursday and it was the first publisher he'd sent it to. He'd never tried that publisher before. Oh, and did you realize that *Few Are Chosen* contains exactly the same number of letters as "Vincent Hooke"? So obviously it all confirms that an exciting new life brimming with success is about to begin. And I'm his lucky charm, a fairy godmother waving her magic wand and making it all come true.'

'But aren't you being a little hard?'

'I can't put up with him any more,' she said wearily, lying back in the chair.

'I thought you'd be pleased.'

'About what? The way he's carrying on – Oh all it proves is that he's just a common little man after all.'

'Oh come. He's excited, of course; but surely that's understandable? When I was published —'

'That was different. You were never carried away.'

'But you've always complained because I'm never carried away!'

'Oh shut up.'

We were silent and I wondered if she was crying, but

164

she was sunk too far in the depths of the chair for me to be sure. She sat forward eventually and gazed at me, her face haggard. 'I used to think he was exceptional, that's the point. An innocent! I thought there was something pure and uncorrupted about him. That's what I loved.' She clenched her hands; her voice hardened scornfully. 'But now it's clear that he's really just like anyone else. You'd think he'd come up on the Pools! There's no dignity, no restraint. . . And what about all his wonderful dedication to serious writing now? His compassion, his anger, his desire to do something about the world? It's all just nothing but a grubby little sordid bourgeois hankering after fame. That's all he really wants! It's all he's ever wanted.' She stared at the floor, her knees spread and her hands hanging clasped between them. 'I used to think he was – Oh I don't know: a man with a mission. Someone you could admire. But all it boils down to is getting himself published and getting his name in the papers, his mug on TV, getting his smug little vindication and scoring over his father – everything cheap and nasty!'

I had nothing to say; there was nothing I could offer to console her. I stayed the night in her guest room. I telephoned Sarah before I went to bed and told her I would be driving Hooke to London. 'You're so considerate,' she laughed spitefully.

I called for him early the next morning. He was still dressing and had not had breakfast. 'Couldn't eat a thing!' Nor could he decide which clothes to wear, though his wardrobe was far from extensive. 'Be casual,' I advised him. 'Show you don't care – an independent, ragamuffin artist unconcerned with the things of this world.'

He got into something at last but it was hardly casual, rather the attire of a dutiful employee applying for some lowly respectable situation – a dull blue suit and those shiny Italianate shoes. I hustled him into the car and we drove off. I would need to drive unremittingly if we were to get to London in time. He glanced at me doubtfully, checked the speed of the car – the speedometer gamely straining

165

towards seventy – and wondered if he shouldn't have taken the train after all. Once we gained the motorway, my exasperation sent the car soaring into the eighties and beyond. 'Watch your speed,' he cried irritably. 'We don't want to be stopped by the police.'

The sun had been shining when we set out, the hills glittering with frost; but as we forged south into the industrial Midlands the sky became overcast and the day was grey and cold by the time we reached London. Hooke dozed, having barely slept the night before; then he would rouse himself, find a bit of paper and jot down a note. He feared the publisher would demand cuts. *Few Are Chosen* was rather long – 131,000 words, to be precise. 'I shall agree up to a point,' he decided; 'as long as it's nothing vitally important. One has to be prepared to make concessions. The main thing is to get published, get myself established. Then I can set my own terms.'

He dowsed his cigarette in the ashtray beneath the No Smoking symbol and settled into another comfortable doze. After Watford, the great brick morass of London began to swarm about us. 'You've made good time,' he said, waking up and staring out of the window. 'God, it's years since I've dared visit this place. When you leave the motorway, drive to Bloomsbury and I'll show you where to pick me up later.'

But I had no intention of risking my car and my sanity in the traffic of central London and I parked somewhere in Golders Green. From there we took a Tube into the city. We lunched in a small crowded Italian restaurant, the sort of place that strives to disguise poor food and sloppy service beneath a veneer of Latin ebullience. It was full of office workers who didn't care how they spent their luncheon vouchers, everyone eating fast and talking animatedly. They were blithely adapted to the haste and pressure of a great city, but I found it intimidating. Compared with London's oppressive power and ceaseless urgency, Liverpool was a seaboard nonentity squatting among the dregs of a notable past and my home town was no more than a picture postcard in a tourist's pocket.

166

Hooke paid the bill – 'Sixteen quid for spaghetti in frogspawn!' We left the place and parted outside, on the pavement of a busy street. People strode past, soberly dressed most of them and seemingly intent on important affairs. Hooke looked thin and hung-up in his blue suit. He carried his drab beige raincoat nonchalantly. 'Wouldn't you like to go instead of me?' he joked, walking off while I was still trying to sort out the ambiguity of his utterance.

We had arranged to meet on the terrace of the National Gallery at six o'clock – 'Better not make it any earlier. He may want to take me for a drink.' I walked about until then, bought something for Sarah and browsed in bookshops. It was some time since I had visited London and it seemed to have changed for the worse. The traffic had thickened until it dominated the streets. The buildings – the shops and theatres, even the great ponderous blocks of congealed history – were grubby and shrunken into sham. Yet despite looking like Rome crumbling beneath the onslaught of a band of seedy vandals; and although I did my best to disparage it, even bringing to bear on it a smattering of offended morality I must have contracted from Hooke, the sheer might of the metropolis overawed me, the grandeur of its reputation; for it was still the centre of power, the great conglomerate of culture and enterprise, wealth and success, with which every provincial has to come to terms, conquer if he can or at least secure its seal of approval.

I arrived at the National Gallery early for I meant to spend some time with the pictures before meeting Hooke. But he was already there and waiting for me. His face told me at once what had happened.

29

It was Ainsworth Crag all over again. His face was mottled with shame and self-loathing. He could barely speak, merely shake his head, and it was obvious that at that moment he simply did not wish to exist. I felt it was my fault. The guilt we experience on such occasions is recognition of our failure to experience another's pain. . . A timely and diverting reflection. He was holding a bulky package which I took to be the typescript of his novel, and when he saw me he made as if to chuck it over the terrace of the National Gallery onto the pavement below, where it would burst open, its pages fluttering up to mingle with the pigeons in their startled flight. . . Another diversion.

I took the package from him and we went for a drink. He stumbled along at my side, not looking where he was going. I had to take his arm when we crossed the road and I hoped people weren't watching. But they were absorbed in their own affairs; it could have been *War and Peace* that had been rejected, for all they cared. The crowd surged about Trafalgar Square and poured into the Underground station. Some – chiefly girls and young men – had a carefree air appropriate to the end of the working day; but the majority were grimly intent upon reaching home, thrusting ahead for a seat on the train, the packed journey to the suburbs.

I found a pub in a side street and drew him into it. It was near Whitehall and full of civil servants of the middle-management grade. They were well-dressed, sprightly and faintly arrogant, sniggering over the follies of their superiors and glinting with inside information, government scandals.

The men eyed the women; the women preened themselves in the presence of the men. There was a good-tempered, sophisticated tone to the place, reinforced by the glamour of solid mahogany in subdued lights, the glitter of glass. I stood with Hooke at the bar, neither of us looking at the other. Then one of the stalls against the wall was vacated and I thrust him into it out of sight. 'I've run out of cigarettes,' he said as I left him.

At the bar I ordered drinks and twenty cigarettes, took them to the table and sat down facing him. He said nothing, his face closed in upon himself. I urged him to drink his whisky and he sipped it absently. By degrees he told me what had happened.

The meeting had gone badly from the start, for the editor had assumed that the author of *Few Are Chosen* would be a much younger man. Someone just down from university perhaps, who had written his first novel. When he saw Hooke – his thinning hair, his mothballed suit – he was forced to make the best of an embarrassing situation and I could visualize his smile as he had done this, his controlled swing into well-mannered deception. Once they began to discuss his novel, Hooke realized that there had never been any intention to publish it as it stood (yet if he had been younger, a promising newcomer. . !) The invitation to a meeting had been meant as no more than an encouraging gesture, the kind of thing a young author with a lifetime before him might have appreciated.

'That put me off my stride straightaway, of course,' he mumbled. And what had made matters worse was the discovery that the editor, far from being, as Hooke had expected, an amiable public-school duffer who enjoyed a good read, was a man with a keenly analytical mind who, after little more than a swift glance through the novel, appeared to know it better than its author did and was at once aware of its shortcomings. The discussion that ensued was onerous and Hooke was crippled with embarrassment. 'I wasn't prepared for it. It was like an exam and I didn't know any of the answers. It was as though I'd never really

169

seen the novel before. It's always been my cursed failing. I never take enough trouble. I don't *think*. I'm too damned conceited and stupid!'

He had raised his voice and I was afraid someone would hear, but no one looked our way. The bar was still crowded and everyone was having a good time.

The editor had been anxious to point out that there were many good things in *Few Are Chosen* – the childhood scenes, the descriptions of Liverpool, the mother's death. But before meeting Hooke, he had assumed these were a young author's imaginative recreations of an earlier period, and he had been impressed. Confronted by Hooke's anxious, aging face he realized it was merely autobiography watered down into fiction; and probably concluded he was landed with the sort of hopeless has-been every publisher's editor comes across from time to time – an indefatigable author with ten or twenty unpublished novels behind him; not necessarily untalented but incapable of viewing his work objectively and learning from his mistakes.

And the editor was so mercilessly intelligent – 'One of the most intelligent men I've ever met.' He was a decent chap with no wish to mortify his visitor; but he was also a professional and genuinely, detachedly interested in identifying the novel's failings. Where had Hooke gone wrong and why? He was also anxious to justify the decision he must finally convey to the author – that in its present state and bearing in mind the current parlous state of publishing (an editor's stock disclaimer) there was no chance of accepting his novel. He went through the typescript in great detail to prove this, assuming that Hooke would find the discussion both absorbing and illuminating. His attitude was kindly, his approach heuristic; he might have been an admirably perceptive teacher going over a scrappy essay with a dull pupil – What about this character and that situation? Isn't there at times a lack of imaginative penetration and do we need all this fairly obvious moralizing? And Hooke was a sweating dunce failing beneath the ordeal. He had likened it to a school examination, the kind you fail because you

170

haven't swotted for it – Sweating is not swotting – and he was bottom of the class, incapable of supplying the correct answers when tested on his novel, reduced to remorseful concurrence when its inadequacies were tactfully pointed out to him.

It wasn't entirely his fault: he was stupid with grief. He was dazed with panic and couldn't think straight for the feelings pounding him from all sides. All he knew was a desperate ache and the ragged plea in his heart – *Oh please! Oh for God's sake, please publish it*! Because while all this was going on, he could not entirely rid himself of the notion that there was a contract in the editor's desk with his name on it, drawn up and awaiting his signature. He could almost see it nestling there. As though, despite every indication to the contrary, the editor wasn't irrevocably committed to rejection and might yet change his mind should Hooke make a sufficiently strong case; but that rejection was inevitable once he discovered that Hooke didn't really know his own work; that he was, in short, neither as talented nor as intelligent as might be expected. . .

It was this that had crushed Hooke finally: the tormenting conviction that success had been within his grasp but that he had been incapable of securing it, thus ruining the best chance of his life.

'But it's only one publisher,' I insisted automatically. 'And the fact that he was interested enough to want to meet you – surely that's at least halfway encouraging? You can make a few – a few necessary alterations and send it out again.'

He said nothing. I suggested another drink and he stared at me dully. He said that he would get them and made as if to rise – 'No, that's all right.' I got up. 'I've plenty of money.'

'Of course, you have, you've sold your shop,' he snarled. 'You've plenty of money, plenty of everything.'

He decided he didn't want another drink. 'D'you expect me to sit here like some hopeless fool, drowning my sorrows?' He got up. 'Let's go home,' he said roughly, lurching ahead of me out of the bar. But in truth he had no home to go to.

The crowds had dispersed and there were few travellers now in the Underground station. We took a Tube to Golders Green and found the car. I started the engine and headed north. I was weary; but the heroic piquancy of the situation – carrying my dying comrade home from the battlefield – kept me alert and responsible. Hooke was silent for long intervals, staring through the windscreen at the night slashed frantic with headlights; but from time to time he gave vent to his feelings. Once he said: 'How am I going to face Marion?' This was always to be his worst moment, returning defeated.

I found some reassuring answers; lying came easily. He sank into silence. Then suddenly he cried: 'And I told my father about it!'

I concentrated upon my driving; the remorseless boredom of the motorway. He fell into a doze and his face was anguished when he awoke and it all rushed back upon him. 'Christ!' he yelped. 'The way I talked about the cuts I was prepared to make —'

I drove on and on, my eyes smarting with fatigue, my mind set hard like concrete. It was close on midnight when I finally drew up outside Marion's shop. He got out of the car, absently mumbling his thanks. The typescript was on the seat and I thought he had forgotten it; but he meant to leave it behind. 'Do me a favour,' he said. 'You've done me so many already – reading it and telling me how good it was, encouraging me!' He flung a hand at the novel. 'Just get rid of the bloody thing for me.'

'But it's only one publisher! Don't say you're going to give up now? I thought you were made of sterner stuff.' I laughed witlessly.

He turned away.

I drove to Marion's house, my head drooping with exhaustion. She let me in. 'They didn't want it, did they? He would have phoned if the news had been good.'

'I don't want to go through all that again,' I groaned.

172

'Poor precious!' She put her arm about me. 'I suppose I ought to go to him. . . What do you think?'

'Oh, I think he'd rather be left to himself tonight.'

'Yes, that's best. I'll see him tomorrow.'

She made coffee, scrambled eggs, and sat with me at the kitchen table while I ate. The house was still and there was an immense silence in the night outside. We talked quietly, smiling at each other. Soon I began to feel at home and at peace.

30

I stayed the night at Marion's and spent much of the following day there, mooning about. Then I drove back to Liverpool, reaching the flat soon after Sarah had returned from work. Mounting the dreary stairs, I might have been Hooke returning home to her with yet another dead baby in his arms. I had his helpless strained smile on my face.

She did not greet me with particular enthusiasm; her attention was entirely concentrated upon learning what had happened. It was as though I was transparent or merely the frame that contained the drama of his latest exploit.When I told her of the rejection, she brooded miserably. 'Poor old Vincent. He never has any luck.' She wanted to know every detail of his meeting with the editor and by the time I had finished, her compassion had enlarged to righteous scorn. 'It's their bloody fault! They just don't want anything that tries to be honest. All they're interested in is something that will sell because it's full of weirdo sex – oral and up your bum and anything that dispenses with love.'

Her primitive response offended me. Also I was jealous. Confused, moreover, by her wrathful allusion to sexual tom-foolery, which seemed a subterranean outburst – 'You can't blame the publisher; it simply isn't a publishable novel. I can see that now.'

'Oh you can, can you?'

'The point is, it falls between two stools. It isn't written well enough to be taken seriously; on the other hand, it lacks the readability that would make it successful on

another level. He wants – Oh so desperately! – to write a
great novel. But really it's like someone trying to play the
Eroica on a mouth organ.'

'That's just your opinion.'

'It's the editor's as well.'

'And obviously you're influenced. I've often felt you
weren't independent enough in your judgement. Just because he's a publisher and probably wears an old school
tie and speaks with the proper accent —'

'God, you're stupid.'

She laughed. 'Is that the best you can do?'

'When I attempt a more sophisticated explanation, you
don't seem able to understand.'

'That's the second time you've called me stupid.'

She faced me, writhing with a troubled fury that brought
out the lines in her face. Yet despite the fact that she was
the elder, it was as though she was my daughter and I must
love her with the wisdom and compassion of a parent. She
was an impudent girl squirming with wilful folly, knowing
she was in the wrong yet incapable of admitting it. I wanted
both to spank her and hug her – at least to reach her and gain
her acceptance. But there were all the years she had spent
with Hooke, the major portion of her life, and all they had
gone through together, the urgent ineradicable faith it had
engendered. She could not let it go. She had to defend him
to the last, defending and justifying the past.

'If it's really so bad, why did you go and encourage
him in the first place? You must've thought it was worth
it.'

'But I told him,' I explained eagerly, 'there were problems
he would have to solve. And I expected him to take much
longer over the rewrite. He was too impatient. He couldn't
wait to be published. It's all he really wants, you know.'

'What problems?' she muttered. 'What problems?' Twist-
ing her hands together.

'Why success eludes his hero. That's the main problem.
It's his own problem, too; his only problem, as far as he's
concerned. But all that happens in the novel – Victor

Hogarth leaves his wife; his father dies. Oh and he falls down a mountain.'

'His father?'

'Victor. Victor falls down the mountain. Then suddenly he is capable at last of writing the sort of novel no publisher would dare reject. It's simplistic, to say the least. He dodges the issue and it's wholly unconvincing.'

'So. . .well. . .' She was unhappy, uncertain how to proceed. 'Are you going to destroy it now, the way he asked you?'

'No, I won't take the responsibility. I'm fed up with being the agent of his fate.'

She bucked up. Perhaps she thought my refusal implied some lingering belief in the value of his work. 'Anyway, it's only one of his novels, and maybe not the best. He probably made a mess of it, trying to please your sister. You can't just sum him up and brush him aside when you've read only one of them. And you didn't even read that one properly.'

I broke away and went into the study. She followed. I stood over the metal trunk staring at it. 'I'm quite prepared to read everything he's written,' I quavered self-righteously. 'I doubt very much whether it would cause me to change my opinion.'

'Wait till you've read them before you decide.'

'I can't read them,' I pointed out with some satisfaction. 'The trunk is padlocked and I'm not going to ask him for the key.'

She went away. I found her in the living room. She had taken a squat vase from the mantelpiece, upending it over the palm of her hand. A small object fell out. 'You have a key,' I said thinly.

'He left it with me, in case I should want to open the thing and brood over his stuff when I no longer had him. In the event of his death, they were to be my property. I could start sending them out all over again and – who knows?'

Somewhat to my surprise she was eager to make love that night and there was a joyous fury in her passion –

176

Do you love me? The following day after she had gone to work, I unlocked the trunk and removed the manuscripts. Discounting numerous rewrites and extra copies; leaving aside a sheaf of short stories, a couple of incomplete plays, great wads of notes and what appeared to be an attempt at a philosophical treatise entitled *How To Live*, there were nine novels, ten if you included *Few Are Chosen*. He had written the first when he was twenty-three and had completed the latest when he was forty-five. Ten novels in twenty-two years. It wasn't exceptional. George Gissing had written and published twenty-seven books in twenty-six years. I had produced one in five years.

I set them out in a low wall across the floor of the study; then I made a cup of coffee and stood drinking it, gazing at the wall of manuscripts. It might have been the tumulus erected over the slain bodies of an army of mice. . . I was apprehensive, of course. What if they were all really terribly good? Even one or two of them. After all, only one publisher had read *Few Are Chosen* and he could well be wrong. I could be wrong. Hooke could be right.

I set to work. I read the earliest novel first: three hundred pages crammed with an eyesore of words. When I had finished I replaced it in the trunk and took the next from the wall. It was late in April before all the novels were back in the trunk; early May before I had recovered from the ordeal and no longer had Hooke's voice yammering in my head for page after page, his characters jolting back and forth like Punch and Judy; and always the burden of his conviction that no matter the brutal indifference of publishers, he was a man with a mission, engaged on a project of Tolstoyan dimensions.

It had me shaking my head like a wise old mediocrity perched on the sidelines, watching a deluded fanatic rush to his doom. Yet despite everything, I felt a troubled envy for the existence behind the tattered barricade of manuscripts: the lonely heroic endeavour, the dedication of life to something greater than oneself – posterity, God's stand-in.

Whilst reading I was fully occupied, a man locked in his

177

study and wrestling with words, Hooke in reverse. I had no time for idle distractions, I neglected the adventures of my famous friends in the review pages and Sarah was pleased not to find me sprawling bored and unemployed when she came home from work. Usually I was still in the study, bent over the desk, and she would greet me with a sweet little kiss, tempered in passion so as not to disturb my concentration. And when I had finished for the day, joining her in the living room, she would glance up brightly from the *Guardian* she had been mangling. 'How's it going?' she would ask. It was a testing time for her.

At first I would say little; I reserved my judgement. But as I finished one novel and then another, it was difficult to keep my conclusions to myself; for as the wall crumbled and the novels, like so many conjuror's rabbits, disappeared back into the trunk, I grew stronger and more confident, and I did not spare her, I wanted her to know the truth even if it meant the end of us.

I wanted her admiration; I wanted the woman to acknowledge my superiority. Sometimes when I came to her after finishing a novel, rising from the desk and chucking the manuscript into the trunk, I felt that I must be glowing as though sheathed in gold. I was a young man – younger than Hooke anyway – and I was sure of myself, intellectually ruthless and morally pure. My sole allegiance was to the truth and the sternest of literary standards. I was their representative – there was nothing *personal* in it – and I judged and condemned with the sanction of their authority.

My approach was sensitive and apologetic, however; I didn't want to hurt her feelings, destroy the man entirely. I gave him his due and always found something to praise – the childhood scenes, etc. 'The trouble is,' I then went on, furrowing my brow concernedly, 'he can't keep it up. His aim is to criticize the modern world – too much weirdo sex, drugs for God, meaningless affluence and the world drowning in shit, ideological fanaticism – and all right, if that's what he feels he must write about. The trouble is' –

178

removing my spectacles and polishing them industriously –
'he doesn't demonstrate it dramatically but confines himself
to moralizing comment. As a result, what you get is less a
novel than a sermon.'

She made as though to protest. I raised my hand and
wafted it about like the conductor of a spectral orchestra.
'Novels are about relationships; but Vincent isn't really
interested in people. His characters lack autonomy. They
are usually there to illustrate a point, and because of this
they exist in a kind of bleached social background that lacks
the authenticity of common life. You see? He doesn't want
to know how people really behave or the way reality really
is. The novels are written, in fact, to shield him from that
awareness.' I watched it all going into her face.

'And that's why he's never succeeded?'

Sometimes to reinforce a point, I would quote from a
manuscript. 'Just listen to this; he's describing the city – *The
sewerlike streets, the houses like old men reeking of grime.*'
I was aware of the sound of my own voice. My articulation
was beautifully precise, my tone silken and almost caressive.
'Then we move on to a shopping-centre – *The wide thighs of
the shops luring simpletons into the great cunt of commerce.*
Notice how he laces his morality with prurience. Here's
another: *The turbid river like an open sewer* – back to the
sewer, you see – *beneath a sky the colour of dead men's
buttocks.*'

'You're just picking out bits,' she protested. 'That's not
fair. He was trying to write about the misery of life – for
some people.'

'I don't object to his loathing of the world; the point
is, it's fearfully overwritten. He took great care with his
prose, I've no doubt; but he never saw it for what it
was. He wasn't sufficiently hard on himself. And he never
learned what to leave out. He could never resist a resounding
phrase, a melodramatic image, whether it contributed to the
narrative or not. What mattered was that it contributed to his
opinion of himself as a serious and significant writer. That's
what he expended most of his imagination on, I'm afraid.

179

Writing was an end in itself, a process of self-reflection not a means of communication. In fact he rarely seems aware of the reader and he isn't in the least concerned to entertain. Yet that must always be an obligation, surely, whatever the level? But despite the fact that his novels are highly conventional, he isn't interested in telling a story. He really wants to preach, fling his words over the world and remake reality in his own image. He never gets beyond himself, that's the point.'

'What are you getting out of this?' she asked once.

'Well, at least I'm learning how not to write a novel.'

And teaching her the truth of Hooke was exciting, a kind of smoothly savage seduction. She fought against it, striving to uphold his honour. She would run to the trunk and pluck out a novel, show me a page – Wasn't it a powerful piece of writing? (Perhaps he had once read it out to her and she had loved his mastery, flushed with the glory of being the wife of a genius.) Of course I conceded the point: it was indeed an effectively written page; for I wanted the game to last. But I was always going to win, for she had only isolated pages to offer, chance fragments of Osiris, glittering scraps of the past; whereas I possessed the untried power of (comparative) youth, the fearless purity of one who had never known failure. I removed my glasses and was a hard young man bearing down on her, catching her at every turn, scattering her wits with unanswerable arguments, incontrovertible evidence. I would not let her escape, I forced the truth home. She recognized, hopelessly, that I possessed the truth; it was like a rampant penis obdurately grinding its way into her.

Ultimately she submitted, she acknowledged my superiority, she lay helpless before me. 'Of course I was always a bit afraid he was kidding himself,' she admitted, her face pale and straight.

Later I found her in the study. The trunk was open and she was sitting on the floor beside it, the manuscripts piled about her. She smirked guiltily when she saw me and at once got to her feet. She came to me and held my arms, searching my face. Her body seemed to sway towards me unresistingly. 'I meant to tell you before. . . I think I may be going to have a baby.' Her eyes were wide and staring.

31

I wanted to think, but not consciously or logically. The thinking I had in mind was a matter of holding consciousness absolutely still: an absence of thought suspended over a void. It was not the province of the conscious mind – speculating, sorting things out, busily engaged in concrete computation: a grasping, mastering, masculine operation. My preoccupation was passive, receptive, feminine – the imagination.

I took my mood to Wallasey one afternoon and trailed it along the promenade. I had become fond of the place since first visiting it with Hooke and I often walked there, alone and relishing its loneliness, the long deserted stretch of the sea wall, the open sky and the idle glutinous river. I thought of the day we had been here together and what he had told me of his youth, his difference. He had hoarded his difference against the pain of loss.

On a sudden impulse I went and visited his father. I knew the address – I had found it among some papers in a drawer of his desk – and soon I was entering the council estate, walking through it to the avenue of private dwellings beyond. I passed council houses he had somewhere described as *smeared in pebbledash the colour of dung, as though some celestial cow had wandered that way once and shit all over them.* Writing is a throbbing bruise. It's also good for revenge and I wondered if the description would have pleased his mother. Supplementary to her gratified snigger there might have been a tiny wince for the scatological reference. A child standing in the gutter raised a toy gun and fired at me, aiming at Hooke. His mother placed a fond

182

hand on my shoulder restrainingly. 'You are *different*,' she assured me.

I climbed the rise beyond the estate and came upon the avenue. *Few Are Chosen* was my guide. There were trees set at regular intervals just as he had promised, and each house had a neat front garden. In the garden of his father's house the flowers were small stunted growths, waxen in texture and crouching close to the earth. In the centre there was a tiny lawn mowed to within an inch of its life.

His elder sister opened the door and let me in once I announced that I was a friend of Vincent's. Her name was Madge but Hooke had never been sure whether it stood for 'Margery' or 'Margaret'. She was a lean sallow-faced woman, about fifty, and she had looked after her young brother and younger sister when their mother had died. Now she looked after her father. It was her life.

I was Hooke returning home, aware of oppression, resentment and frustration as I crossed the threshold. In the hallway waiting to greet me was a grandfather clock with a smarmy legend printed round its dial (*Time Wasted Is Existence, Used Is Life*), a photograph of Lord Baden-Powell at a Scout Jamboree, and the Scout emblem itself, embroidered in green wool and framed in knotty pine, looking like an over-ripe phallic symbol. And down that narrow carpeted staircase they had carried my helpless, weeping mother, carting her off to the hospital to die.

The house was hushed and orderly, a small polished shrine of domesticity. Madge was the attendant priestess. A kindly one.

She showed me into the front room and Graham Hooke, switching off the TV, welcomed me with his harsh abrupt laugh (*My father's laugh*, he had written, *that withers the world*, overwriting as usual). The old man was supposed to be ill, he had had several heart attacks, and he sat in an armchair, with a plaid shawl about him; but he didn't look like an invalid. He was a squat muscular man with a hard round head shaved to match his lawn. The shawl could have been a sweaty towel covering the shoulders of a veteran

183

boxer who had survived a gruelling bout in the ring, which he had doubtless won on points by virtue of a scholarly straight left. I was prepared to like him and he was pleased to see me. *A young gentleman*, he may have concluded, taking my accent into account, my bland spectacled gaze and my tastefully casual attire, my tall and clean-limbed appearance. 'A friend of Vincent's?' he queried with some surprise.

'He was concerned about your health,' I lied. 'Asked if I would call and see how you were.'

'Really? Oh well, I'm . . . as you see.' He gestured defeatedly. There was a hollowness in his voice despite the stoical gleam of his tanned face browned by the outdoors he loved, and the dogged set of his scrubby-haired head.

'Oh but you're much better than you were,' Madge insisted. 'And you're going to get better and better.'

'How the devil do you know?'

'I know. And the devil's got nothing to do with it.'

She glanced coyly at a statuette of St Theresa, the Little Flower, which stood in a corner of the living room. Then she went off to make some tea.

'It's not a matter of pain,' her father told me with a wry smile. 'It's the disgrace. The body letting you down. Age!' He plucked at his shawl. 'And our old friend, the Angel of Death.'

I murmured something reassuringly banal. The ornate clock on the mantelpiece ticked surreptitiously. It had been presented to him when he had retired from teaching, he said. He recalled his days in the classroom, the loutish kids he had taught. 'They were always in wellingtons,' he said. 'You had to fight them off with one hand while trying to instil some manners into them with the other.' He chuckled sourly. 'Ah but they weren't so bad really, if you could win their respect.' He had done it with a cane apparently, a masterly pedagogue who had succeeded in converting a hateful task into a bracing challenge, being simple minded enough to mistake his hatred for fondness.

There were framed photographs on either side of the clock and if I tilted my spectacles, thus mysteriously increasing

184

their magnification, I could make out Hooke as a young man, his expression shifty with embarrassment. There was also a picture of a dark-haired woman with a crooked smile, her face disappearing into death. The other photographs were all of boy scouts engaged in some jolly campfire activity or other.

'I used to run ten miles a day,' Graham Hooke said.

'Along the promenade?' I enquired inanely.

'Sometimes took Vincent along. But he could never keep up with me.'

Madge returned with a tea tray. As I had feared, there were homemade scones spread thickly with butter. Fortunately her father ate most of them. 'And now it seems he's going to be published at last,' he said between mouthfuls. 'You'd have thought he'd won the Nobel Prize, to judge from his excitement.'

'What's his book about?' Madge asked eagerly.

'Success and' – I refused another scone – 'failure.'

'He's an expert on the latter,' his father sneered.

'What do you know about it?' Madge burst out, red in the face. 'You've never read a thing he's written!'

'Because he would never let me!'

'I've never read anything neither,' she confessed to me with a shamed smile.

'How's Sarah?' his father asked. 'Has she taken him back?'

'They're getting divorced, I believe.'

His father shrugged. 'As they were married without the blessing of the Church, I don't suppose it matters very much.'

'He's better off without her,' Madge said. 'I've nothing against her personally, I'm sure she was as good a wife as she could be. But she kept him away from his religion. She never succeeded in settling him down. Never gave him any kids.'

'I miss Sarah,' her father said. 'She had some life in her, though there was never a blessed thing we agreed about. Her political opinions were puerile.'

Madge removed the tea things and he lay back wearily in his chair. I glanced at the clock and thought about leaving. The old man seemed to have fallen into a doze – 'Yes, ten miles!' he said suddenly, opening his eyes. 'Every single day. Eventually I had to reduce it to five. But I always kept myself fit, *mens sana in corpore sano*. Now I daren't move for angina. It doesn't make sense. None of it does.' He closed his eyes.

Madge returned and I said I must go – 'Oh I'll just come along with you,' she said. 'I have to go to the shops.' She glanced coolly at her father. 'Simon's going now, Dad,' she said loudly. The old man opened his eyes and seemed amazed to find himself where he was. When he said goodbye he held onto my hand with a tenacious grip.

I left the house with Madge. She seemed amused and mildly excited, walking by my side. We went down through the council estate and she asked if I was acquainted with the new woman Vincent had found. 'He says they're going to be married! A real lady, he said she was.'

I smiled and said nothing.

'It looks like everything is coming out right for him at last,' she went on. 'I've been praying for years that he'd get published. It just shows what persistence will do. Don't take any notice of me Dad; he's really in tucks about it. If only me Mam could have lived to see the day. She always said he'd be famous.'

'Really?'

We halted some way into the council estate where there was a row of shabby shops. I wanted to return to the promenade. 'Her death,' I said. 'He found her dying, didn't he?'

Her solemn, rather dingy face gazed into mine. She placed her hand on my arm. 'I don't suppose he ever got over it. Not really. And then there was her prophecy.'

'Her prophecy?' In my mind, Hooke's mother merged with the Little Flower.

Madge lapsed comfortably into a storytelling posture.

186

Her hand remained on my arm, her face monopolized the recital. I loved her simplicity. 'Well, she got taken to the hospital, of course, and we were all there, gathered round her deathbed. It was terrible, watching her suffer. Me Dad was in tears and you could have stuck pins in our Vincent and he wouldn't have noticed. But then at the end —' Her face softened with a mysterious smile: 'All her sufferings seemed to be over, the hard life she'd had; all the saints and angels were gathered about her and she was at peace in the arms of Our Lord. And at the very last it was Vincent she wanted. Not me Dad; and not me or our Betty, of course. He'd always been her favourite. So we made way for him and he went to her side; she put her arm about him. Then she made her dying prophecy,' Madge concluded impressively. 'She told him he would be a great man some day. It was like a promise, as though she was already in Heaven and could see the future. So there you are.'

I left her and strolled down to the promenade, carrying my thought like a brimming vessel. I leaned on the railing and gazed at the thick breathing heave of water. The sun was somewhere to the left, veiled in thin cloud, stationed over the ocean. There was a stillness everywhere and I was Hooke staring at the river in which he had drowned his God, his mother rising eerily from the depths brandishing her prophecy. *A great man some day!* He had not written of it in any of his novels. Perhaps he had forgotten – the way, much of the time, you forget you have a body with hands and feet, heart and lungs, everything needful to see you through life. And I was Hooke at forty-five with the waste of a lifetime draggled about his ankles like a comedian's baggy pants.

I felt that I understood him finally; I knew how it was – the loss of God and the death of his mother, her momentous prophecy fomenting his heroic delusion; and then the years of prolonged struggle as he sought to live up to it, the increasing burden of failure and shame. . .

The brimming substance in my closely-guarded vessel overflowed. It was the headiest champagne, sparkling and frothing. *I had it!*

187

32

When I had mused at the promenade railing long enough
– once, that is, I had become conscious of musing and had
begun to admire the mood – I returned to Liverpool. Sarah
saw something in my face and wanted to know what it meant.
She waited for me to confide in her, smiling tentatively. I
told her of visiting Hooke's father.

'How was he? I should go and see him, I suppose. It's
been ages.' She laughed. 'He's a sly old monkey. Whenever
I used to go there with Vincent, when his Dad kissed me he
always sort of angled himself so that he got a good feel of
my breast. I suppose it's something they teach you in the
boy scouts.'

I would have liked to have told her of the excitement
that had seized me after Madge had unwittingly given me
the final clue, the momentous item that caused everything
to fall into place – Inspiration! And my desire to put it all
down on paper. But she had once told me I wasn't a novelist,
hadn't the temperament; I was too analytical, had not been
hurt in the right places and was probably invulnerable. 'Did
anything else happen?' she persisted. 'You look like a tall
thin pussy that's swallowed a mouse.'

'I had a chat with Madge afterwards.'

'What did you talk about – the Little Flower? I used to
enjoy a chat with Madge. I always felt younger and prettier
after it.'

I escaped to the study and opened my notebook. I
wanted to write a novel, but it must not be a fictionalized
biography; I did not want to have to include all the boring

bits about Hooke. Yet I wanted to convey the essence of his life and I knew that this was largely metaphysical, a gaudy myth founded on self-deception. The Catholic Church had shown him how to do it.

I was restless with excitement and couldn't keep it to myself, so I went to see Marion. It was nearly summer and the town was crowded, the streets swarming with tourists who would put up with the drizzle drifting down from the hills so long as there was something to photograph and something to buy. A number of them had found Marion's shop and she was busy at the counter; but when she saw me, she left the work to her assistant and took me out to lunch. Her response was brusque when I apologized for calling during working hours: 'I was glad to get away. I really loathe the place now. I think I'll sell it like you did yours.' She walked swiftly, her head raised and her hair floating, a white raincoat swirled about her. 'Have you come back for good?'

'Not yet.'

We lunched in the vegetarian restaurant and over a parsnip goulash I told her something of the novel I hoped to write. 'The story of a man who makes a myth of his life, a nonentity who confuses ambition with talent because he can never escape the need to make existence meaningful. His life is one long nostalgia for the security he once enjoyed with Mum and the Church of Rome. He feels he is chosen, singled out, different: a great writer. And to safeguard the delusion, he builds an elaborate metaphysical contrivance about himself, by means of which he constantly interprets reality to his own advantage. So, everything that happens to him is *meant* to happen: his mother's death, falling down a mountain – they're all turning points, signposts of fate; and everything is inevitable, fatefully conspiring in his evolution as a great writer. Life is no more than a means to that end. Even when things go badly with him, when his novels are rejected time and again, he despairs momentarily but then he bounces back again, convinced that his suffering is necessary, an ordeal, a forging of the soul; a Purgatory he must

189

undergo before he can finally attain the Paradise of success and eternal fame. It's a perfect system he's created, impermeable to reality. And he can never escape from it.'

I paused for congratulations; but Marion seemed preoccupied, her face full and sullen above her plate. 'What happens to him at the end?'

'Oh I haven't got that far yet!' I laughed, animatedly forking the butter-slippery new potatoes served with the goulash.

I wasn't even sure how to begin. Should I start *in media res* and present the reader with a hopelessly deluded character clinging desperately to the belief that he is a great writer or should I begin at the beginning with a boy staring up at a mountain that is really a molehill? As for the end. . . 'I suppose he'll go mad, commit suicide: something like that.' I popped a potato into my mouth.

'Vincent's gone away, you know,' she said. 'He's gone for good.'

I stared, gobfaced, half a spud lodged in my mouth. 'Oh it was inevitable,' she insisted briskly. 'It was all over, before he went to London; and when he came back, he could hardly face me. A very painful time for both of us. So in the end – he didn't tell me he was going; he just slunk off. He left me a letter full of tender regrets and noble renunciation, as though he was doing me a favour.'

She smiled tragically, a lovelorn heroine. From an adjoining table, Brian Hargreaves observed her heavily.

It was early in the evening when I got back to Liverpool. Sarah had prepared a meal and we ate it at the nasty rickety little table in the living room. I told her the news about Hooke and she stiffened with anger. 'So she's got rid of him, has she? I thought she would, once his novel was turned down.'

'It wasn't like that!' I glowered at my plate, loathing the turgid proletarian mess that confronted me. 'She didn't tell him to go – unlike you. She knew nothing about it. He simply took himself off.'

'Well, where is he now?'

'I don't know. He didn't leave a forwarding address.'

'Oh Christ. . . I wonder what will happen to him?'

'Incidentally —' I stabbed at one of the fish fingers on my plate. 'Would you mind very much if I went off for a while?'

I did not look at her but she was burningly there. 'You want to go away?' Her voice wobbled. If you measured it on a graph it would be a decidedly wavy line. I thought about speech production and methods of measuring it scientifically. A continuous scroll, I suppose, with sensitive needles registering the finest tremor of feeling. 'What do you want to go away for?' she cried accusingly.

It was Marion's idea. Why didn't I come home for a while? I could live in the apartment she had made for Hooke. I could write my novel there undisturbed. 'I'll be back long before the baby is due.'

Now I was examining the bright orange crumb-coating of the fish fingers, the dense texture and grey-white sheen of the mashed potatoes – 'There isn't going to be a baby.'

I looked up. She smiled resignedly. 'It was a false alarm.'

'Well . . . we'll keep on trying.'

'There won't be much opportunity if you're going away. Why d'you want to go?'

'There is some work I'd like to do.'

'Well, you can do it here. I won't disturb you. What work?'

I ate one of the fish fingers then told her my plan. If it meant the end of us. . . So be it. The phrase troubled me: *So be it!* The catch-all cliché of bad faith. 'The fact is, I'd like to try and write a novel.' I was watching the needles registering my own speech production.

'Is that all?' She laughed in relief. 'Bloody hell, Simon – you gave me a shock. Well, why shouldn't you have a try? I think it's a great idea.' She gazed at me wonderingly. 'You'll do it too, I'll bet, you competent bugger. What's it going to be about?'

I repeated the summary I had given Marion, simplifying the concepts where necessary. 'Of course the character isn't *really* Vincent. It's an imaginative extrapolation. By that I mean —'

'I know what 'extrapolation' means. Are you going to put me in it?' she asked warily.

'Oh no. I couldn't do justice to you, my sweet.'

'Don't be hard-faced.'

I made no further mention of going away and she was happy, feeling that she had secured me. When we made love that night her eyes were shut, her ardour was prayerful.

I returned to my notebook. Gradually a narrative furnished with characters occurred to me. I had a family for my hero. In *Few Are Chosen* Hooke had made an ogre of his father; his sisters were stereotypes. But I wanted to convey my own impression of Graham Hooke – a man whose rugged campfire principles prevented him from ever communicating successfully with his son and gaining his love. Also I wanted to write of the unsuspected purity I had discerned in Madge, the sacrifice of her life in the care of others.

It all came so readily, so naturally! Suddenly I was an imaginative writer, a novelist, and I wanted nothing more. It was all I wished to do with my life. I was hooked.

There were problems, but I worked at them patiently and a solution suggested itself sooner or later. What poor old Hooke should have done, of course. . . It was more difficult to overcome the mild but persistent embarrassment I felt, arising out of the fact that I was planning a novel about a writer writing novels – a done-to-death theme no publisher would welcome. Yet how otherwise could I make my point? Other artists – painters, musicians – are obliged to demonstrate a singular practical skill; but virtually everyone can write at some level and the activity is essentially private. As a result, self-deception comes easily. Moreover, in writing about someone who believed himself to be an artist, I felt I was touching a common truth. It seemed likely that many who felt powerless and alienated in the modern world would like to be artists, for the artist alone is an autonomous source of power. He creates out of himself. And because his work is his life, he may be seen –

despite asthma, blindness, consumption, poverty, madness, a missing ear – as an enviably integrated personality. He is not alienated from himself. He is self-sufficient.

In June – 'You've been working too hard' – Sarah carried me off to Scotland for a brief holiday and hauled me up and down the Highlands. She showed me the world's beauty from the top of a mountain, the boundless receding rhythm of the heights, green-golden turf and burnished rock flowing away beneath a sunset. 'Oh God, I love all this,' she sighed. My response was not as enthusiastic as Hooke's would have been; I was preoccupied, detained in the doldrums of Liverpool with my luckless hero. But she understood and made allowances. A writer's work is never done. 'You just can't get away from it, can you? Vincent was like that.'

In the evenings, in the bedroom of the small hotel I had insisted on paying for – she had wanted to camp in a fragile tent in that wilderness – we made love studiously. The stable pregnancy she hoped for hadn't yet materialized and sex was now devoted to that end. Her attention was divided between her womb and myself, and she expected wonders from both.

She was tenderly possessive, watching me closely, her manner fraught with expectation. Eventually her loving, gently insistent pressure began to get on my nerves. It was like running a race and falling behind. And I was frightened when suddenly and for no reason – it was a day quite like the one that had gone before – I found myself unable to think and suffering the sort of blankness Hooke must often have endured. The novel had got away from me; it had gone and was lying dead in a ditch somewhere. The characters, the incidents I had invented, my powerful themes – they had all receded into an opaque substance that was merely words and meant nothing. I felt nothing for them. All I had was a terrible sense of deprivation and a disorientating, panic-stricken helplessness. Then the hopeless conviction pressed on me – it was all useless, I wasn't a writer. It was all a dreadful sham.

Sarah was watching and I couldn't hide my fear from her.

193

My fear of her. But she was a seasoned campaigner, familiar with such crises, and she reassured me. 'All it means, you know – well, it means the planning stage is over. It's time you actually began writing the book.'

She regarded me speculatively. 'That's the hard part,' she added.

33

I didn't feel I was quite ready for it. The novel I meant to write was a mountain rearing hugely above me, its summit wreathed in mist, and I was still circling the base searching for a practicable route, scanning the brute stone face for handholds. In less fancy terms, I hadn't yet worked everything out; I wasn't sure how the story should develop, I didn't know how my hero would end. To get the truly tragic sting I should have him discovering, when he is too old to make amends and change his life, that he has deceived himself – he is not a great artist, he will never be even a moderately successful writer and there is no longer the possibility of becoming anything else. He has ruined his chances, and in a secular world deprived of God they are all he has. A life that might have been spent contentedly enough – the worthy life of a man who accepts his limitations and devotes himself to the satisfaction of moderate desires – has been squandered on daydreams of an unreachable glory. Then suicide or madness.

That was the aim, the final appalling discovery I had in mind. But how to get there? I was faced with a climb of eighty or a hundred thousand words and Sarah was waiting for me to begin the ascent. Her smile hovered before me, a smile full of meanings, some of which I preferred not to interpret. The subtle and gently oppressive weight of a woman's smile! It is like a feather but enough of them will smother you. I was exposed to her and afraid of losing her esteem; her contempt would be unbearable. I had to prove myself – to her and to Hooke and to myself. But his example – for all its failure – unnerved me: his trunkful of writings, his dedication to the task carried on day after day in this study, at this desk where I sat with a blank sheaf of paper. And were his novels really as second rate as I had assumed? Perhaps I had persuaded myself that they were, eager to convince Sarah and in the process steal the love and admiration she had cherished for him. Having done so, I was faced with the task of doing better, becoming the successful Hooke she had always desired.

But this was all prevarication. I was simply afraid of getting down to work and committing myself to paper.

One morning I awoke early. Sarah slept soundly at my side. She lay on her back and was snoring softly; it sounded like a tiny motorboat puttering out over a moonlit lake. . . Bear in mind that I had not known her very long. In any case her snores were not preventing me from sleeping. I wanted to get up, as though someone was calling me. Making a mug of coffee I took it to the living room window and gazed out over the city. It was just dawn and the ordinary urban birds were singing their heads off, producing a shrill silken rustling that came from everywhere at once. The city lay silent beneath a spreading sky that promised a fine day – the barren streets, the stoical rows of houses and the people living within them, their simple trust in life. A sudden unaccountable love assailed me. I went to the study and sat at the desk. After a moment's thought, I began my novel.

I worked steadily, a finger of each hand prodding the keys of my electronic typewriter. How Hooke would have jeered could he have seen me. I sat like a bespectacled mantis poised above the smoothly designed facade of the machine. It had a little screen which displayed the typed line before printing it, an ingenious invention enabling me to change my mind from word to word. It was a chess computer that would never answer back.

By degrees I filled the screen with words and the machine printed them. Something emerged out of nothing. We were off! When I reached the end of the page an electronic device remembered to roll it out of the typewriter. Then it was but a moment's work to place another sheet of paper against the platen, press a button, and the machine rolled it into place. Indefatigably. Urging me on, as it were; for it was always ready for more words, eager to serve me. And if I made a mistake, it was easily erased; the machine was conscienceless and imperturbable. Thus we came to share a comfortable conspiracy.

In turn one typed page was laid upon another in a box provided for that purpose. My hero lay there, the character who was not entirely Hooke, pressed close by his parents, his philistine upbringing and the Church that had given him his first taste of the sacramental, the steadying power of ritual, a belief in miracles. But I did not spend long on his childhood. I had hoped to make of Graham Hooke a father forever denied his son's loving companionship; but somehow it was difficult to fit in. In any case I no longer felt much for the idea. It was the same with Madge, the purity of her self-sacrifice. Perhaps I had been mistaken. Was she really anything more than a dour and simple-minded old maid. . ? I wanted to get on to the colourful tragedy of my hero's self-deception.

I worked every day, many hours a day, feeling virtuous and authoritative, typing a page and going over it, typing it again and getting it right. When she arrived home from work, and at regular intervals during the weekend, Sarah would bring me a mug of coffee and stand for a moment at the desk, shyly, like a schoolgirl, watching as I prodded the keys and the words flicked onto the screen.

I did not produce them as rapidly as Hooke would have done, counting the total each day and entering it in the diary he kept for the enlightenment of posterity – *Good day's work: 4,778 words*. But that did not seem to bother Sarah. She assumed I wrote slowly because I thought more carefully than he had done. She was pleased with me and always prompt with encouragement, though she never asked to see what I had written. Hooke had taught her to keep her place and wait until the great moment when the

197

completed novel would be ceremoniously presented to her; the novel – whichever it was: third or fourth or seventh – he was convinced would finally be published.

'How long d'you think it will take you? Oh but take all the time you need, love,' she added hastily. 'Don't rush it and spoil it.'

Every night I dug at her womb, her cosy little screen waiting to be imprinted. Urgency and suspense took much of the joy out of it. And then there was a week's rest when her system rejected all our labour in a flow of blood.

When I had finished work for the day I would often walk alone about the streets, dazed and happy more often than not and feeling like a conqueror. I strode about as if I owned the place and knew all its secrets. Sometimes I entered a pub and observed the locals speaking their racy gutter poetry, my notebook at the ready – *Lickle feller he was, with a head like a rosarybead. I said 'Yew what?' He said 'Yew heard: get your cards. It's your lucky day. We're sending you ferra rest-cure on the Dole.' So I wen' up the road, saw the gaffer at the udder place. No chance. You need a letter from the Holy Ghost to gerra job der. . .* But generally I simply walked about inside myself, admiring the hazy architecture of my novel. I had changed metaphors; I was no longer climbing a mountain but building a palace, intoxicated with the beauty and daring and strength of the scheme.

My hero was engaged upon a similar enterprise; he had left home and was writing his first novel, though in his case all that was going up was a flimsy castle of dreams to shelter his inflated opinion of himself. Frederick Welch I called him – I don't know why; the name simply came to me. I had concluded his early years with the death of his mother. And her prophecy, I had to have that. Now he was in London writing his novel, a scrubby provincial steaming with ambition; and I was in Liverpool writing the first novel I would actually finish. We walked the city streets together and I came to know him well, his precious self-deceiving fantasies. I recognized them as if they were my own, and they were everyone's in some measure: that wild and splendid inner world which is always ready to beguile us. I was Frederick and we had our dreams of fame in which we starred to the world's applause, behaving with becoming nonchalance when, for example, we delivered a speech of thanks upon receiving the Booker Prize. We appeared on TV chat shows – the kind that aspire to be serious – and selected our favourite records for Desert Island Discs. We were celebrities, our photographs hung in the gallery of the review pages. There were also the voices I heard that Frederick heard – the cheers of a horde of reviewers, the purring tone of some eminent critic appraising our work, the level-headed discourse of a biographer recording the artistic trials and triumphs of our life.

Self-deception! Soon the theme possessed the voracity of a mad dog straining at the leash, eager to swallow up the world; and I was God's spy, uncovering incriminating evidence everywhere. In religion obviously – Who wouldn't deceive himself to escape the pains of death? In politics – No leader could survive without it – and throughout history, in heroism and self-sacrifice, tyranny and rebellion; in human relations and in our subjective interpretation of the natural world. Man was no more than a self-created conspiracy. And I would have to include all of this somehow, introduce more characters and cover the social spectrum, invent images and incidents to illustrate the theme. . . It was at this point that I began to realize I was writing a great novel.

The convolutions of my hero's psychology fascinated me and I wanted Sarah to share the joy I found in creation – which was essentially a matter of discovery. 'I shall call it *A Sheltered Life*,' I told her. 'You remember once telling me about Nietzsche and living dangerously, you and Vincent? All right, he took chances: but did he really live dangerously? What Nietzsche meant was the risk of ultimate moral and intellectual exposure; but Vincent never came close to that. He was all the time sheltering himself with self-deception, and that is what my hero does. For instance, he doesn't go to university, because higher education with its insistence on objectivity and truth would threaten the opinion he has of himself. He shuns education and shelters his delusion. He will educate himself, he says; but in doing so, he chooses only those areas of learning that are easily within his competence; he restricts his reading to those books that do not present a serious challenge.'

'You always speak in such complete sentences,' she said.

Was she bored?

'And he chooses his acquaintances on the same principle,' I went on. 'He makes sure he doesn't brush up against anyone too intelligent – His wife!' I yelped, the idea suddenly occurring to me. 'When he marries, he makes sure it's some good loyal undemanding woman who won't see through him. Where are you off to?' I cried as she turned abruptly away.

I caught her and held her. 'Oh you silly muggins! I'm talking about my novel. It's fiction!' I stroked her tenderly. 'Vincent's real tragedy, you know, is that he never appreciated the one undeniable success in his life – his marriage to you.'

'Do you really mean that?'

'Why else should I say it?'

'It's just that sometimes you seem more concerned with the style than the feeling, as though you were writing it out in your head and admiring it.'

An interesting idea. Maybe I could use it for Frederick. But I could not attend to it now for I was caught up in a new problem and harassed by the thought that I would have to build extra rooms and towers, add a dungeon to my palace and a cluster of attics to accommodate further complications swarming out of my theme and demanding admittance. I would have to take Frederick's wife into account, the misery of her childlessness and the emptiness of her future; the fact that there was to be no return on the love she had lavished in the past, the years with Frederick having deprived her of any promising alternative life. . . I left Sarah and went off to sorrow over the destruction of an ardent girl brimming with love and hope, transformed by failure into a crabbed old bitch.

On the other hand, wasn't his wife partly responsible for Frederick's failure? Having joined her fond delusion to his, she had hardened it into imprisonment, increasing his anguish with her foolish insistence upon the fulfilment of the impossible. . . Ideas and inventions, proposals and counter-proposals reeled and writhed about me and I was burdened by the obligation to include everything. My palace rose and distended grotesquely with a thousand rooms and a multitude of turrets, towers in danger of toppling and walls rearing crazily, the subconscious growling in the dungeon and a monstrous three-headed ego raving in the attic.

The novel was expanding beyond my control, protean and intimidating, a genie escaping from its bottle and filling the world. But when I tried to talk to Sarah about it, laughing my anxiety – 'There is so much I have to include!' – I felt like a tethered balloon riding helplessly above her. She gazed up at me incuriously.

34

It wasn't like me, she said. Her smile reflected some inner amusement. 'All this excitement. You're like a girl at her first party. Calm down, for God's sake. The world isn't going to end just because you're writing a novel.'

'I'm sorry.'

'You used to be so cool and collected; you never got carried away. You've changed in other ways too.'

It was true. When I looked in the mirror I saw a face lean with strain which seemed to shine unhealthily. I was often unshaven and my hair needed cutting; it hung lank, and when I fingered the crown it seemed to be thinning there. I no longer cared what I wore and put on the same clothes every day until Sarah insisted on a change. Marion would have raised her eyebrows, her eyes widening in tender mock alarm; but I was impressed by my reflection, proud of the visible proof of my labours. The world should know that I was engaged on a superhuman literary task. It was all that mattered. My life was enlarged to the dimensions of a novel. Every day when I finished work I carefully counted the words, entering the total in my notebook. In time this had the unforeseen effect of making me aware that I was writing fewer words each day. 'And when are you going to give me a baby?' Sarah wanted to know.

She went to the medical centre for tests and they showed there was nothing wrong with her. 'It's not me that's at fault. I'm not too old. They said I was good for a couple of kids before I dried up. They want to have a look at your sperm.'

'What do you mean?'

'Your sperm. If you produce some, I'll take it to them now.'

When I objected, she smiled knowingly. 'Are you afraid of discovering it's your fault?'

'I quite fail to see that a moral interpretation is justified. You're too impatient.'

'Come on,' she murmured, closing with me. 'I'll do it for you, if you like. All they want is a sample.' She unfastened my belt and unzipped my trousers, pulling them down. She had a small bottle in which to collect the semen.

'Oh look, this is ridiculous —'

But she had her hands on me and I was helpless, embarrassed, fascinated. If you can imagine a mother masturbating her teenage son then you have a fairly accurate idea of the situation. We were in the living room, standing together, and my trousers and underpants were draggled about my ankles. She was fully dressed. I removed my glasses and she took them from me. Then she stooped over me, with something crone-like in the hump of her bowed shoulders. Her face was hard and pure with concentration. Her small thin hand squeezed and jerked my dick in a clumsy amateurish fashion – 'Come on, for God's sake!' But the thing, mulishly flaccid, refused to rise into an erection.

I gazed about the room wondering how it was that one knew the expression on one's face without seeing one's reflection. The nerves must transmit to the mind the chosen configuration of facial muscles. . . What they transmitted in this instance was a martyred expression. 'What's up with you?' she giggled maliciously. 'Have you nothing left?' Rubbing and pulling at it, the bottle ready in her other hand. 'Have I made too many demands on you?' Her facial muscles were ranged in a suffering expression.

Finally she went down on her knees before me, clasped my dick in her warm mouth and sucked angrily, her teeth closing about me, her face crimson. 'Look out!' I cried, the sperm foaming within me like a horde of tiny travellers at rush hour cursing and crowding as they fought their way out of an Underground station. She wrenched her face away. She

203

held my dick like a hose and tried to direct the ejaculation into the bottle. But the idiot had not studied the logistics of the problem beforehand – a funnel, for example, would have aided matters considerably – and as a result most of the sperm went over her hand. A blob clung to her skirt, there was another on her shoe, a smear on the floor – 'Oh God!' she yelled and with a shriek flung the bottle away.

She rushed to a chair and crouched in it, her face in her hands, sobbing uncontrollably. I went in search of a towel, my trousers clutched somewhere about my thighs, walking in a lamed slithering manner, my penis poking and lurching like the prow of a ship in a storm.

I went back to work, shaken and unnerved, feeling oddly weakened as though in drawing off the sample she had leeched the essence of my inner strength. But this was probably a cowardly excuse. My typewriter was convinced of it. The little screen, facing me impassively like the slot of a confessional, refused to grant absolution and yield its customary quota of words. I was stuck. A writer's block. Those who don't write think of it as a mysterious ailment, the intellectual equivalent of writers' cramp. But those who write feel guilty, knowing the block is the symptom of some profound problem that has been ignored and will no longer suffer neglect.

Sarah, recovering from her demoralization, caressed me sympathetically: we were both victims of a cruel fate. 'It will come right,' she assured me (*Vincent had them all the time*). 'Probably you need a break.'

I was already broken, although I refused to admit it. I would have liked to have gone away, visited Yorkshire. I was homesick for the hills and river-strewn valleys glowing now with the wealth of summer. To be free of these dreary imprisoning streets! And the small friendly town of rugged stone which I had scorned and left precipitately, eager to test myself in the city, glamorizing the dump. I wanted to go home. But I daren't face Marion for I could not have discussed my novel with her; it would be like hunting for survivors after a disastrous earthquake.

204

To discover the problem and unblock inspiration, to repossess the clarity and force of my original vision, I knew that I ought to read through what I had written, searching for faults with zealous objectivity the way Hooke should have done with his hopeless novel. After typing each page I had placed it in the box and had not looked at it again. But I was afraid to read what I had written.

And Sarah was watching, waiting. At first she seemed merely puzzled; she repressed disappointment, hoping for the best. Then by degrees she stiffened into embarrassment and seemed to creep about on tiptoes as though afraid of alerting me to her presence. She averted her face – out of compassion? – and we had little to say to each other. In bed she no longer expected to be serviced with regular copulation. She seemed to have abandoned her plans for a baby and she grew indifferent to sexual love.

In desperation, longing to be writing again, to have that peopled world in my head once more and, best of all, to feel again the glory of a conqueror for whom everything was possible, I faced what I felt were my limitations and bravely renounced the grand inflation of my theme, the unrelenting exposure of universal self-deception. I hauled them down, the massive walls, the glittering towers – It was like punishing myself in the hope of propitiating fate. I reduced everything to the scale of my hero, brought him back to Liverpool, gave him a loyal wife as deluded as himself and set him to writing further novels. They were all rejected.

And what more was there to say? It was failure. It went on and on, terrible in its monotony, the way failure does. I knew there was a great deal more to say, there was all the suffering core of Frederick's Hooke life; but I could not reach it, my imagination failed in the attempt. I could not measure up to it. My experience was too meagre, my sympathies too shrinking, to encompass that grimness. In retaliation I became bored with my novel and its hero.

But I dared not admit this to Sarah and for a while I managed to deceive her. Though I might spend most of the day lounging in the living-room reading light pornography or walking about the city staring glumly at the pictures in the art gallery, the boastful battery of books in the central library, the dog-eared remains of someone's love in the secondhand bookshops; or mingling with a crowd of distracted shoppers in the town centre or pacing the cobbled quay of the Albert Dock recalling the time when I was happy and hopeful – when Sarah returned from work I was always at the desk in the study, bent over the keyboard of the typewriter like some intrepid space explorer launched on a momentous mission.

But I couldn't fool her for long, for she could see that the shallow stack of typed pages had not increased recently. Possibly she read them in secret anyway and had found nothing more to read. Gradually her smile narrowed and hardened with, it seemed, a stifled air of triumph.

It made me resentful and reckless. I no longer cared what she thought; and when she came home in the evening – brisk and indignant after having fought all day for the survival of her misfits – she began to find me sprawled indolently in the coffin of the couch reading something undemanding, watching television or simply staring my failure in the face. She would stand above me then with her head on one side, regarding me as though I was an amusing oddity.

Finally, with the air of one leaving his prison cell and marching either to doom or liberation, I took up the slim sheaf and read what I had written: as Hooke must often have done, hoping against hope. Perhaps after all I was in for a pleasant surprise. But I soon discovered that what I had produced was really no better than he could have written. In fact you might have mistaken one for the other. I was Simon Cleaver writing about Frederick Welch who was mostly Vincent Hooke, and we all sounded the same. We had failure in common.

But strident images of doom or liberation were quite out of place. Once the worst was over, I felt something that would eventually widen into rueful relief; and I was my bland dispassionate self once more when at last I told

Sarah the truth. 'I can't do it. There's no point in kidding myself. It's a story only Vincent could have written, and he can't write it. He has written it with his life.'

'What do you mean?'

'I was afraid you might not understand.'

'Well, you can't do it: that's easy enough to understand.' She laughed in my face. 'And when I think of the way you tore into him, reading his novels like you were God Almighty and dismissing them as hopeless crap; all the time convinced, of course, that you could do miles better!'

She stood before me in the living room much as she had that first night, slight and fair-haired, my plucky little cabin boy. 'The point is,' I ground out patiently, 'it isn't really a tragedy. The agony of an unpublished writer? When you place it alongside the giant agony of the world, the real tragedy people suffer every day – and you know as much about that as anyone – it's little more than an absurdity, a grim farce. Who on earth gives a damn whether a second-rate writer gets published or not?'

She stood her ground, searching my face with her pained smile. 'You got it all wrong from the start. You never really understood. It shows how little you know about life and the way people manage it, the way they survive. You decided his life was a tragedy; and now that you can't write it that way, you go to the opposite extreme and call it a farce. That shows how much you have to learn, how immature you really are.'

She paused as if inviting me to defend myself. I said nothing. She went on. 'He never thought of his life as a tragedy and neither did I. He loves life! He doesn't pity himself. He doesn't go round claiming the world owes him a living and it's all the fault of the rotten publishers. He may be a fool but he isn't a snivelling creep, and his life isn't a tragedy.'

'What is it then?'

'It's – a life; no worse than many another and better than some. The life I shared with him – it had a pattern, its ups

207

and downs, just like any other life. There were needs and they were satisfied, sometimes. There was companionship, true friendship at times, even love. He may have deceived himself about being a great writer – all right, he deceived himself. What's that – a fucking mortal sin?'

She turned away. 'At his best he was a man you could love and admire, even for his foolishness. I admired him! Because he was brave and good.'

35

I went to the United States – a caprice, a sudden whim, a long holiday. Sarah thought it was a good idea. She did not suggest accompanying me. She kissed me goodbye, temperately but not unkindly, and did not expect to see me again. Marion welcomed me back, wrapping her strong arms about me. On the day of my departure, she drove me to Manchester Airport. 'And when you get back, we'll be able to settle down together.'

New York was magnificent and terrible, roaring with beauty and violence, a millionaire's Liverpool. The shriek of fame was deafening; the review pages in the newspapers were slabs as thick as tombstones. I went to Boston and enjoyed the cosy parts, then travelled north through New England hunting for chipmunks in the unending forest. I stayed in motels with sanitized toilets and a TV that hiccuped commercials. The people I met were friendly, generous and frighteningly naive.

Gradually, among unfamiliar sights and mild adventures – the waitress in Concord who loved to stuff me with ice-cream – the agitation of the last few months fell away and I began to feel cool and uncluttered once more. But I would never be the same again. My youth was over and I bore about with me always a vague oppression. It was regret and guilt, I suppose, but chiefly the awareness of mortality.

On the long flight back across the Atlantic, the sun beaming unweariedly above the clouds, I thought of Hooke and was uneasy, wondering what had happened to him. I would have liked to have seen him again, to renew if only briefly and for the last time, our constantly misfiring relationship – his eagerness to be friends and my reluctance to accommodate him; my vain attempt to place him finally and accurately, to fix in some tidy frame his personality shorn of all irregularities, reduced to a manageable stereotype. And all I had learned while failing in this.

Marion wanted me to share her house; there was room and there would be more once Willy graduated and went off in pursuit of his own life. I compromised, moving into the flat above her shop, though I generally dined with her for she loved to serve me with succulent meals which steadily eroded any nostalgia I may have felt for cheap Chinese take-aways and fish fingers. We rarely spoke of Hooke. But I could not escape him for I was sleeping in his bed, sitting at his desk, living in the featureless, rather insipid rooms he had inhabited, where he had written and suffered, the apartment contrived from a storeroom and tethered to a shop.

I didn't like the place, I couldn't work there. Marion was under the impression that I was still writing my novel and it was some time before she discovered that I had destroyed it in a fit of fury and shame. 'But I'll write another,' I assured her. 'I'm not going to stop now I've got the bit between my teeth.'

The hackneyed phrase convinced her I was done for. But she did not reproach me with failure. Nor did she seek to encourage me. She had had quite enough of men who wanted to be writers and she feared I might end as Hooke had done. 'Did he tell you about the slush pile?' she asked warningly.

'You mean his trunk full of novels?'

'Not exactly. I'm talking about the day he went to London.'

There was something he had not told me. Marion made a cautionary tale of it and I was Hooke once more struggling and failing to pass his examination. At the conclusion of the interview, the editor had risen to his feet, murmuring platitudes and holding out his hand in farewell. Hooke had clung to it (*Oh please!*) and the editor had drawn him along to the door, allowing him to leave the office first. Hooke had wandered off down a narrow corridor stacked with boxes of published novels awaiting distribution. Searching for the way out, he had opened the wrong door and had discovered a dim little room that appeared to be a broom cupboard. But instead of mops and pails, the place was piled high with manuscripts, hundreds of them, stacked on shelves and heaped on the floor, many still parcelled as they had been posted. The editor said it was called the slush pile. A pile of slush. Every day, he explained, they received dozens of unsolicited novels, hundreds in a year; and every publisher in London received as many, if not more. In London and New York, in Berlin and Tokyo, Paris and Baghdad there was a slush pile in every publisher's office in the world. 'Then for the first time, you see,' Marion said, 'he realized that he was not unique.'

He was indistinguishable from hundreds in Britain and thousands throughout the world; a doomed tribe of authors, unknown and never to be published, sitting at their desks and writing their hearts out, day after day and year after year, scribbling furiously or typing like maniacs, deluging some hapless publisher with their manuscripts, their love stories and domestic dramas, their historical romances, their imitations of Hemingway and Joyce and John le Carré, their science fiction and childhood reminiscences, their lurid fantasies and raving pornography – a wild storm of impossible, unreadable novels blasting through a publisher's door and ending in a thick drift of paper in a broom cupboard.

'I don't want you to end on a slush pile,' she said in conclusion.

'Why did he tell you this?' I wondered.

'Oh I suppose he wanted me to tell him it wasn't true – he was unique, he was different from the others.' She smiled patiently. 'I couldn't do it. He went away soon afterwards.'

I thought of him – the appalling discovery he had made – and felt that I must help him. I went to the college where he had worked. The place looked like a small untidy factory. It

211

was November, a dark day, and all the rooms were lighted. I found the main office and made my enquiry – 'Vincent Hooke?' They told me that he had left at the end of the summer term. No one knew where he had gone. He had left his temporary lodging in the town and there was no forwarding address.

'Why did you want to see him?' Marion asked. 'Isn't it best to leave well alone?'

'But we don't know what's happened to him! He may even have – well, killed himself.'

'Vincent?' She placed a generous slice of broccoli quiche on my plate and offered a bowl of dazzling coleslaw. 'He's too vain for suicide.'

'That's pretty unfeeling,' I protested.

She raised her eyebrows. 'It wasn't meant to be. There's a lot to be said for vanity. It's what keeps you alive, half the time.' She poured the wine and raised her glass in a toast. 'Here's to vanity and a long, selfish life! Now listen to the marvellous idea I've had,' she went on, setting down her glass.

Her inspired plan for our future. England was dead and putrefying – D.H. Lawrence's prophetic fulminations had finally reached the commercial classes – so we would go abroad. She would sell her house, find a good money-grubbing manager for the shop, and we would live on the proceeds – my fortune added to hers and invested shrewdly – in some renovated farmhouse in Provence. 'Isn't that a lovely idea?' She would wear her hair long and soft, let her clothes flow in careless and becoming lines. She would take up painting – an easel outdoors, a huge straw hat, the abounding countryside. We would eat well, drink lots of wine and care for no one else. A bohemian existence in plentiful sunshine. And I could visualize my part in it: I would be the charming and ineffectual dilettante brother she would care for and sigh over, bully tenderly and keep with her forever.

I went to Liverpool for the day. I had not been there since leaving Sarah but little had changed and the city readily forgave me for having run away. *Everyone would like to*, it admitted tiredly, *but despite the shite, there is something here that does the heart good.* Sentimental old Irish bitch. I walked the murmurous streets, recognizing the battered cars in the gutter, the shuttered shops and broken pavements, wrecked buildings, wrathful graffiti. And the people living among this: the poetry of their phlegmy language, their irrepressible swagger. It was invigorating. The place was uncouth and inspired, knee-deep in dreams and disaster; its back turned on the mainland, its grubby face staring into the west, yearning for sight of the Atlantic.

I made a few tentative enquiries about accommodation: there were some desirable apartments for sale in the huge houses that bordered the park. I went to a job centre and learned of a temporary position with the council writing publicity material that would overflow with words like *Future!* and *City of Opportunity!* With my Oxford degree and my experience in mendacity, I stood a good chance of getting it.

Finally – I had meant to all along, keeping it in reserve like a Christmas present I hadn't yet opened – I called on Sarah, climbing flights of stairs through smells and gloom to the top-floor flat. It was late in the day and she would probably be at home. Something fluttered in my chest as I rang the doorbell. Hooke opened the door. 'Simon, how nice to see you!'

He was pleased for all the wrong reasons.

36

Of course he had bounced. I should have expected it.

He brought me into the living room and called out to Sarah. When she came in, curious to see who it was and absently touching her hair into place, I imagined I could smell the fresh tang of toilet soap on her fair skin. She smiled angrily when she saw me and almost immediately went away again to make coffee (dolloping spoonfuls of the stuff into a jug, sloshing boiling water onto it. It would taste vile but I wouldn't notice). 'Yes, we're back together again, as you see,' Hooke said comfortably.

He seemed in good health but looked older, as might an explorer who had returned from some perilous journey which, though it had cost suffering, had left him leaner and harder, wiser: a man who had learned to sum up the world with a quizzical glint. He was neatly dressed in dark trousers, an open-necked shirt of primrose hue and a woollen waistcoat. The bald spot on his crown had not increased significantly and could still be concealed by a cunning arrangement of his fine dark hair. Hardest to bear was his suppressed air of sprightly complacency.

He asked after Marion – 'She's quite over it by now, I trust?' – and used the opportunity while Sarah was absent to explain why he had broken off the relationship. 'I had to get away and a clean break was best. Hard on both of us, but at least it was honest. An admission of defeat. . ? No, I can't believe that. We gave a lot to each other. I shall never regret having known her. But I could never have lived up to her expectations, you know. I'm just not made for that sort of life. If I'd stayed with her much longer, she'd have made me into – Oh with the best of intentions, with all the love in the world! But she'd have made me into a dilettante, comfortably ensconced in an idle and no doubt charming but really quite meaningless existence.'

He paused to recover breath, lighting a cigarette as he did so. Sarah brought in the coffee and sat down. They sat beside each other facing me. I wanted an explanation, felt I was entitled to one. 'How —?' I began, but Sarah was in charge. 'Well, how are you, Simon?' Her smile was firm. 'How was America?' She was a schoolteacher demanding some rote-learned recital from a dimwitted pupil.

I told them about America. Some of my observations amused them but I felt that, on the whole, they would have preferred a more penetrating and censorious account of the corrupt kingdom of capitalism. Then Sarah got up and fetched her big coat, the one she had worn that day on the landing stage. 'I promised to go and see me Mam,' she told Hooke, who seemed surprised. She turned to me, and for a moment – but it may have been no more than a trick of the light – her slender face was waspish. 'You'll excuse me, won't you?'

She left the flat. Hooke smiled and lit another cigarette. He spoke of the terrible time he had endured after leaving Marion – though leaving her was little more than a convenient marker in time; what mattered was his humiliation in London and the ruin of his hopes. He had found suitably self-punishing lodgings in a gloomy house in Halifax and had striven to piece his life together again. Gradually he had recovered the compensations which never failed him at such times – long walks in the country, improving but not too challenging literature and an earful of classical music, Beethoven for defiance and Bach for spirituality. He grew philosophical. He had begun to believe that perhaps after all life was possible, provided one expected little of it. He had felt that he should try once more to find contentment in a virtuous ordinary life. He would devote himself to teaching, bend his unruly will to the demands of duty.

215

But then he had bounced, he couldn't help himself: it was a wild loving leap back into the past and what he called his true self.

'I'm an impulsive creature, always have been. I thought of the life I had in mind – safe, dutiful. A good life certainly, for those who have nothing else. But what horrified me was the thought of living on as a teacher and nothing more, mildly wanking myself into futility with my feeble compensations and rigidly refusing to write ever again; using up the rest of my life in that way, doing my duty as a teacher, humble and conscientious, pretending to be ordinary. And what would happen at the end?' he cried, staring at me. 'I would come to the end of that harmless existence; I'd look back – a white-haired old has-been, a timorous, benevolent, burnt-out old cliché of a pedagogue. Oh my father would have been proud of me! But I would have been in hell, Simon, howling and gnashing my teeth, hopelessly lamenting the years I had wasted in a good meaningless life – when I could have been writing! Failing, probably. Yes, all right – failing! But at least living to the fullest extent of myself. You see the point?' he enquired anxiously.

He had given in his notice and had bounced out of teaching, quivering with the desire to re-write *Few Are Chosen*. But what if I had destroyed the typescript as he had directed? He had gone to Liverpool and called on Sarah – 'When was this?' I asked, bewildered.

In July, he thought.

'But she never told me!'

'You were out at the time – walking the streets or getting drunk or something. It was when you were trying to write your novel.' He chuckled indulgently. 'Anyhow, I had a chat with her, found the manuscript and took it away with me. She probably felt there was little point in telling you: what you didn't know wouldn't hurt you. I worked at the book in that grotty room I had in Halifax. But happy, Simon! For a while anyway. And then – September, it would be – Sarah called on me and told me it was all over between you. We decided not to get a divorce after all, and —' He

216

smiled expansively. 'Here I am! Back with Sarah, back in Liverpool.'

He was picking up a little part-time teaching and Sarah's salary took care of the rest. 'She is so loyal and strong,' he sighed fondly. 'She knows what's best for me.'

'And so you're writing again?' I squeezed the words out bravely. 'That's good. You'll have learned a lot from the trip to London. I think they were right to reject the novel, you know. It fell between two stools. You were trying to write beyond yourself. But now, if you – er – moderate your ambition and write within your limitations . . . Well, you can get a lot done that way.'

My conclusion was lame because he seemed indifferent to what I was saying. The smile curving round the cigarette he was lighting suggested that I was being presumptuous and patronizing. 'What happened with the novel *you* tried to write?' He leaned back – he was sitting in the sunken couch – and regarded me amusedly. 'What was it about?'

'Didn't Sarah tell you?'

'She didn't seem to know. How much did you write?'

'Oh I never got much further than the quotation I chose for the title page.'

'What was that?'

'A thing of Sartre's: *You can get rid of a neurosis but you are never cured of yourself.*'

'Interesting,' he commented idly. 'But you really tried to write novel?' He blew out smoke. 'Did Sarah put you up to it?'

'Oh no. It was my own idea. She was against it, if anything. She thought I was trying to be you.'

He laughed goodnaturedly – At Sarah's assumption? At the absurdity of anyone trying to be him? I would never know. He referred to my novel with patent insincerity. 'I'll bet it was as good as anything I could have done. Why did you give up?'

'I couldn't solve the problems. I hadn't worked everything out.' I stared at the floor. There was a whitish stain on the carpet that might have been the lingering remembrance of my misfiring sperm.

'Will you try and write another?'

'Oh yes.'

'That's good. Don't give up heart.' He ashed his cigarette, pleased with the charity he had dispensed.

I felt it was time I left. He came with me to the door. I wished him luck with the rewriting of *Few Are Chosen* – 'Oh I've put that aside,' he said. 'I'm working on something different now, much bigger and more important.'

We shook hands and I went down the stairs through the old house for the last time. It was dark outside and the night was cold but I felt warm as I got into my car and drove away. It should have been a comedy, I realized: the story of a man who never understands that the success he longs for lies precisely in the myth he has made of his life, for it has given his existence a largeness denied to most lives. That was the way I would write it, I decided.